The One They Called "Quiet"

L. J. Bolar

VANTAGE PRESS
New York

Published by Vantage Press, Inc.
516 West 34th Street, New York, New York 10001

Manufactured in the United States of America
ISBN: 0-533-11208-7

Library of Congress Catalog Card No.: 94-90383

0 9 8 7 6 5 4 3 2 1

Prologue

From the spring and summer months of the year 1965, during the Watts riots in Los Angeles, up to 1968, the year Dr. Martin Luther King, Jr. was murdered, police had been on a black male shooting spree. Few friends and relatives of these known victims raised questions as to why the victims were killed. The officers involved usually stated they had had reason to believe their lives were in danger.

The victim would always have a weapon in hand, usually a knife. And the victim would wind up with a bullet wound in the back. To friends and relatives, the victim was generally known not to own or carry a weapon. So once again the question would be raised, where had the weapon come from? Then it would later be discovered that the weapon the victim was accused of having had come from the police lost-and-found lockup room. So how did it get in the victim's hand?

From California up the coast to Seattle, the dispute between the police and blacks continued. From 1969 to 1972, the shooting of blacks got out of control. Most of the black killings happened at night. A black would be walking home alone and for no apparent reason be stopped by an officer and wind up killed. At the inquiries the killings were always justified. Blacks, however, felt the police thought they had a license to shoot blacks whenever they got an urge to kill someone.

It took the Watts riots to ignite the fuse because blacks

didn't like the incident that happened in California. In Seattle it took Martin Luther King, Jr.'s death to set off a chain reaction. In various ways blacks began to fight back against the police. Like a reported stolen car found on a deserted or dead-end street. When an officer in a squad car answered a call and investigated, he was ambushed. Or when a complaint was called in on a marital dispute, an officer who answered the call would find himself going to a vacant house. He would be gunned down walking up the walkway or when he got up on the porch. Or a squad car might be driving down a street. A car would pull up beside it and those inside would open fire. There were other incidents against the police that were not mentioned.

The trigger-happy police who had been shooting blacks were taken off the streets and put behind desks. The higher-ups in the police department felt that getting these men off the streets would stop the attacks against the police. But the damage was already done. Certain groups of blacks had declared war on the police.

These few incidents the police kept out of the papers. What news the papers did print was what the police told the papers to print. But the radio and television carried the news. The police kept certain incidents out of the papers because they were afraid the attacks on them might inspire other blacks to take up cop killing. It got to where three or four police officers would ride in the same car because on two occasions an officer somehow got trapped on a dead-end street and was forced into an all-out gun battle.

Certain police officers decided to form their own group. They were going to fight back against the blacks, who'd declared open season on them. To them all blacks were open prey. Certain blacks were singled out. They were arrested at their homes, picked up from their jobs, or just picked up while walking down the street. When these blacks were taken down to the police department, they were thrown into a small, dim-lighted room and were interrogated brutally. They were questioned with fists and feet and billy clubs. After being beaten into unconsciousness, blacks were put in isolated cells away from the other prisoners. And through the courts, blacks were railroaded into prisons. Most of these blacks may not have had anything to do with the certain groups of blacks that had been going around killing cops.

There were a few blacks who never made it downtown to the police department. They were found somewhere on the outskirts of town, lying in a ditch. The causes of these deaths were unknown. The police placed these cases in the unsolved-murder files, and no more was said about them.

This is a true story of such incidents, but the names are fictitious because none of the people—the friends and relatives of the victims and the blacks who attacked the police—wanted their names mentioned.

1

Quiet, a young black in about his middle twenties, stood six feet tall and weighed 185 pounds. In 1967, he was drafted into the army, and he spent sixteen months in Vietnam. He was discharged in 1969. During his tour in Vietnam, Quiet spent most of his time with the infantry units. He was in a quartermaster unit known as the 506th. Most quartermaster units in Vietnam were assigned an infantry unit to do their laundry. But Quiet's unit was different. They spent most of their time with the infantry units to which they were assigned. Quiet's quartermaster unit was assigned to three different infantry units during his stay in Vietnam: the First Infantry Division, the Fourth Cavalry Division and the 173d Airborne Division.

Although Quiet wasn't involved in any actual fighting, he did enough to know what it was all about. Many times when the infantry units went out on a search-and-destroy mission, they had to have a few quartermaster men with them. For what purpose Quiet never understood. He just went when he was ordered to.

On some of these missions into the jungle, a few guys, fresh from the States, got weak stomachs at the sight of blood. But the men who had been in Vietnam for six months or longer had become used to the killings on these search-and-destroy missions. As for Quiet, not many things bothered him, least of all blood. A few of the infantry men wondered about Quiet because he stayed mostly to himself, except when it came to some type of recreation.

Sixteen months Quiet spent in Vietnam waiting for the day he would go home, back to the States. Then one cold rainy day, it was time for him to return to the States. He felt he had served sixteen months of hell in a war that no one understood.

The following morning there was a roll call for the men whose time was up. It was rainy that morning. Soaking wet, Quiet stood in formation, along with two thousand other men. The master sergeant held a list of names of the men who were leaving Vietnam the next day. He called the names out in alphabetical order. They were to turn in their weapons and army issues, then report back to their tents for further orders.

The sergeant was more than halfway down the list on the second page before he got to Quiet's name. When Quiet heard his name called, he went back to his tent, collected his army issues, and headed for the supply tent. In the supply tent another sergeant sitting in front of the entrance was checking off the men's equipment as they brought it to be turned in.

Standing in front of the sergeant's desk for a long period of time, Quiet stared down at his weapon. While the sergeant was checking off the list of equipment Quiet had brought in, Quiet mumbled, "I don't ever want to hold another weapon in my hands again."

The sergeant at the desk told him, "Take a long look around, cause it'll be your last; you're going home."

Quiet was in a daze. But when he heard the word "home," he came back to the present. *Home, he thought, is a good word.* Quiet handed the sergeant his rifle, then went back to his tent.

Quiet relaxed in his tent for the rest of the day, waiting for the next roll call. It came about ten o'clock that night. This roll call was for the men to board an army bus bound for the Tung-sun Nu airfield to catch their flight.

When the bus pulled onto the airfield, Quiet saw a

planeload of troops just getting off the plane as he was getting off the bus. A few of the servicemen were teasing the new recruits; Quiet felt only sorrow for them. *They don't know what they're getting themselves into,* he thought.

Moments after the jet took to the sky, a few of the servicemen began to compare experiences they had had in Vietnam. Many of them stretched the truth. Quiet felt he could tell which ones had had any actual experience with the Vietcong and which ones hadn't. The latter were silent. While listening to the smooth-running sound of the engine, Quiet laid his head back and looked out the window.

The plane was above the clouds, soaring through the air. *What would it be like if men could walk on clouds?* he wondered. The clouds looked like cotton. But yet it rained hard. The wind banged against the windows. In the distance, lightning streaked across the sky. It was the one thing that put fear in Quiet's bones. Farther away, the sun was trying to peek through the clouds, but the clouds refused to let it shine. Up here Quiet felt he was almost in heaven, but yet so far away. *Where is heaven?* he asked himself, *if it's not on earth?*

In the dark, like a flying spaceship, another plane was carrying a load of troops, but in the opposite direction. The jet was heading for Vietnam. Once again Quiet felt sorry for the men who were going to replace the ones going home. A tear rolled down his cheek. All Quiet wanted to do now was go home.

After ten hours of flying, the jet landed in Honolulu, Hawaii for refueling. When the jet stopped, most of the servicemen got off to look around. The pilot announced that the stop would be for at least six hours. The mechanic had to check the jet over and give the engines time to cool off. So Quiet went to sleep.

After eighteen hours of flying, the jet finally landed at Travis Air Force Base, just outside San Francisco, California. There were 350 servicemen aboard. When the jet landed, Quiet and the other servicemen debarked. They formed a line in front of a large building. Inside the building were six tables for the men who were being discharged from the army. After getting his discharge papers, Quiet was put in another group of men who lived north of California. Those living in Portland, Olympia, Tacoma, and Seattle were to be cleared at a base in Washington, Fort Lewis. They boarded a bus that would take them to the San Francisco airport. There they caught another flight to the Sea-Tac Airport, which was located in Washington between Seattle and Tacoma.

Once again Quiet was in the air, but for the last time. The jet flew along the coast. Over the mountaintops you could hear the jet cutting through the wind. The windows were covered with streaking rain. Below, fishing boats were scattered along the coast. The waves were as high as rooftops. Every so often the jet would jerk and a lump would rise in Quiet's throat. It went down again when the jet settled.

After about three and a half hours of flying, the jet landed at the Sea-Tac Airport, where a bus for Fort Lewis was waiting. As Quiet was getting off the jet he saw a squad of police and security officers on the grounds. A curious expression came over his face. He boarded the bus. From there the bus drove the servicemen to Fort Lewis Army Base, about twenty miles from the airport. When the bus pulled onto the army base, it stopped in front of a building. Once again Quiet joined a line in front of the building. It was longer than the one at Travis Air Force Base; it extended from the building to the outside on the sidewalk and on around the corner. Quiet wondered where all these people had come from. He figured he would be standing in line for a long time. Inside the building there were two tables for clearance. Quiet got to it that morning; he didn't get cleared until later that afternoon.

When Quiet and a few servicemen finished signing their clearance papers, Quiet went outside and walked to the Greyhound bus depot, located on the other side of the base. A bus left the depot for Seattle approximately every forty-five minutes. Quiet waited in the depot about an hour till the bus arrived. Seventeen passengers boarded the bus for Seattle. Twenty passengers were going to Tacoma.

Fort Lewis was about forty miles south of Seattle. Tacoma was about thirty miles from Seattle. The bus left the depot, and it took about twenty minutes for the bus to pull into the depot in Tacoma. It stayed about fifteen minutes before continuing to Seattle.

Tacoma, a brother city to Seattle. Going through Tacoma, Quiet noticed quite a few changes in parts of the city. A vacant lot on the outskirts of town, where neighborhood kids used to play ball, was being built upon. Quiet and his team used to come to Tacoma and play a Tacoma team in that vacant lot during his high school years. The cities around Tacoma seemed to be growing. Buildings were being put up everywhere.

Two years had gone by, and the few cities seemed to have grown into almost a space age.

The bus was traveling on Interstate 5, a main freeway that runs from the Canadian/Washington border to the border between California and Mexico on the West Coast. To the sides of the highway were mileage signs telling drivers how far away they were from the next major city. Quiet looked out the window. A sign read: 16 MILES FROM SEATTLE. The exit was for Kent and Des Moines. From the freeway you could see bits and pieces of the Kent Valley. Trees obscured most of the view.

Kent Valley used to be farmland. As the bus rolled through Kent city limits, Quiet saw quite a few buildings sitting on the former farmlands. As a young boy Quiet used to come to the Kent Valley with friends or with his family, to pick the vegetables and strawberries for the farmers to take to market. The money Quiet made from picking the vegetables helped out the family, 'cause they were poor. At times Quiet had enough money left over for dances and dates. But the farmlands were no more.

Many parts of the farmlands had new office buildings sitting on them. Big businesses had bought up the farmlands and placed their establishments there.

Looking east toward the distant clouds he saw the Cascade mountain range. It ran from Canada to California. Quiet could remember, when he was growing up, the many weekends his father took him to the mountains, him and his three brothers. But none of the three other brothers was as interested in nature as Quiet was. So Mr. Jones, Quiet's father, never took them as often. Mr. Jones and Quiet went on many camping and fishing trips. Along with them went a big German shepherd named Shep. The dog was owned by Mr. Jones.

Quiet could remember the first time he saw Shep. Mr. Jones was coming home from work one night around midnight when he saw a black movement in the street, just up ahead in the neighborhood. The little black puppy was under Mr. Jones's truck before he came to a screeching halt. For a split second Mr. Jones thought he ran over the little puppy. But when he got out of his truck the puppy ran up to Mr. Jones, being friendly, and the man started playing with him. The puppy couldn't have been more than a few weeks old. By the way the dog was acting, Mr. Jones could tell the puppy wasn't weaned yet. So Mr. Jones picked the puppy up and put him in the truck. He took the puppy home. One of Quiet's older brothers, Earl, named the puppy Shep. The puppy grew into a large black shepherd. Not a speck of white showed anywhere. Later, Mr. Jones discovered that one of his friend's dogs had had a litter and one of the puppies was missing. Out of good faith, Mr. Jones's friend let him keep the dog.

With Shep along for the journey, Quiet felt safe. On two incidents Quiet remembered Shep got him out of trouble. One summer Quiet and Mr. Jones went camping for the Labor Day weekend. Mr. Jones had taken a week off, so he could spend three days of it in the mountains, fishing and hiking. Quiet's three brothers stayed home with Mrs. Jones. Mr. Jones, with Quiet's help, set up a tent near a rapid-running river where they had camped many times. They spent the rest of the day fishing. Early the next morning, before sunrise, Quiet soundlessly got up and dressed and went outside the tent. The morning was cold. But it seemed it would be a warm day. He wanted to take a short hike before Mr. Jones woke up. When Quiet got a few yards away from camp, Shep tried to follow, but Quiet sent him back, then continued. Without realizing it, Quiet was soon quite a ways from the tent. As the sun was beginning to make more of an appearance, he felt the day warming up.

Quiet knew better than to go off into the woods alone, being aware of the dangers they possessed. But many times Quiet had gone off into the woods alone and had never been inflicted with anything he couldn't handle. But this was the farthest he had ever gone away from camp.

Quiet walked through the woods until he came to a small clearing. The cold was beginning to burn away as he went and sat down on a large rock that overlooked a valley. There were many trees in the valley, with a river running between them. On the other side of the valley, mountains peeked through the clouds. *This is beautiful country,* he thought, *God's country. The wealth of people will ruin it, like they almost did to the plains buffalo. It would have happened if the government hadn't stepped in and stopped the slaughter.*

As Quiet sat at the edge of the clearing admiring the countryside, he heard the snap of a twig behind him. Quickly he turned around and saw a cougar slowly approaching him. When Quiet saw the cougar he quickly got up and picked up a stick and pointed it at the cougar. The cougar paused for a moment when he saw the stick, then showed his fangs. Moving from side to side, the cougar began to come closer. Quiet held the stick pointed at the cougar until he stopped at the tip of the stick. When the cougar advanced, Quiet poked the cougar a couple of times to make him back off. The cougar took a couple of swats at the stick as he backed away. Again the cougar growled as he took a couple more swats at the stick. Then the cougar tried to circle Quiet, but he managed to keep the cougar in front of him.

As the cougar became more aggressive, there was another crackle in the woods. When Quiet first heard the snap, he thought it might be the cougar's mate to come and give assistance. Quiet knew he was in trouble. But then he heard a couple of barks. This made Quiet feel more at ease. It was Shep coming to his rescue.

When Shep made his appearance, the cougar ran and jumped on a high rock. Shep ran to the rock and started barking. He tried to jump up on the rock, but it was too high. As Shep made one leap after another, the cougar could see that the dog was almost reaching the top, so he began to try to keep Shep from jumping too high by striking at him. But when Shep went back to the ground to attempt another jump, the cougar tried to jump on Shep's back. Shep moved away when the cougar missed and attacked.

As Shep attacked, the cougar met him with fangs and claws. The cougar nicked Shep on the nose, then chased Shep around the clearing. When the cougar came too close, Shep quickly turned around and went at the cougar, cutting him across the nose and taking a nick out of his ear. This made the cougar give Shep respect. But Shep didn't come out of the entanglement unmarked either. He had a scratch on his left side and a scratch mark down the middle of his face. The cougar also gained respect from the black beast.

Around the neighborhood, Shep was known for killing alley cats. But the cougar was the biggest neighborhood cat he had ever seen. Shep knew he had to put all his experience together to fight this big cat. This cat was bigger, stronger, and faster than the other cats Shep had faced.

With a number of barks, using his body as a shield, Shep intimidated the cougar while trying to catch his tail. The cougar spun around and came at Shep with teeth and claws. But Shep moved back and from side to side and nicked the cougar on his ear. Once again Shep gained respect from the cougar. For the few moments the two animals tussled, the cougar knew there was also a person in the area. To the cougar, man meant weapons.

The cougar made his attack on Shep by rushing him again and again with teeth and claws. This forced Shep to move back again and again and maneuver from side to side to find a way to counterattack. But the cougar's attacks caused Shep to get off balance and gave the cougar just enough time to make an escape, by jumping up on a large rock, then jumping up on one rock after another, each one higher than the previous one. Shep tried to follow the cougar until he saw him heading up the mountain at top speed.

In all Shep's fights, Quiet had never seen him so angry. Shep seemed as though he had a hatred for cats. Seeing Shep trying to follow the cougar up the high rocks, Quiet called him back. Shep hesitated for a short moment, then came back off the rocks. They headed back to camp. When Quiet got back to camp, he had some explaining to do when Mr. Jones saw the scratches on Shep's face and body. Mr. Jones made it plain to Quiet that he was never to leave camp alone again.

The second incident came about two years later, when Quiet was about fourteen. It was on another warm summer day when Quiet and Mr. Jones had gone to the same river fishing for trout. It was late afternoon and Quiet and Mr. Jones were in the river fishing when a bear cub wandered into camp. Shep saw the cub and started playing with it. The cub looked to be about four to six months old. To Quiet, that meant the mother bear wasn't too far away. So Quiet decided to take the cub far away from the camp before the mother bear came looking for it.

Quiet rushed out of the river and tried to get the bear cub. The cub resisted until Quiet managed to get a hold on it, the cub constantly calling for its mother. Quiet started running with the bear cub in the opposite direction from where the cub had been and to the nearest part of the woods. Quiet was about fifty yards away from camp when he saw the mother bear come charging out of the woods from where the cub came. Then he heard Mr. Jones holler, "Put the cub down. Put the cub down, Son!" But the only thing Quiet wanted to do was get the bear cub far away from camp.

When Quiet neared the woods, he heard his father holler again, "Drop the cub! The mother is coming after you." But Quiet never missed a stride. When he got to the woods he dropped the cub and headed in the other direction, looking for an easy tree to climb. But the mother bear was gaining too fast. So Quiet felt he had to run for it unaware that when the black bear made her appearance, charging out of the woods, Shep had already made his move. Shep was following Quiet with the cub when he heard Mr. Jones call. As the bear came charging, at first sight Shep crossed in front of her at top speed. But that didn't draw the bear's attention away from Quiet. Shep turned and went at the bear again, but this time he crossed in front of the bear and cut her on the nose. The bear became angry and went after Shep. He attacked the bear as though she were another dog and got slapped. The power in her slap wasn't like anything he had felt before. When Shep hit the ground he recovered quickly before the bear came to finish him off.

From a distance Shep heard a voice. "Get away from her, Shep!" It was Quiet's voice.

When the bear heard Quiet's voice she went charging again. The next time Shep came between Quiet and the bear, the dog distracted her with irritating barks. This gave Mr. Jones enough time to come out of the river, go into his tent, and get his 30-30 Winchester rifle. When he came out he fired a couple

13

of shots over the bear's head. When the bear felt the wind of the bullets she headed back to the woods to join her cub. . . .

By this time the bus had reached the Seattle city limits. Up ahead on the freeway was a sign that said: MEN AT WORK. DETOUR! An arrow pointed the way through town. As the bus continued through town, Quiet noticed many new buildings being built on the south end. "This town has sure changed a lot since I've been away," he mumbled.

The Greyhound bus finally pulled into the depot. Quiet and the other passengers got off the bus, went into the baggage claims department, and got their luggage. Some of the passengers went into the lobby, but Quiet went outside. There he saw quite a few cabs parked in front of the depot. Most of them were the Yellow and the Farwest cab companies. He took a Yellow cab to where he had once lived.

Before being inducted into the service, Quiet had been living with his three brothers in their parents' house. At that time Quiet was twenty-one. At the age of eighteen he had lost his father to cancer. Two years later, Mrs. Jones also died of cancer. They were buried in the Evergreen Cemetery in Renton. Every year the four brothers visited the graves on Memorial Day. The parents were buried beside each other. Quiet could remember what his father had told him and his three brothers on his deathbed: "I don't want you four brothers fighting among one another. I want you four to always stick together and to share and share alike." The words seemed as though they were uttered only yesterday. At this time Quiet was twenty-four.

The cabdriver drove through town. The sun faded behind the clouds. The day was becoming gray. That was the sign of a rainstorm coming. Light drizzle began to fall. People rushed every which way trying to get out of the coming bad weather. Dark clouds began to obscure the view of the tall buildings. All of a sudden there was a streak of lightning. Then came the thunder. Rain started pouring. In a few minutes people who couldn't get out of the rain would be soaked before they got where they were going.

When the cab reached the outskirts of town, the clouds had hidden the view of the Olympia Mountains. Only one mountain stayed in view of the city: Mount Rainier, its peak revealed through the clouds, Washington State's most famous mountain. Most people loved it during the spring and summer season for camping picnicking, hiking, and barbecuing. Mount Rainier also had other recreation. In certain parts of these seasons, it was good for hunting deer, elk, and black bear.

As the cab was getting closer to home, Quiet began to wonder about his three brothers and how they were getting along. *They will be surprised to see me, I know,* he thought. *Have they changed since I've been gone? Or are they still the same? When I left they were hot-tempered and ready to fight, though they were never rowdy. I wonder if life has been good to them and made them slow down some. My brothers never caused anyone any trouble; they just never knew how to run from it. I used to be the same way, until I went into the army. That slowed me down a lot,* he thought.

Leaving the bus depot, Quiet had told the cabdriver to take the downtown route. It was a longer route, but for some reason Quiet wanted to see how much of the downtown area had changed. Where there were once houses, trees, and waterfront now small office buildings were sitting. From one end of town to the other was all business, no more residences. Going up Jackson Street was the same as downtown. The only residences left were apartments, just a few, and hotels. A freeway bridge ran overhead, and new unfinished bridges were being constructed from the downtown area to the Floating Bridge. That route would run past Quiet's address.

Quiet's home was located on the lower part of the Beacon Hill district, where a residential street led to the Floating Bridge. When the cabdriver pulled up in front of Quiet's home, Quiet got out. The meter on the cab read: "$10.95." Quiet paid the fare and gave the driver a five-dollar tip. The cabdriver helped Quiet with his bag, then got back in his cab and drove away.

After the cab pulled away and went around the corner, Quiet stood in the middle of the street, looking at the house. It hadn't changed much, though it looked as though someone had taken the time to do some remodeling. It didn't look old anymore. The original color was still there, red like a barn. Quiet picked up his bag and headed toward the house and up the thirteen stairs from the street, then on up the stairs to the house. When Quiet got up on the porch he rang the doorbell but got no answer. He didn't have a key, 'cause he had given it to his brother Wyatt when he went into the service.

As Quiet sat down on the porch the rain had stopped. But the streets were still wet. Slowly, night was coming. Traffic with its headlights was running up and down the streets. He looked down at the neighborhood street. Once again Quiet went back into his memory bank. When he was a young boy, the street had never had a heavy flow of traffic. Up and down the blocks, neighborhood kids used to play ball of all kinds in the street. Quiet could still hear his mother's voice telling him and the other kids to stop playing in the street. But the street was the nearest place around to play any type of games. Other kids from other neighborhoods, mainly from across town, would bring their dogs over to fight Shep, who was a good fighter. He never lost a fight. He was well known in the Beacon Hill area for whipping dogs brought up against him. But Quiet was careful not to let Mr. Jones know about it. It would mean the belt for the boy. Now, cars used the street as a thoroughfare. It wasn't safe for kids to play in streets anymore. But yet a few still did.

It's a good thing the porch has a roof, thought Quiet, because the rain was beginning to come down heavily again. So Quiet got up off the steps and walked underneath the roof. He walked over to the banister and placed his hands on it. Through

16

the mist of rain he got a good view of Franklin High School. He remembered the first day he started school. In 1963 there were only fifty-one blacks there, including teachers. The rest were whites, Orientals, and a few Filipinos and Spanish. A few whites were hassling some blacks who started at Franklin that year.

Quiet remembered that morning he went though the process of enrolling in his new classes. When lunchtime came, he was stopped outside by three whites as he was on his way to a hamburger place. This place was the Beanery, where many students went when they didn't go to the lunchroom inside the school building. The Beanery was just across the street. The tallest of the three whites did the talking. He tried to scare Quiet out of his lunch money. The scene had attracted a crowd of other students. Some of the whites who had come to Franklin with Quiet from junior high knew of his reputation for fighting and knew what to expect. When one white grabbed Quiet by his collar, he expected his two companions to back him up. But Quiet quickly dropped the white student with a punch to the midsection and a three-way combination that sent him on his back. When the other two students saw this, they backed off. Then Quiet continued on to the Beanery.

Later that afternoon when school came to an end, Quiet was at his locker putting a book away when a neighborhood friend approached him. His name was Louie, and he was an Italian boy Quiet had grown up with. Louie lived down the street from Quiet. Quiet smiled when Louie came up to him, but the grin faded away when he saw the expression on Louie's face. "What's up?" Quiet asked.

"Three white boys are going to beat up on Earl, because they saw him talking to a white girl in the hallway. They're waiting for him down on the football field. Earl was still in the gym when I saw him a few minutes ago."

While Quiet was in action in Vietnam, Earl had written Quiet, telling him of Louie's death. Louie's death came in action just three months after he came in country. The night Louie was to catch a flight to Vietnam, he had stopped by Quiet's home and had a talk with Quiet's three brothers. Louie was sad. Quiet was almost ready to come home, and Louie was about to leave. The three brothers sympathized with him, 'cause Quiet had felt the same way about leaving Louie when he had to go.

Quiet didn't say a word as he closed his locker and let Louie lead the way. The gym was about a half a block down the hill from the school. When they got outside it, they saw the three white students standing at the top of the steps leading down to the track and football field. Louie pointed at them, and Quiet started walking toward them. When Quiet got to the first set of steps that led to the gym, Earl was just coming through the doorway. He didn't look Quiet's way as he headed toward the football field. Going across the football field was a shortcut to going home. Earl took this route every day.

As Earl approached the steps that led to the football field, the leader of the three whites stepped in his path. "You was talking to a white girl. We're going to teach you niggers to stay with your own kind," he said as he grabbed Earl by his collar. Before the white student had a chance to say another word, Earl punched him in the stomach and an uppercut followed and the student went down. When Earl did this, the other two whites went at him and started throwing punches.

While Earl was fighting off the two whites, Quiet and Louie came off the steps and went to his aid. When Quiet got up on one of the whites, he grabbed him by his hair, pulled his head back, and threw a number of punches that left him motionless. At the same instant Louie had the other white on his back and was putting his foot in his face. "Mashed potatoes," Louie was saying repeatedly. As for Earl, he had no problem with his opponent. He was already sleeping. The fight was over; the three students went home. The students on the football field never noticed the incident.

Once again the rain had slacked off. The traffic was thinning out. Streetlights came on. When Quiet came back to the present he scanned his eyes toward Mount Baker Hill District and on toward the tunnel that led to the Floating Bridge. For many summers as far back as he could remember, Quiet, with a few friends, had walked through the tunnel going to the Mount Baker Beach. Around summertime it was always full of people. Some went to swim and some to take a sunbath but got burned in return.

The rain had finally stopped. Puddles of water had left traces in the front yard. The streets were wet. As the dark began to fall, the streetlights became brighter. Just then, a brown '65 Chevrolet pulled up near the curb in front of the house. Curiously Quiet looked at the car. He felt it might be a friend of one of his brothers, but when the person got out of the car, it was Quiet's younger brother, Wyatt.

Wyatt was five feet, eleven inches in height. Two years younger than Quiet, he weighed about 165 to 170 pounds. He had a nice complexion with a neat natural. Wyatt got out of the car and walked toward the house. But when he got to the bottom of the stairs, he saw Quiet on the porch. "Hi, Bro!" Wyatt said joyously. "When did you get back?" He rushed up the stairs. "You're good for surprises." When Wyatt got up on the porch, the two brothers looked at one another for a split second. They smiled, then hugged one another. "Glad you're home. Let's go in so you can take them army duds off and get comfortable." Wyatt unlocked the door, and both went into the house.

When they got inside, Wyatt noticed Quiet looking at the portrait of his brothers from when they were younger. "Earl and Clinton are sure going to be glad to see you."

"Where are they?" asked Quiet.

"They're married, you know," said Wyatt, "but they always come by. They'll be by sometime tonight." But then Wyatt changed the subject. "Want to go to a party? Or have you forgotten how to dance?"

"You never forget what you really learn," Quiet said as they went from the living room to the kitchen. "Whatcha got to munch on?"

"You know we never cooked for ourselves. Our women do most of our cooking."

As Quiet was going through the cupboards and refrigerator, he saw they were almost bare. "Yeah! I see what you mean. I'll go to the store and get some groceries."

"No need, Bro! I'll go. Just tell me what you want," Wyatt volunteered.

"Just food. Now I'm going to take a bath," said Quiet as he went into the bathroom. After Wyatt left the house, Quiet started running his bathwater. As the tub was filling up he took off his clothes and lay in the water.

About an hour later, when Quiet was done taking his bath, Wyatt had just walked through the door. "I got some chicken to fry," he said as he put the groceries on the kitchen counter. As Wyatt dumped the groceries on the counter, Quiet saw a box of rice, a loaf of bread, a little jar of coffee, and other small items.

"I didn't mean for you to go shopping. I just wanted something simple. What about something to wear?" Quiet asked as he came into the kitchen with a bathrobe on.

"Hold on while I find you something," said Wyatt as he walked out of the kitchen and headed for his bedroom. Moments later he came back with a pair of brown dress slacks, a casual sweater, and a pair of stylish black leather shoes. "Put these on," he said. "We're going to that party tonight."

While changing into the clothes, Quiet said, "I see a lot of changes since I've been away, including the remodeling of the house." Then he went to the cupboard and pulled out some cooking utensils and set them on top of the stove.

"Since you've been away, the city's been growing, Bro!

Most of the businesses came from out-of-state, like New York, California, and Colorado. But even with all these jobs going around, it been even harder for blacks to get a decent job. I work at the Boeing plant in Renton. I went to school to become a machinist, but my supervisor has me keep the metal shavings off the machines and keep the floor swept. The whites do the machinery work. I feel like a flunky."

"Have you talked to your supervisor about this?"

"Yes, but he says there's nothing he can do. I even went to my supervisor's boss. And he agreed with my supervisor. They both believe that I'm too incompetent to operate the machines."

"Why don't you just quit and get another job?"

"It's not that easy for a black man, Bro! A black woman has a better chance of getting a job than a black man. You've been away too long. Not only the city has changed, but the people, too. Wait till you've lived here awhile. Then you'll understand what I'm saying."

"I understand exactly what you're saying," said Quiet disgustedly. "There's almost every type of person in the service you'll meet. I know how people are. I just hope the police department hasn't gotten any worse."

"Worse isn't the word for it. The way the police department enforces the law, we don't need the police; what we need are vigilantes. In '66, after you went into the army, the police went on a black-killing spree. You remember Charles Davis?" Quiet nodded. "Right! He got gunned down in the downtown area. The newspaper said the police report indicated that he attempted to rob a bank not far from the police department. That's like committing suicide."

"Was he trying to rob a bank?" asked Quiet curiously.

"Charles had better sense than that. You remember Johnny Washington? He got killed in a car wreck trying to outrun the police."

"Why were the cops chasing him?" interrupted Quiet.

"A traffic warrant was issued against him," answered Wyatt. "All he had to do was pay the traffic ticket," added Quiet. "Then none of that might've happened."

"Okay," Wyatt said, smirking. "You don't believe the police are as bad as I think. Remember your good friend Billy Williams?" At the name "Billy Williams" a hard lump clogged Quiet's throat. "He's dead, too. Shot in the back trying to attack a cop with a knife."

"Attacking a cop with a knife," repeated Quiet doubtfully. "I've never known Billy to ever use a weapon. He hated weapons. He was no troublemaker. You know how it really happened?"

Wyatt walked over to the kitchen counter, opened up a cupboard door that was over the water faucet, pulled out a glass, and got himself a glass of water. "Yeah! I know, Bro!" he said sadly. "Billy didn't have a knife. But that's what the police put in their report.

"Clinton and Earl work at the Urban League office trying to get blacks into the trade unions. Most of the trade unions deny blacks because they say blacks are incompetent. So Clinton and Earl's office called a rally at the Volunteer Park one weekend. The police called the rally unsanctioned, so they came in to break it up. Two cops jumped Clinton. They were trying to beat him up and take him to jail downtown. Billy pulled one of the cops off of Clint, and another cop shot him in the back. Billy was trying to keep Clinton from getting hurt."

"Was there an investigation of the incident?" Quiet asked curiously.

"Yes," said Wyatt angrily. "The inquiry justified the cop shooting. They believed the policeman's life was in jeopardy."

For a split second Quiet became hatefully angry and just such an expression came over his face as Wyatt noticed. Then slowly it faded away. Billy Williams had been another neighborhood friend raised on the same block as Quiet and his three brothers. Billy used to live a few houses up the street and around the bend.

Slowly Quiet walked out of the kitchen and went into the living room and sat down on the couch. He leaned his head back and trained his eyes on the ceiling. Then his thoughts went back to his childhood days with Billy, who was one of the few kids at school who gave Quiet respect and wanted to be his friend. At this time Quiet was in the fourth grade. While Quiet was growing up, a few of the kids in the neighborhood and in school used to pick on him and make fun of him whenever they felt distressed. One late spring, a week before summer vacation, Quiet got into a fight with a sixth-grader named Dino, known around the school as a bully who took advantage of younger kids. That morning Dino's mother gave him a dollar to buy his lunch. The change he had left over Dino spent.

Mrs. Jones had given Quiet a dollar bill to buy his lunch also. The change Quiet had left over he was going to take home. But later that day after school, Quiet and Billy were walking home, about a block away from the school, when they saw Dino and two of his friends coming from around a parked car across the street. Dino had been stopping kids going that way ever since school got out. Dino approached Quiet and grabbed him by his shirt collar and demanded, "I want your money."

"This is my mother's money. I can't give you that," said Quiet, frightened. "I'll get a whipping."

"I don't care whose money it is. I want it." Then he punched Quiet in the stomach. As Quiet doubled over, Dino said, "Are you going to give it to me, or do I have to take it?"

"Why don't you leave him alone?" said Billy, who was standing next to Quiet. "He told you the money belongs to his mother."

Dino turned to his two friends. "You two keep that one's mouth shut, while I work on this one."

The two boys walked over to Billy and stood on either side

of him. When they did this Billy took his books and bashed the boy on his right in the face and threw a left hook at the boy on his left. After they started fighting, the two boys wrestled Billy to the ground. When this happened Quiet ducked his head and rammed Dino in the stomach. As Dino doubled over, Quiet gave him an uppercut, which sent Dino sailing backward. For the short moment Dino was put out of commission Quiet went and pulled one of the boys off Billy and punched him in the eye. Billy rolled on top of the other boy and punched him in the nose. When Quiet and Billy got back on their feet they started running down the hill, rocks following them. . . . Quiet remembered Billy was always a happy-go-lucky fellow, always jolly.

About forty-five minutes later, Wyatt came into the living room. "The food is ready," he said. "Want me to fix you a plate?"

Quiet sighed as he looked out the window. It was pitch-black. The windows were steamed. Only spots of lights showed that the streetlights were on. A light drizzle pattered against the windowsill. The sound of the wind whistled through the trees. Still a few cars were driving up and down the slushy streets. Although the night was young, most people were getting ready for the weekend. Some were getting ready for a night out, and some were staying home watching television.

Quiet slowly rose off the couch and walked to the kitchen table. Wyatt thought he knew what was bothering him. Wyatt felt the death of Billy Williams had shaken Quiet. Wyatt sympathized with him.

"I can't go to the party with you tonight. I don't feel up to it," Quiet said.

"Sure, Bro!" Wyatt assured him. "I understand. Well . . . Anyway, how has it been with you?"

"Pretty good, I guess," said Quiet disgustedly.

Around nine o'clock Wyatt left for the party. Quiet stayed

home and watched television. The television was upstairs in the middle room.

The upstairs had three rooms: a back bedroom, a middle bedroom, and a front bedroom. The middle bedroom had always been used as a recreation room. When they were kids, Clinton had the back bedroom and Earl slept in the front bedroom. Quiet and Wyatt slept in the bedroom downstairs, next to their parents' bedroom, just to the side of the front door from where the living room lay adjoining the dining room. A hallway led to the kitchen on the right side and the bathroom to the left. But since the boys had grown up, Quiet had kept his old room, Wyatt had moved into his parents' bedroom, and Clinton and Earl got married and moved out.

While watching television, Quiet fell asleep on the couch, where he was stretched out. About three o'clock the next morning he felt someone shaking him. Slowly Quiet opened his eyes and saw two blurry male figures standing over him. When his vision cleared, he recognized Earl and Clinton.

Clinton was about six feet, two inches tall and weighed about 195 pounds. He was the oldest of the four brothers, four years older than Quiet. Usually Clinton wore a suit. His complexion was about the same as Wyatt's.

Earl was two years older than Quiet, with a well-blended complexion also. He was six feet tall and weighed about 185 pounds. All four brothers wore neat naturals.

"Hi, Bro!" said Clinton as he sat down beside Quiet on the couch. "I saw Wyatt earlier. He told me you were back. How have things been?"

Quiet, sounding exhausted as he slowly rose off the couch, said "Good! Good!" as he rubbed his face. "Where's Wyatt?"

"Probably with his lady." Clinton paused for a moment. "Now that you're back, what are you going to do with yourself?"

Quiet leaned his head back against the couch. "I don't

know yet," he said tiredly. "Maybe try and get my old job back at Boeing. I'll see come Monday morning."

"Things have changed since you've been away," said Earl as he came into the conversation. "Ever since Martin Luther King started the black movement, it's been harder for blacks to get jobs and keep them. You know that as well as I do. Best you try and keep the one you have at Boeing unless you find something better. A few blacks are forced back to the streets, those who had jobs and lost them. And those who were already in the street went to jail or prison for some type of crime. Robbery, burglary, you name it. It seems that the whites are trying to get as many blacks off the streets as they can. And some of these dumb blacks can't see it. Some of them don't think of coming to us unless they get in trouble, when we ask them for support."

"And those who don't go to jail or prison usually end up in a pine box with a cop's bullet in them," added Clinton as he came back into the conversation.

"I know what you're saying, Clint, Earl!" said Quiet. "I heard what happened to Billy. Wyatt told me."

Clinton and Earl stayed up the rest of the night with Quiet, telling him about other incidents that had happened while he was away.

Clinton and Earl lived on the other side of town, known as the CD (Central District). Clinton lived on Twenty-fifth and Denney, an all-black neighborhood. Earl lived two blocks away on Twenty-seventh and Denney, four houses down from the corner. Clinton and Earl worked at the Urban League, an organization begun to help get blacks in trade unions. When there was discrimination on these jobs, the black workers turned their complaints in to Clinton and Earl's office and they filed a grievance with the National Labor Relations Board (NLRB). Then the Board would take the grievance to the courts.

2

Came Monday morning around nine o'clock, Quiet caught a bus downtown, to the Boeing employment office, located on Second and University Avenue. When Quiet walked into the office, he approached the information desk. The Boeing employment office was about the size of an auditorium. It was full of people. All the chairs were in use. Some of the people had to stand against the walls. Most of them were blacks, ages ranging from eighteen to sixty. The rest were whites, Orientals, and Mexicans.

A short middle-aged bald man was sitting behind the desk, a few gray strands of hair just above his ears. He wore thick glasses with black frames. The man didn't raise his head but said, "We're pretty well filled right now."

"I want to fill out an application," said Quiet.

"What are you applying for?" he asked sarcastically.

Trying to keep his composure, Quiet said, "I want my old job back. Machinist."

"Whatcha do? Get fired or laid off?" the man smirked.

"Neither. I was drafted into the service." Although Quiet had understood what his brothers told him about the situation blacks were in, he hadn't realized it was this bad. He felt he hadn't given the middle-aged man a reason to be sarcastic with him. Anger was burning Quiet's insides up. He wondered how a person like this bald guy got a job like this serving the public.

"This what you want, boy?" said the man smartly as he gave Quiet an application. "This is for rehires. Take it over to that table and fill it out," he said as he pointed. "And put it on the receptionist's desk when you leave."

Quiet took the application from the information clerk, went to a table and filled it out. When he was done filling out the application he laid it on the receptionist's desk. Then he went back to the information clerk, said, "If I didn't know any better, I'd have thought you were being nasty," and left the employment office.

When Quiet got outside the building he walked back to the bus stop. There were quite a few people standing there. It was around noon, and the day was humid. People walked up and down the streets, women with their knee-highs and low-cut shoes. Some were going to lunch, and some were going back to work. From two blocks away Quiet saw his bus coming. His mind became full of thought, and he felt that he needed to go somewhere and think. When the bus came, passengers boarded. After the last passenger boarded, the bus waited for Quiet, who looked at the bus driver for a short moment, then waved him on. Feeling disgusted, Quiet started walking down the street.

Many times as small boys Quiet and a few neighborhood friends had walked from their homes to the downtown area. During those times it was all fun and games to run into stores causing some disturbances with the customers and the employees, then getting chased out. But when they got a chance, they would take a few items, like candy, toys, or whatever seemed easy. Quiet was never known for taking big chances. At times he would get caught by the police and taken to the youth center, a place where juveniles were kept. The white friends Quiet was with would be taken by the police either to their homes or to the outskirts of town and then sent home. Quiet's parents would always pick him up from the youth center, and then Quiet would get punished for stealing or just for getting caught.

Quiet, walking through town, went past a few construction sites he had noticed riding in the cab. Counting all the construction workers, he saw there were many whites and a handful of blacks. On one particular construction site Quiet noticed a black laborer scooping up loads of trash off the ground and throwing it into a dumpster. The trash was supposed to be thrown from floors of a high-rise into a dumpster below, but some of the trash missed the dumpsters and landed on the ground. As the black laborer scooped a shovelful into the dumpster, dust began to fly. Some of the dust flew into a white carpenter's face. He became angry and walked over to the black, saying, "Watch where you're throwing that shit or I'll put you in it."

Walking one block after another, Quiet finally ended up in Chinatown, which wasn't too far from his home. Many days ago, as far back as Quiet could remember, Chinatown used to be part of his old stomping grounds. Many of his Oriental school buddies used to live in Chinatown. But as he was walking through Chinatown today, it seemed like none of it had changed. It still looked the same. Still the same type of people lingered there: drunks, bums, and Orientals.

When Quiet turned a corner he came in front of a Chinese theater that used to be called the Atlas. It used to be the cheapest show in town, showing a lot of good movies. He looked to see what was playing. The printing was in Chinese, but he understood what the movie was about by looking at the posters.

While Quiet stood in front of the theater looking at the titles, he heard shouting coming from down the street. A black in his late teens came running toward him, carrying two whole raw chickens in his hands. A middle-aged Chinese cook was chasing him with a meat cleaver, hollering something at the young black in Chinese.

From around the same corner came two Caucasian police

29

officers, running. They passed the Chinese. Then one of the police officers stopped and drew his pistol. When Quiet saw the police officer draw his pistol he ducked behind a parked car. When the young black came near, a number of shots were fired. The black staggered toward the parked car. Quiet slowly came from around the car and caught the youth before he fell to the ground. The black died in Quiet's arms. It seemed as though he hadn't eaten for days. Easily Quiet laid the body down.

When the two police officers came up to Quiet, the one who had done the shooting said, "Move away from him."

"If I don't, whatcha gonna do?" said Quiet angrily. "Shoot me, too?"

As the police officer held his pistol on Quiet, he asked, "Have you ever tried to use that on someone who could shoot back?"

With hate showing in his eyes, the police officer said, "Don't you sass me, boy!"

"If you don't know the difference between a man and a boy, go home and look at your kids," said Quiet, smirking.

The police officer started to attack Quiet as he stood his ground. But his partner stepped in between them and said to Quiet, "You'd better go."

As a crowd began to form, Quiet slowly backed away, then continued walking. *Killings in the streets are as bad as killings in Vietnam. Many people lost their loved ones there. Who'll cry for this one? And this is not Vietnam. I hated that place. But maybe the United States isn't any better. Sometimes I wonder,* he thought.

Two blocks up the street from Chinatown was the Bailey Gazzert Elementary School. Across the school was the school's asphalt playground, surrounded by a twelve-foot-high fence. Although he couldn't forget the killing of the black, Quiet was awakened from his dazed state by the voices of kids playing on the playground. As Quiet walked up near the fence, he noticed

30

three black youths arguing about who was going to bat first. This brought back an incident that had happened many years ago, when he was going to Coleman Elementary School. Coleman was located on Twenty-third and Atlantic.

Quiet was in the sixth grade at the time. He and a few of his classmates were on the playfield playing soccer when he kicked the ball to the sidelines. A bully from Washington Junior High named Leonard Thomas picked the ball up and started walking away with it.

Leonard Thomas, one of the school bullies when Quiet was going to Coleman, was put back a year to make up sixth grade. Now he was an eighth-grade student in junior high. Whenever Thomas felt angry about something, he would take it out on one of the younger kids.

When Leonard tried to walk away with the ball, Quiet ran over to him and said, "May I have the ball?"

"Take it," Leonard challenged him.

As the two students looked at one another, a teacher from another class, who was watching the incident, came over to the two students and said, "Is something the matter?"

"No," said Quiet as Leonard gave him the ball.

After the teacher walked away, Leonard looked at Quiet. "Don't be here after school," he threatened; then he walked away.

Later that afternoon when the school hours ended, Quiet went from his classroom to Wyatt's and waited for him in the hallway. The class was in the process of terminating. When the classroom door opened Wyatt was collecting his books. He would be the last student to leave the class. At the far end of the hallway Billy Williams was just coming down the stairs. Quiet went into the classroom and helped Wyatt get his books and the three students left the school building.

About three blocks away from school, down the hill, was a recreation center called the Deaconess. On Sundays nearby

31

neighbors used it as a church. A few of the kids from Coleman usually stopped there and played some type of ball games or some other type of game. Basketball was more popular than any other sport at the center, 'cause it had no football field. The basketball court was made of asphalt. Many kids stopped here before going home. Some kids would go home first and then come back.

On their way home Quiet, Billy, and Wyatt stopped at the center. They were playing basketball when Leonard and three other boys approached the basketball court. Quiet, Billy, and Wyatt were playing against three boys from Quiet's class when Leonard made his appearance. But when Quiet saw him, he stopped and walked to the center of the court.

As they stood before one another Leonard grabbed Quiet by his collar. "I said don't be around after school," he said as he punched Quiet in the stomach.

As Quiet stumbled backward and fell to the ground, he said, "You always needed help to pick on someone smaller than you."

"I won't need help to take care of you," Leonard challenged him.

The few moments Quiet stayed on the ground, he thought, *What did I get myself into? This guy is bigger than I am. How do you fight a person like this?* Then he remembered what Clinton said once: "Stay under a person bigger than you. It'll give him less of a target." So when Quiet got up off the ground he ducked his head and rammed Leonard in the stomach. As the two boys wrestled, Leonard tried to get leverage to take swings at Quiet. But Quiet kept a hold on Leonard's shoulders and pressed his body down on his. Leonard tried to push Quiet's head against the asphalt, but Quiet kept his head pressed into Leonard's chest.

As the two boys scuffled on the asphalt, Ike Zimmerman, a young supervisor for the recreation center, came out on the basketball court after he saw the fight from an upstairs window.

When Zimmerman came onto the court, he pulled the two boys apart, "What started this?" he demanded. Both boys were silent. As Zimmerman looked at them, they were breathing like locomotives. "If you two want to finish this, I have some boxing gloves inside." Quiet and Leonard agreed to put the boxing gloves on as Zimmerman led them into the building.

Inside the center the boys drew a crowd from the other students. When they took off their shirts, to Quiet Leonard didn't seem to be much bigger than he was. Although Leonard wasn't much taller, his shoulders were a little broader. The size of their arms was pretty much the same, which gave Quiet a little more confidence that he stood a chance of holding his own.

The two boys walked into the center of a floor mat. While Zimmerman was telling them the rules, Quiet remembered a few things Clinton had taught him the few times they had sparred: "Keep your jabs in your opponent's face. That will keep him off balance and make him telegraph his next move. Then you can counterattack it, like a pro." When Zimmerman was finished telling the boys the rules they went to their corners.

Zimmerman rang a small bell, and the boys came from their corners. Leonard rushed Quiet with a flurry of wild punches. Quiet ducked his head, then came up swinging back. When the two boys got in a clinch, Zimmerman separated them. Once again Leonard came at Quiet with a flurry of punches, but this time as Leonard came in, Quiet dropped him with a straight right. When this happened Quiet gained respect from Leonard, who got up off the canvas and started leading with his right. Quiet came over Leonard's right and once again dropped him to the canvas, with a left cross. When Leonard got back on his feet he started pawing Quiet with his left. But Quiet kept Leonard at bay with his jabs. As Leonard came in close, Quiet jabbed at his nose, then let a hard right cross follow.

The fight went on for seven rounds, and both boys were

33

exhausted. Zimmerman stopped the fight and called it a draw. From that day on Quiet and Leonard were friends. . . .

Quiet walked onto the playing field and approached the boys. "May I help?" he said with a smile.

At first sight of a strange man, the boys became a little frightened. But the sound of his voice made them feel he might be a friend.

Kids of many nationalities were playing together. A black youth who was at bat and refused to give up the bat said, "They won't play fair. I nicked the ball and he said he struck me out."

The pitcher was a white student. "I did strike him out."

"Wait a minute," interrupted Quiet. "Where's your umpire?"

The kids became silent for a moment. Then the pitcher spoke. "We don't have one."

"I'll tell you what," assured Quiet. "Suppose I be you guys' umpire."

The kids agreed and went back to playing ball. Quiet umpired for the kids until it was time for them to go back to class. But while the kids played ball, they accumulated a crowd from the other kids in school and the teachers. Normally the teachers didn't let any strangers mingle with the kids. But for some reason the kids seemed to be having more fun this time than they had ever had before.

At that moment Quiet felt good inside. He felt as though he was doing something he really liked for the first time since he'd been home. *This is where I should be,* he thought. *With kids. Maybe I can give them something no one had a chance to give me: a destiny. Kids of all nationalities can play all day without seeing colors. Only when they come home do their parents teach them prejudice. If there is a way I can find to change that, I will.* When the playing field was empty, Quiet went home.

When Quiet got home, he saw Wyatt sitting in the living room on the couch. "Why aren't you at work?" he asked.

"I got in a fight with a white boy," said Wyatt disgustedly as he got up and started walking toward the kitchen.

Quiet followed behind him. "What started it?" he asked curiously.

As Wyatt was going through the cupboards, he said, "I came in this morning a couple of minutes late, and my work partner, acting as though he was my boss, started threatening me about my job. Then he grabbed me by my shirt and pushed me into a table. So I let him have it."

"But we're not kids anymore. You're supposed to know how to get around that kind of stuff."

"What would you have done if someone put his hands on you?"

Quiet paused for a moment as he looked at Wyatt. "I don't know." He walked to the kitchen stove. "Now whatcha gonna do?"

"Find another job, I guess," said Wyatt grumpily, "go see my brothers. But I hate to depend on my family with something like this. Especially when I can do something for myself."

"Yeah," agreed Quiet. "I know what you mean." Then he walked out of the kitchen and went on upstairs. He lay back on the couch and stretched out, staring up at the ceiling. He lay there for a moment, then heard tires coming to a screeching halt in front of the house. Car doors were slamming. There were flurries of footsteps coming across the street, up the stairs, and around the house. For some reason this told Quiet that the police were outside. So he quickly jumped up off the couch and hurried downstairs. But by the time he got downstairs, Wyatt had already let the police into the house and they had put handcuffs on him. Wyatt's arms were behind his back.

"What did he do?" Quiet demanded.

There were four detectives and six uniformed police officers. "If you know what's good for you, you'll stay out of this," said one of the detectives who was leading Wyatt out the door.

"It took ten of you to come after him," said Quiet angrily. "What is he charged with?"

"Assault!" said a uniformed police officer.

"It's all right, Bro," said Wyatt reassuringly. "This way I'll be in jail for only a short while, then I'll be out. This way no one gets hurt. Take care of the house while I'm gone."

Seeing his brother being escorted to a squad car, Quiet felt helpless. He felt that there was nothing he could do. He remembered how once when he was thirteen Mr. Jones told him of certain incidents of whites coming into a black's house and taking away the son or father and lynching him in his own front yard or from a nearby tree. At times they were just carried off and that was the last you heard of them. Other blacks would just watch through door openings, curtains, or half-raised windows. They wouldn't help, 'cause they were afraid they might be next. Once the white police got a black downtown in the elevator, they were subject to getting beat up before they got upstairs to the jail.

Quiet watched the police and the detective cars pull away. *I'd better get some bail money,* he thought. So Quiet borrowed Wyatt's car and drove up to the Beacon Hill Pacific Bank, where he had his combat pay from Vietnam sent, and drew out some of his savings.

Meanwhile, when the police got Wyatt downtown two uniformed officers escorted him into a police elevator. The elevator was about halfway between the jail and the lobby when one of the police officers stopped it. When this happened Wyatt became frightened. "Whatcha stopping for?"

The police officer reached in his back pocket and pulled out a thin pair of gloves. "We're gonna teach you niggers about putting your hands on white people. You need to be taught some manners," he said as he grabbed Wyatt by his collar and threw a punch to his midsection. As Wyatt was going down, the other police officer kicked him in the chin.

36

"Don't mess up his face. We don't want him marked," said the first police officer.

When Wyatt fell to the floor both police officers started kicking him in the stomach and ribs. After he passed out, the police officers resumed taking him up to jail. When the two police officers got Wyatt upstairs to the cells, a jailer asked when he saw them carrying Wyatt out of the elevator, "What happened to him?"

"He got in a fight," said the first police officer.

When Quiet got downtown he drove around a couple of blocks looking for a bail bondsman's office. Inland, Lacy O'Malley Associated, Nation Wide, and Seattle bond companies were all on the same street: Third Avenue. But when Quiet turned the corner to find a parking place, he saw the Overland Bond Company as he pulled Wyatt's car in front of it. Instead of trying to decide which one was the better bail bondsman, Quiet got out of the car and went inside the office.

When Quiet walked into the office, there was a short, chubby black man in his middle fifties sitting behind a desk. "May I help you?" he said.

Quiet explained to the bail bondsman about the police coming to his house and arresting Wyatt. The bail bondsman told Quiet to wait in his office until he returned with Wyatt.

It had been around noon when Quiet went into the bail bondsman's office. Now it was a few minutes after three o'clock, and still the bail bondsman hadn't come back. Quiet began to wonder what was keeping him so long. Then suddenly the office door opened. Quiet felt relieved when he saw the bail bondsman and Wyatt walking through the door.

When Wyatt entered the office, Quiet said, "Oh, no!" humbly as he looked at Wyatt's face. "What did they do to you?" Wyatt was silent. "Come! Let me take you home." Before they left, the bail bondsman gave Quiet a court date when Wyatt was supposed to appear.

37

When they got back to the house, in the bathroom Quiet put ointment on Wyatt's bruises. "I'm sorry, Bro," he said sadly, "I didn't give you any help. It'll never happen again. That I promise."

"That's all right, Bro!" said Wyatt reassuringly. "If you had interfered they'd have killed us both. Told you, Bro. Things have gotten worse since you've been away."

"I'm beginning to see what you mean," said Quiet as he walked out of the bathroom.

Two days later, while Quiet was lying in bed one morning, the telephone rang. Quiet got up and went downstairs to answer it. "Hello," he said.

"Is Mr. Jones home?"

"Speaking," said Quiet.

"This is Mr. Smith from the Boeing employment office. You don't lose your job when you go into the military. Boeing wants you to report to Gate 35 tomorrow morning and pick up your badge from the guard. Then go to Building 1040. A Mr. Scofield will put you to work at your old job."

When Quiet got done talking, he went to the bathroom and washed up. Then he went upstairs and pulled a brown corduroy outfit out of his closet, went to his dresser, pulled out a set of underclothes from the drawer, and laid them on the bed. He got dressed and then went back downstairs to the bathroom. As he stood in front of the mirror combing his hair, he mumbled, "I need some wheels. But where do I go? Think I'll get a newspaper and find what kind of buys I can get. Then I'll wheel on down to Boeing's tomorrow and see if that's changed, too. From what I've seen so far, nothing would surprise me."

After leaving the bathroom, Quiet went into the kitchen and fixed himself some breakfast. When he was done eating his breakfast, he grabbed his coat and walked to the store to get a newspaper. The store was about a mile from the house on

Fifteenth Avenue and near a shopping square. While at the store, Quiet bought meat, rice, a loaf of bread, potatoes, and other items. When he was finished shopping, he went back home.

When Quiet got home he went to the kitchen and made a pot of coffee. Then he went to the dining room table and started scanning the newspaper. In the want-ad section he saw a '62 Corvette for sale for $2,500. being advertised by a private owner. A '63 Ford Galaxy was being sold through a private owner also, for $1,600. There were many other cars for sale, but not what Quiet wanted. At this stage Quiet didn't know what he wanted. So he turned one page after another until he came to the auction section. The auction section didn't state what types of vehicles they had for sale but only where the auction was being held and the time, from 11:00 A.M. to 5:00 P.M.

Quiet got up for a moment to go in the kitchen to fix himself a cup of coffee. But just as he sat back down at the dining room table, Earl and a friend walked through the front door.

"How's it going? You remember Aaron Mitchell?" Earl said.

Quiet got up from the table and shook Mitchell's hand. "We go back a long way," he said with a smile.

"Clint told me you were back," said Mitchell. "I ran into him over the weekend. I found Earl at the Urban League. He was on his way here, so I asked if I could come along."

"Whatcha got planned today?" interrupted Earl. "If you have nothing important planned, why don't you ride around with us?" he suggested. But as he noticed the newspaper turned to the classified section he asked, "Whatcha looking for?"

"Some wheels," said Quiet. "Glad you came by. I need you to run me out to Renton. There's an auction I want to go to. How much time do you have?"

"Practically all day. I have a couple of complaints to see about on a job. Then I'll be free the rest of the day until I go back to the office. There's some type of discrimination going on out

39

there, and the complaint was put on my desk. So I have to look into it."

Quiet closed the newspaper and leaned back in his chair. "Do you get these complaints all the time?" he asked.

"At least two a day is about average. We may get up to twenty complaints in one day. But all from different jobs. that's why we have so many people in our office, to handle these complaints. We are in and out of court constantly, and still problems are not solved, just delayed. Blacks don't have a chance in a white man's court."

"So where do you go from there?" asked Quiet.

"Demonstrate."

"You mind if I go on one of these jobs with you?"

"What about the car you was going to see about?"

"There's an auction; it doesn't start till 11:00 A.M."

Just then Mitchell pulled out a card from his wallet and handed it to Quiet. Quiet looked at the card. It was a dealer's license. "I can help you out if you want me to go to the auction with you."

Quiet agreed.

"Are you ready to go?" interrupted Earl.

"Yes," said Quiet as he got up out of his chair.

Without wasting any more time, the three men left the house. When they got outside, they got into Earl's car, a Ford Fairlane.

The first job site was located in Bellevue and was a small Seattle First Office Bank Building just off Bel-Red Road. A black apprentice electrician and a black apprentice carpenter were on the job with five white iron workers, seven white carpenters, and three white laborers. It was about ten o'clock that morning when Earl pulled up on the job. The building was still under construction.

Quiet, Mitchell, and Earl got out of the car and walked around the job. They saw the black carpenter carrying a box, picking up trash. The black electrician was digging ditches around the building. As the two brothers and their friend approached the black apprentice carpenter, Earl asked, "How's things going? Are you having any problems?" When Earl started talking to the carpenter, an odd look came over his face, a look with a question mark. So Earl identified himself.

"You see what I'm doing," said the carpenter. "Cleaning up. I never had a chance to use a tool since I've been on this job. I've been here three months already, and all I've done was flunky for these whites. There's two white apprentices under me, but they're using their tools. I'll be a journeyman soon." Quiet could almost taste the bitterness in his voice.

While Earl, Quiet, and Mitchell were listening to the apprentice carpenter, the black apprentice electrician walked over to them. He began speaking. At the same instant the Caucasians became leery of the three blacks talking to the two black craftsmen. They began to gather together. Quiet noticed the two middle-aged Caucasians walking toward the five blacks. *They must be the bosses,* Quiet thought. One Caucasian was wearing a carpenter's tool pouch, and the other was wearing an electrician's pouch.

"What are you doing way out here?" said the electrician foreman sarcastically.

"We came to talk to your man," said Earl.

"Anything you got to say to him, you say to me."

"All right! We got a complaint about discrimination. We came to see why."

"Me and my boy don't have any kind of problems we can't handle."

As Earl was explaining to the electrician foreman why he and his two companions had come to the job site, the carpenter boss came over to join them. Without finding out what they were talking about he started talking sarcastically. It seemed as though he tried to get Earl angry. He made a few minor threats but retreated when he realized that Earl had pulled out a notebook and was writing down what he was saying.

"The blacks are not as good as whites when it comes to doing technical work. They are troublemakers. Their grades are below average. It's a proven fact that whites are smarter. What the blacks need is someone to put them in their place, and we're the ones who can do it. We outnumber the blacks ten to one. It's about time they realize this."

As the carpenter foreman seemed as though he was going to take a swing at Earl, Earl moved out of his reach and said, "If you take a swing at me, I'll have you in court so fast you won't have time to apologize."

"Hey-ey!" said the carpenter foreman. "We're in this to-gether. Why don't we come to some type of an agreement?"

Earl just smiled and walked away from the carpenter fore-man and got back in his car. They headed for the other job site.

The second job site was located on the east side of South Renton. It was a Safeway store in a shopping mall under con-struction. There was the same problem on the second job as there was on the first, a black and white dispute. Once again Earl got the blacks and the white bosses together and had a discussion with them. Again Earl made notes of all remarks. On some of these jobs police were called in to stop riots before they got started. But usually it would be a black or blacks who were arrested, those who seemed to be the troublemakers.

When Earl was through with his investigation, Quiet asked him to drop him off where the auction was to be held. It was around noon when Earl dropped Quiet and Mitchell off near the auction's parking lot. Quiet wanted to look at a few cars before going into the auction building. In the parking lot there were other bystanders looking at the cars that were up for auction. The lot was 200 square yards in size. There were many vehicles. Almost every parking stall was filled. The majority of the people were middle-aged or elderly. A few were between their late twenties and early forties.

While walking through the lot, Quiet saw almost every American-made vehicle from 1903 to 1967. The starting bids on the old cars were from $1,500. But Quiet was more interested in the later-model cars, the '62s and on up. The '62s started at $200. The '63s were $300 and up. The '64s were $400 and up. The '65s were $500 and up. The '66s were $600 and up. The '67s were $700 and up.

Then there were the luxury cars, like the Cadillacs, Lincoln Continentals, Rolls Royces, and Mercedes-Benzes. Starting bids were from $2,500, regardless of what year.

While working his way toward the building, Quiet noticed a brown '66 Plymouth Roadrunner parked near the first few stalls near the entrance to the building. The auction building was about the size of an arena. It was located at the far end of the parking lot.

Quiet examined the car carefully. The upholstery and the tires were new. The engine was sprayed clean. The keys were in the car. So he got in the car and started up the engine. It was very quiet and ran smooth. The reading on the speedometer was 4,089.5. "I like this one," he mumbled.

Just then Mitchell approached the car and saw Quiet sitting behind the wheel. "I see you like the car," he said. "I'll try to get this one for you."

Then a voice came over the loudspeaker, "The afternoon auction will start in a few minutes. If you wish to make your bids, please come to the building."

"That means us," said Mitchell. So Quiet got out of the car and the two men walked toward the building.

When Quiet and Mitchell got to the entrance of the building, there was an usher checking the license of dealerships before the bidders entered. When the usher looked at Mitchell's license, he didn't bother to see if Quiet had one. A few female ushers escorted the two men to seats in about the middle row of the building. Ushers were placed at each end of the row of seats to identify the bidders. The ushers were in the aisles.

The auction attracted a large crowd of people. It was almost like everyone had come to watch a ball game.

The first few vehicles that came up for bidding were a '62 Cadillac, '65 Ford Galaxy, '62 Dodge Dart, and '66 Ford Fairlane. Then came the Plymouth Roadrunner, along with five other cars. The Roadrunner was up for bidding first. The opening bid was $600, said the auctioneer. A man in his thirties raised his hand. Quiet raised his hand.

"Six-fifty," said the auctioneer. Another man raised his hand. He was in his thirties also. Quiet raised his hand. But it seemed as though no one really wanted the car. The last bid was $750. "Going once, going twice, gone three times. Sold!" said the auctioneer. Then an usher drove the car to the sold lot, which was on the other side of the building. Quiet and Mitchell left the auction building and went to the sold lot. There Quiet went to a sales booth where Mitchell had to produce his license and give the money to a clerk. Then the clerk gave Mitchell the bill of sale and the keys. He gave them to Quiet, and they got in the car and drove out of the lot.

As they were going back toward Seattle, Mitchell wanted Quiet to drop him off back where he had parked his car in the Urban League's parking lot. "I thank you for doing this for me," said Quiet.

"Remember when I was going to rob a bank and you talked me out of it? Then you took it upon yourself to buy us groceries and paid some of our family bills," said Mitchell. Quiet was silent, as though he couldn't find the right words to say. "Well, I owe you for that and for other things," Mitchell continued. "You've always liked dogs. I have a dog you can have if you want it. If you find the time, come on by." Mitchell wrote down his address on a piece of paper and gave it to Quiet.

After Quiet took Mitchell to his car, he headed home. When Quiet got back to his house, he saw Wyatt in the living room sitting on the couch watching television. "How are things going, Bro?" he said.

"Not so good," he said disgustedly. "I went down to the Urban League office to see Clint. He said everything was filled up right now. He'll call me when there's an opening on one of the trades."

"Why don't you wait till after court, then go back to Boeing?"

"I don't want to go back to Boeing if I can get something better."

Knowing how he felt, Quiet changed the subject. "Come to the window and see what I got," he said as he pulled back the curtains.

"What is it?" asked Wyatt curiously as he got up off the couch and walked toward the window. "Man! That's bad!" He looked at Quiet. "Mind if I drive it? I want to see what it feels like." Excitement was in his voice.

"Sure!" said Quiet as he handed Wyatt his keys. "But bring it back in one piece. I never had a chance to enjoy it." He sounded worried but confident that Wyatt wouldn't let anything happen to his car.

"Don't worry, Bro! I'll be careful," said Wyatt as he was leaving the house.

Quiet watched Wyatt drive away. He could hear the screeching of his tires as Wyatt changed gears.

About an hour later, Wyatt came back, screeching his tires in front of the house. Quiet's heart jumped up into his throat until he saw Wyatt running up the stairs. When Wyatt walked into the house, he said with glee, "That car rides smooth."

"Where'd you go?" asked Quiet curiously.

"Up and down Rainier Avenue. Around Mount Baker and down to Empire Way. Then back around the Beacon Hill area, then home." With excitement in his voice, he said, "How about us driving over to our bros' houses and letting them see your new ride?"

"Okay!" agreed Quiet. "Wait till I change clothes." He headed upstairs. He was upstairs only a few moments before he came back down, wearing his Levi jeans. "I'm ready," he said. Then he and Wyatt left the house.

Quiet drove away from the house heading eastbound, taking the car across the Floating Bridge viaduct and on toward the Floating Bridge through the tunnel. A curious look came over Wyatt's face as he said, "I just want to get the feel of it before going to our brothers' houses."

Quiet cruised around Mercer Island. Then they headed for Bellevue. They drove through the downtown area, looking at many women walking up and down the streets. Most of them were doing some type of shopping. Some were just enjoying the little sunshine they had left. The day was warm.

Leaving the downtown area, the men cruised through the back streets in the residential area. There were a few middle-aged women working in their flower gardens. Some were walking up and down the streets to a destination.

Driving on through other neighborhoods, Quiet noticed through the windows a couple of young women doing house-cleaning.

"Why are we driving through these back neighborhoods?" asked Wyatt curiously.

"Homely women make the best girlfriends," said Quiet. "Let's head back to Seattle." Quiet turned the car around and headed back to the downtown area.

Quiet drove the car back through the downtown area and on to Eighth Avenue heading to the freeway that led back to Seattle. But when they came to the city limits, a Bellevue police car had followed them for about six blocks. "Don't look now, but we're being tailed by the police," said Quiet. As he was about to enter the freeway, the squad car flashed its lights. Quiet pulled to the side of the curb. The police pulled their car up behind him.

Two uniformed police officers were in the car. The driver took out his ticket book, got out, and approached Quiet's car. "May I see your driver's license?" he said.

"What did I do?" Quiet questioned him.

"Don't try to sass me. And let me see your driver's license," demanded the officer.

"Hey, Bro!" interrupted Wyatt. "Let him see your drivers' license, so we can go."

Although hate stared in his eyes, Quiet reached into his wallet and pulled out his driver's license and handed it to the police officer. The police officer took the driver's license and went back to the police car. He ran a check on Quiet's license. The other officer just rested in the car. Moments later the officer walked back to Quiet's car and handed him his driver's license, "That's all you had to do in the first place. Then there wouldn't be any trouble," he said.

Quiet put his license back in his wallet. "What I was told was you're supposed to have a reason for stopping someone." Then he continued on to Seattle.

Later that afternoon Quiet pulled his car up in front of Earl's house. A young, attractive woman came out to meet them. She was Carol, Earl's wife. She met the two men about halfway up the walkway. "When did you get that?" she asked with amazement as she examined the car. "That looks nice and clean."

Quiet was silent. He smiled and Wyatt laughed as they watched Carol go through the car.

"Where's Earl? Still at work?" asked Quiet.

"Yes," answered Carol. But she never stopped acting as though she were driving. "When Earl gets home why don't you take us for a ride?" Quiet agreed as he, Wyatt, and Carol went into the house.

Time ticked on by. Around six o'clock Earl came. When he entered the house, he asked about the car parked in front. But when he saw Quiet sitting in the living room he knew whose car it was. Earl asked Quiet to let him look at the car. So Quiet went outside and showed his car off to Earl. After Earl admired the car, Quiet offered to take them by Clinton's house so he could see the car. Earl, Carol, and Wyatt got out of the car and went to Clinton's doorsteps. Earl knocked on the door. Clinton answered. When he saw Quiet sitting in the car, he came out to see it. He was amazed also. Later that evening when Quiet and Wyatt were through with their visiting, they drove Earl and Carol back to their house, then went back home.

Around nine o'clock the next morning, Quiet pulled into the Boeing development parking lot looking for a place to park. Almost every stall had a car parked in it. He had driven all over the parking lot before he found a stall to park his car. After Quiet parked his car, he got out and walked to the guard booth, which was about two blocks away. Quiet identified himself and the guard gave him a temporary badge to enter through the gate. Then Quiet went to Building 1040, as he had been told by Mr. Smith.

When Quiet got inside the building he noticed a lot of changes had been made. As Quiet remembered Building 1040, it was a machine assembly shop. But since Quiet had gone away the building had been under construction. The whole inside was remodeled. The assembly shops were still on the floor, but two more floors had been added. In the far corner section of the building were offices that led to the second floor. That was where the bosses' secretaries were. Then two flights of stairs led to a third floor, where the supervisors could keep an eye on the workers below. Quiet didn't like this setup, 'cause he never liked anyone looking over his shoulder.

Walking through the plant, he saw that the few machines not being used were greased and covered with some type of canvas. A partition separated the machines that were being used from the ones that weren't. At one time there were many people working in the machine shop, but now it seemed as though there were only a handful. After going through the plant, Quiet felt it was time he find Mr. Scofield and see where he was going to put him. So Quiet headed upstairs.

Still on the first floor, all the employees had new faces. None of these people had he ever seen before. As he looked up, he saw the second floor was full of offices surrounded by a glass window. Three front offices overlooked the plant in the machine assembly area. The side window overlooked the other areas of the plant. The offices were those of the supervisors of the plant. On the third floor were offices only, where the supervisors kept the employees' records. Each office had its own secretary.

Quiet went upstairs and took another tour, as he was looking for Mr. Scofield.

He didn't know what Mr. Scofield looked like or what type of person he might be. When Quiet couldn't find Mr. Scofield upstairs, he headed back downstairs into the machine shop area. He walked among the employees. They looked at him as though he were an alien from outer space. Although they were silent, the looks on their faces raised many questions.

Quiet was about halfway through the machine area when he saw a young bald Caucasian in his late thirties shouting at a middle-aged black woman. The woman's face had a few wrinkles. Her hair was gray, as though she had many worries.

At first glance, the middle-aged woman reminded Quiet of his mother. There was a great resemblance. At the sound of the young man's voice, a hateful chill rapidly flowed through Quiet's body. Eyes turned fiery red and narrowed. The look of anger spread across his face as few employees noticed. But casually Quiet walked over to the young man.

The young man was scolding the black woman for accidentally knocking over a can of some cleaning fluid on one of the workbenches. The woman's job was to keep the workbenches clean and ready to be used. Unknown to Quiet, the man snatched a broom out of the woman's hands and shook her by the shoulders, scolding her at the same time. When Quiet approached the bald man and the woman, he grabbed him by the back of his collar and pulled him away. Then he looked at the woman. She seemed frightened. "Go back to work," he said coldly. The woman wondered who this stranger was. But with no arguments, she did what Quiet said. As Quiet looked back at the bald man, there was silence. The expression on his face never changed.

"What the hell do you want?" demanded Mr. Scofield, frightened. "Who are you?" The question mark spread all over Mr. Scofield's face but thought it was best not to pressure the black stranger. But second thoughts told Mr. Scofield to try to calm him down and take away part of the anger he held inside. "You come to work here?" he continued.

The angry expression slowly started fading away from Quiet's face. Then he broke the silence. "I came to see a Mr. Scofield."

"That's me," said Mr. Scofield with relief.

Quiet paused for a moment at the quick change in attitude. He became defensive as though he had a decision to make. "A Mr. Smith from the Boeing employment office called me yesterday morning and told me to come down here and see you about getting my old job back." Quiet looked at Scofield and said, "You don't need me," and started to walk away.

"Wait a minute. Wait a minute," said Scofield quickly. "Forget about what you've just seen, and let me see your referral slip."

Quiet was wearing a jean outfit. With hesitation he reached in his jacket pocket and pulled out the referral slip and handed it to Mr. Scofield.

As Mr. Scofield took the referral slip, he said, "You know I have to confirm this. Company policy. I'll be right back." He then went upstairs to his office.

Scofield called Mr. Smith down at the Boeing employment office. Mr. Smith told Scofield to hire Quiet, because he was a Vietnam vet. Moments later Scofield went back downstairs into the machine area. "He said it was okay. Are you ready to go to work?"

Quiet looked at the black woman with sorrow. But as he turned toward Mr. Scofield, there was uncertainty across his face. "I guess so," he said, undecided. So he went to his old workbench, as the other employees' eyes followed until he sat down on a high stool. Mr. Scofield approached Quiet as though he wanted to speak. But they just eyed one another for a moment; then he walked away without saying a word.

Quiet's old job had been making templates for fuel lines, then printing them on the workbench. The fuel lines were traced with stainless-steel tubing, which later went onto either a jet or airplane engine. The diagrams on the table were still there, plus a few added attractions: fuel pumps and the inlet and outlet valves the fluid lines were attached to.

Quiet worked the rest of that morning and until the afternoon, when it was time to go home. His work hours were from 7:00 A.M. to 3:00 P.M. Within minutes after the whistle blew, the machine shop area was deserted. There was complete silence. Quiet waited until everyone rushed out of the building to get in their cars. Then he left, the last person to do so.

When Quiet got outside, it was pouring rain. People rushed to get home. Engines roared; tires lost traction on takeoff. The cars lined up for the exit of the parking lot were two blocks long. Horns blew. People shouted. Cars stopped bumper to bumper at stoplights and signs. When Quiet finally got to his car, the parking lot was almost empty. Two people couldn't get their cars started, a man at one end of the parking lot and a woman at the other end. When Quiet turned his ignition, his car started right up. The engine sounded like that of a dragster. Not too loud, but just enough engine to let him know it was ready to run, anytime. Quiet drove out of the parking lot.

Realizing what he was up against with his rehiring at Boeing, Quiet felt that if he did his job, he wouldn't be tampered with by the other supervisors. Every morning Quiet was always on time for work. He did his tasks neatly. Mr. Scofield walked among the employees. He would always make his last stop at Quiet's bench. He would try to get a conversation started. But Quiet would cut him short by talking about the work he was doing, like how long it took to make the templates, what it took to bend the tubings and attach them to the engines's fuel lines, and so on. Then Mr. Scofield would go about his business.

Quiet kept good attendance at Boeing up until the time when he was going to go to court with Wyatt. He called Mr. Scofield and told him why he wouldn't be in that day. Wyatt's court time was nine o'clock. While Quiet was in the bathroom getting himself cleaned up, Wyatt was in the kitchen cooking bacon and eggs for breakfast. A pot of coffee was sitting on the kitchen counter.

Just then, the front door opened. Clinton had used his door key to let Earl and himself into the house. Each one of the brothers had his own key to the house. They came to help give support to Wyatt as he was going to court. Whenever the four brothers got together, it was like a family reunion.

While the four brothers were sitting at the dining room table, Quiet could remember a time in '59 when he and his brothers were together. It was spring vacation. Quiet was in the ninth grade, and he and some of his fellow students had decided to have a baseball game down at the Collins playground, which was two blocks down the hill from Washington Junior High.

Quiet was pitching to a boy named Levi Harris, who was at home plate. When Quiet threw the ball, he hit Levi in the hip. Levi accused Quiet of doing it on purpose. They were about the same height, so Quiet didn't feel too afraid. Levi ran out to the pitcher's mound with the bat in his hands. Both boys squared off, which attracted a crowd. A couple of boys in the crowd started instigating the two youths.

At the playground was a guardian for this reason. He was at the other end of the playground refereeing younger boys playing football, until Louie came and told him of the incident that was about to take place. Without wasting any time, the guardian hurried to the baseball field to see what the dispute was about. When he got there, he could see punches were about to be thrown at any time. All the kids had a lot of respect for the guardian. So he talked to Quiet and Levi. They shook hands, made friends, and continued playing ball. . . .

Later that day on the south end of town was a house party, at Carol's parents' house. (At this time Earl and Carol were going together.) Earl had brought Quiet, Clinton, and Wyatt to the party with him. Earl was in the eleventh grade. Carol was in the tenth grade, and Clinton had already graduated. They were going to Franklin High. At the party were mostly friends of Earl's and Carol's. Clinton knew some of them 'cause they were in their sophomore year when he was a senior.

Although Quiet was a good dancer, he was shy around girls. Each time a girl asked him to dance, he would turn her down. The living room lights were dim. It was too dark to recognize anyone on the floor dancing. It was crowded. From the living room Quiet went into the kitchen looking for a little privacy. The kitchen was full of students also, sitting around telling jokes and talking about old times.

Quiet was standing near the doorway of the living room and the kitchen watching the students dance. The kitchen was stuffy and Quiet wanted to get some fresh air. So he left the doorway, worked his way through the kitchen, and went outside, through the back door.

Unaware that Quiet was going outside, Levi, along with his

two older brothers, was just coming into the kitchen light when he saw him. "There's that troublemaker," he said, pointing. They waited a few moments, then followed.

When Quiet got outside, he stood on the back porch, which had a few steps leading to a large backyard. But to the right a few more steps led to the sidewalk on the street that ran past the house. With his hands in his front pockets, Quiet walked off the back porch and stepped onto the sidewalk. Slowly pacing back and forth on the sidewalk, he heard someone coming through the back door. It was dark. Five shadows were coming down the steps. Quiet didn't recognize the young men until they came under the streetlight. He then recognized Levi, but not the others.

Levi's two older brothers and one of the friends went to Garfield High. The other friend had already graduated from Garfield.

When Levi approached Quiet, he said, "You don't have that honkie flunky to save you this time."

At the same instant Wyatt was in the party looking for Quiet. He went to Earl and Clinton, who were in the living room dancing, and asked them if they had seen him. "No," they replied. A slow song was playing. Wyatt continued toward the kitchen. A guy was standing in a corner next to the kitchen sink with a girl. The sink was left of the kitchen door. Wyatt asked him if he had seen Quiet. The guy was out of Earl's class, but he didn't know Quiet. So when Wyatt described what Quiet was wearing, he told Wyatt he had seen Quiet go outside, and some others went also.

Curiously, Wyatt went outside. But when he got outside and stood on the front porch he heard scuffling. The struggle seemed to be on the sidewalk. He walked to the edge of the porch, leaned over the banister, then saw Quiet trying to fight off the five guys. But they overpowered him quickly. When Wyatt saw this, he jumped over the banister onto the sidewalk and went to Quiet's aid.

Quiet was on the ground. With a flying leap, Wyatt dived on Levi's and his friends' backs, forcing them to roll off Quiet. As they scuffled on the ground, Quiet managed to get up first. But Levi's older brothers started throwing punches. For a while Quiet was upholding his own as he threw punches back. Then Levi joined his brothers.

On the ground Wyatt tried to use one of the guys as a shield to keep from being beaten up by the other one. But Wyatt managed to wrestle himself back onto his feet. When he did, he came up behind Levi and pushed him into Quiet's punch, which caught him on the jaw. Levi fell back into Wyatt's arms, but Wyatt swung him backward into his friends' arms as they were coming up behind him. The two brothers kept trying to throw punches. Quiet kept one brother in front to use him as a shield as he tried to fight off the other one. Then Wyatt got beside Quiet and they both were throwing a flurry of punches to slow the two brothers down. Then Levi and his two friends joined in the flurry of punches. Within moments Quiet and Wyatt were overpowered.

While they were in the house the music stopped playing. Someone turned up the lights. Then Clinton started looking for Quiet and Wyatt. Joan, Wyatt's girlfriend, was standing next to the phonograph, going through some records. Clinton walked over to her. "Have you seen Wyatt or Quiet?" he asked.

"He was here a few minutes ago looking for Quiet," she said. "The last time I saw him, he went in the kitchen." Joan's complexion was dark but like shining bronze. Her hair was silky black and came down to her shoulders. She was about five feet five. Puppy love! She was in the sixth grade.

Earl was standing next to Carol while she was helping Joan going through the stacks of records, trying to find something to play. "What's up?" he said curiously.

"Wyatt came through here looking for Quiet when I was dancing. Now both of them are gone," said Clinton.

"Yes," agreed Earl. "Wyatt came to me asking if I'd seen Quiet."

So the two brothers got together and went into the kitchen. When they got in the kitchen, there were quite a few people the brothers didn't know. But the person standing in the corner with a girl was a jogging friend of Earl's. So Earl went over to him and asked about Wyatt. The guy told Earl that he wasn't sure if the guy he had seen go outside was Earl's brother. But he told Earl where he saw them last. Without wasting another moment, Earl and Clinton went out the back door.

When Clinton and Earl got on the back porch, they heard scuffling coming from the sidewalk. The cursing and noises of struggle made it seem that a fight was in progress. So quickly they rushed to the end of the porch. Leaning over the banister, they saw Quiet and Wyatt putting up a battle, which they were losing, against five guys. The fight was just below the banister. So Earl and Clinton jumped over the banister and landed right in the fight. Whatever started the fight never crossed their minds. All they could see was that their brothers were outnumbered. So they evened up the odds.

Clinton started fighting the friend who had graduated. Earl went after the other friend. Wyatt was fighting Levi and Quiet took on the two older brothers. The fight became more even and the battle was turned around. The fight drew a large crowd from the partygoers inside. "Them bad-ass Joneses," said someone from the crowd. This was the last time Quiet could remember getting together with his brothers. Fighting side by side, the four brothers had whipped the three brothers and their two friends.

3

While Clinton and Earl were sitting at the dining room table eating their breakfast, the doorbell rang. Quiet got up and went to answer it. It was Joan. As she stood on the front porch, Quiet remembered her as a young girl, but now she had grown into a nice-looking young woman. This was the first time Quiet had seen Joan since Carol's party.

When Joan entered, Quiet stood up and away from the table. Joan ran into his arms. "I'm so glad you're back. Wyatt told me you've come home," she said as she went and stood by Wyatt. "Now all you brothers are back together again. I came to go to court with you." Wyatt tried to talk her out of going to court, but Joan insisted. So she left the house with the four brothers. They drove away in Quiet's car.

Around nine o'clock Quiet, his brothers, and Joan stood outside the municipal courtroom. Quite a few people were sitting outside the courtroom. There weren't enough seats to go around. There were three black men and two black women. The rest were white. Two public defenders, dressed in expensive suits, were going around talking to their defendants. As for Wyatt, he had no defense.

Wyatt saw the man he had been charged with assaulting, sitting on the end of the bench near another hallway. He had a lawyer sitting with him. Wyatt looked at the man for a moment, then turned his head as the elevator bell rang, attracting his

57

attention. As the doors opened, two uniformed police officers stepped out. Quiet recognized them as two of the police officers who had come to the house to arrest Wyatt. The two officers eyed Wyatt as they walked past. Quiet noticed the expression on Wyatt's face, an expression of hate. Quiet felt these two officers had beaten Wyatt up while they were in the police elevator. *That's the reason Wyatt had them bruises on his face,* Quiet thought. The two police officers went into the courtroom. Moments later the courtroom clerk poked his head through the door, saying, "Come into the courtroom. The judge is ready to start." Then the door closed behind him. People got up from where they were sitting or standing around and went into the courtroom.

When all were sitting in the courtroom, the clerk said, "All rise," and the judge came out of his chambers into the courtroom and took a seat behind his bench. "You may sit down," the clerk continued.

As everyone sat back down, the judge said, "Can we have the first case?"

"May we have a Miss Washington take the stand please?" said the clerk.

Miss Washington was a young black woman who looked to be in her late twenties or early thirties. *Very attractive,* thought Quiet. She was sitting about in the middle of the courtroom. She got up from her seat and walked down the aisle and on up to the witness stand. The clerk swore her in; then she took her seat.

"Miss Washington, is that your maiden name or your husband's last name?" said the clerk.

"My husband's last name," she answered.

"State your case," said the clerk.

While Miss Washington was stating her case, Quiet went back into his memory bank, thinking of her last name. He went back to a time when he was in third grade. It was around the middle of winter. Christmas and New Year's had passed. Just around the corner was Valentine's Day. One evening Quiet was sitting at the dining room table doing his homework. Mr. Jones was sitting on the couch in the living room reading a newspaper. He noticed something was bothering Quiet, but he did not ask about it.

Finally, after fighting his curiosity, Quiet got out of his chair and went into the living room. "Daddy!" he said nervously as he stood before him.

Mr. Jones put the newspaper aside as he gave Quiet his attention.

"Where did we get our last name from?"

When Quiet asked Mr. Jones that question he became a little angry, but then he said calmly, "It's a damn shame the schools don't teach black kids about their history. Your last name is a slave name. When blacks were brought over here, they were sold in this country as slaves. Blacks came from Africa. They lost their homes, their native lands, everything, including their self-respect. All that was taken from the blacks. Even some of the black tribes sold blacks to the whites. When they came over here, whatever white bought a black, that was the name he used."

"But, Dad," interrupted Quiet, "how could so many blacks be tricked into slavery?"

"It wasn't hard, Son!" continued Mr. Jones. "Families believed they were going to a promised land where life was better. Parents were tricked into sending their kids to a land where they would have a better education. Some were trapped like animals and brought here. Then there were those who were promised they could sail around the world and visit other countries but were sold into slavery. You see, Son, it's not hard to trick someone."

"In school, Dad, we're taught that we are free," said Quiet. "We're not slaves anymore."

"Your freedom is just on paper. As far as the whites are

concerned, we're still slaves. When blacks were supposedly freed, some were recaptured and sold back into slavery. Once again they had homes and families broken up, family members sold separately, scattered throughout the South. Some never saw their families again."

"Didn't the blacks try to get away or fight back?"

"Some blacks escaped, but those who were caught were hung, were tortured to death, or got shot by a firing squad. Our white government wouldn't stop the killing of blacks until a few handfuls started fighting back. Then there was death on both sides. Through the years we were brainwashed to turn against one another. Some of us have caused our fathers to be killed, our mothers and sisters to be raped and murdered. Our blood has so many different nationalities we really don't know where we belong. We no longer have a country to call our own. We're just here because this is where life left us, because of our own stupidity. Some blacks who get good positions and do well enough to provide for themselves and their family forget where we came from and how we were brought here and what the whites used to keep us from thinking about it.

"At one time, just before the Depression hit in 1929, the whites tried to get the blacks to pick up arms and fight against them, knowing that we had few weapons to defend ourselves with. Only a handful of blacks had weapons. The rest had machetes, rakes, hoes, and other garden tools to fight with. They would be no match for the artillery they'd face. The whites had all the guns and bullets. The few blacks who went to buy bullets for their weapons had to have a reason. Then it was put on record. Then, and only then, could they use their weapons in certain areas. Whites had everything sewn up. You even had to have permission to use your weapon on your own property.

"In the South when some of them so-called masters died, they bequeathed some of their property to a few blacks who had stayed on after they were freed from slavery. But whites managed to take it away by means of legal papers the blacks didn't understand. It had been years since books were taken from the blacks' hands to keep them ignorant of the facts concerning their rights. Slowly but surely, we finally realized we had rights, too, just like the whites. But we can never use 'em. What the whites needed from us were our weak minds and strong backs to help build the United States to where it is today. I don't expect you to understand what I'm saying, Son. But you'll learn a lot as you grow older. Then you'll understand more of what I'm saying. I'll give you something to live with: Try to observe every little thing you see, whether it seems big or small. Be relaxed, but don't overlook anything. It may help you as you're growing up. Nowadays you can have no friends, just associates."

Hearing Wyatt's name mentioned by the clerk brought Quiet's attention back to the courtroom. "Are Mr. Wyatt Jones and Robert Wiseman present in the courtroom? If so, please come forward," the man said.

Wyatt and Wiseman got up from their seats and approached the front of the courtroom. Wiseman went and sat next to the prosecutor. Wyatt sat on the opposite side with no defense lawyer.

Seeing Wyatt sitting alone, the judge asked, "Where's your defense counsel?"

"I don't have one," said Wyatt.

The judge looked over at the public defender, sitting near the back row with other clients. "Will you take this man's case?"

"Yes," said the public defender. Then he got up from his seat, went to the front of the courtroom, and sat down next to Wyatt. "I'll need a moment with my client," said the public defender. "I'm Ted Bernard," he introduced himself as he shook Wyatt's hand. "Now why don't you tell me what happened?" When Wyatt got through explaining his side to Bernard, the lawyer said "Okay, Your Honor. We're ready."

"Will Mr. Wiseman please take the stand?" said the clerk.

Wiseman got up from his seat and took the stand and the clerk swore him in. Wiseman told the prosector and the court that he worked as a supervisor at Boeing in Renton. His job meant seeing that the employees were on time for work and that they did their job.

"What happened on the thirteenth?" asked the prosecutor.

Wiseman explained, "Mr. Jones came to work late that morning, and I told him if this kept up I was going to have to give him three weeks off. Mr. Jones became very angry and told me I'd better not. I asked Mr. Jones what that was supposed to mean. He said, 'Just what you suppose it means.' I took it as a threat. So I told Mr. Jones that I was going to report this to Mr. Scofield, my boss. Then Mr. Jones grabbed me by the collar and we started struggling. I struggled to get him off of me until the guards came and apprehended him and took him into custody."

"Have you and Mr. Jones ever discussed this matter before?" asked the prosecutor.

"Yes!" said Wiseman. "Many times. But each time we talked about the matter, it got worse."

"Has he threatened you before?"

"Yes!"

"Were there any witnesses present?"

"Yes!"

"I have no further questions. Your witness," said the prosector as he took his seat.

Mr. Bernard stood up in front of his seat. "Did you provoke the defendant?"

"No," said Wiseman.

"No further questions," said Bernard as he sat back down.

"Will counsel approach the bench?" said the judge. Bernard and the prosecuting attorney approached the bench. "This is one of the worst cases I've presided over. And above all, this is the worst defense case I've seen. I don't see any charge against that black. I'm going to dismiss this case. Now you both take your seats."

When Bernard got back to his seat, he told Wyatt, "The judge says if you plead guilty, he'll give you a suspended sentence. The choice is yours. If not, you can serve from six months up to a year in the county jail. It depends on how he feels."

"But he's lying," whispered Wyatt to Bernard. "Mr. Wiseman cussed me out for being five minutes late for work. Then he grabbed me by my shirt collar and pushed me up against a workbench. So I hit him. When I tried to leave, he tried to hit me when my back was turned. We started fighting and that's when he had someone call the guard."

"Well, that's not what the judge believes," said Bernard. "You'd better make a decision quick, because he's about to rule on the charge."

Feeling the public defender was doing a poor job of representing him because he was black, Wyatt felt he had no chance of getting justice. "Okay," he said disgustedly. "I want to change my plea from not guilty to guilty."

"Smart move," said the public defender. Then he stood up from his seat. "I would like to interrupt the court for a brief moment. My client would like to change his plea from not guilty to guilty."

The court granted Wyatt's request to change his plea from not guilty to guilty. Wyatt was fined $100 and a 180-day suspended jail sentence. Quiet, Clinton, and Earl were very angry at the sentence, but no one spoke a word as they looked at one another, then at Wiseman. After the case was over, the four men and Joan left the courtroom and walked down the hall heading for the elevators. When they got to the elevators, Quiet pushed the button. Moments later the passenger-loading bell rang. The doors opened. The men got into an elevator with other passengers coming from a higher floor. After making a stop on every floor, the elevator took them to the lobby on the first floor. The first floor led to Third Avenue. Quiet's car was parked on Second Avenue, in a parking lot around the corner. Leaving the building, they headed for Quiet's car. When they got to Quiet's car, everyone got in and they headed back to the house. When they got back to the house, they sat in the living room and still neither one spoke a word. Joan went into the kitchen and made some coffee.

A little while later Joan came back into the living room carrying a tray with four coffee cups, cream and sugar, and a coffeepot. She sat the tray on the coffee table in front of Clinton. As Joan poured each man a cup of coffee, they looked as though they were statues. They were sitting in the same positions as when they came into the house. Joan put cream and sugar in Wyatt's while the others drank theirs as it was. The silence hadn't broken as each man started sipping on his coffee. *There is no peace for the black man,* they thought.

Quiet was sitting in the love seat. After two hours had passed he got up, walked outside, and got back in his car. He drove away. Later Clinton and Earl followed out the front door. They got in their cars also and drove away. Wyatt and Joan stayed at the house.

Quiet drove eastward across the Floating Bridge viaduct and on through the tunnel, which was a quarter of a mile long. It was dark driving through the tunnel, but yet sunlight glowed at the other end at the opening. Coming out of the tunnel, Quiet made a sharp right turn onto a street that led to Mount Baker Beach. Mount Baker Beach was just off Washington Lake Boulevard. There were three beaches on Lake Washington Boulevard: Mount Baker Beach; Madrona Beach, a mile and a half north of Mount Baker, and Seward Park Beach, about three and a half miles south of Mount Baker Beach.

The day was warm. Many people were on the beaches that day. They were stretched out from one end of the beach to the other. Although the sun was out, it was still too cold to go swimming. Few people were running alongside the road near the lake. They were running to stay in shape. Some people were boating, and some were sitting in the cars in the beaches' parking lots.

Quiet cruised alongside the lake. The water was shining like silk. A dark blue glare followed beyond the horizon, where the sky and the water appeared to meet. There was no ending. Across the lake, tall trees bordered it for miles. The lake seemed to be in the middle of a forest. At the end of Lake Washington Boulevard a road branched off to Seward Park on the left. Another road led back to the arterial streets.

Quiet took the road to his right and ended up in the Seward Park picnic area, where a lot of people came during the summer holidays and on warm summer days and gathered for some type of recreation after they ate. Driving through Seward Park, he saw a lot of countrylike roads. The lake was in sight from every picnic area. Baseball diamonds, tennis courts, and an open space the size of a football field filled the area with other recreational opportunities. But the most popular recreation was volleyball.

Quiet pulled into a parking stall on the west side of the picnic area. Walking a short distance through the woods, he came to a clearing near the water's edge. He sat down on the grass and looked out at the water. "It's pretty," he mumbled. "But dangerous."

Sailboats cruised back and forth away from the beaches. Two men were sailing one particular sailboat about halfway across the lake. One man decided to go diving. Once again Quiet went back into his early years. At the age of thirteen, Quiet had been placed in Luther Burbank Detention School. Luther Burbank was a school located on Mercer Island where boys were sent for getting caught stealing or just if they were unwanted kids placed by their parents. When things came up missing many times, Quiet was accused of the crime.

One day Quiet and three other boys, a black named Ezell, another black named Sims, and a white youth named Roy, went out in a rowboat. They borrowed the fourteen-foot rowboat from the Luther Burbank boating dock and took it out onto the lake, at this point about two and a half miles wide. They were about halfway across the lake when Quiet and Roy decided to dive. They dived off the boat into the water. It was very calm that day as Quiet and Roy swam among the plants in the water. The water was cold and dark as the two boys went deeper and deeper. It looked like a jungle. Not knowing how many feet they were below, and with the air supply in their lungs running out, they decided to go back topside and get a breather. When Quiet and Roy came up for air, they saw Ezell and Sims rowing the boat toward the other side of the lake. Trying to conserve the energy they had left, Quiet and Roy started stroking toward the shore near Luther Burbank. The swim was long, but Quiet had swum farther at other times. When Ezell and Sims finally came back to shore, Quiet and Roy wanted to fight. But the supervisors who were watching them got in between the boys and tried to find out what had happened. None of the boys told on the others. But Ezell and Sims would lose their popularity among the other boys. . . .

Clinton and Earl made it back to the office. There was a note on their desks, asking them to come to the CAMP (Central Area Motoraction Program) house at seven o'clock. Representatives of different trades were having a discussion. The CAMP house used to be an old fire department building located on Eighteenth and Cherry, across the street from the Providence Hospital. When the fire department decided to destroy the building after they abandoned it, people in the community raised a petition to save the building for public use. So the building was turned over to the Urban League. Now the Urban League used the building for meetings of various trades.

Near seven o'clock Clinton and Earl met outside the CAMP

building. They discussed for a few moments what the meeting would be about, then went inside. The meetings were primarily about the same thing: black and white disputes and racism on the jobs. Each craftsman went into a certain room and told various experiences he had on jobs, then prepared himself for going into the auditorium. These meetings let new workers know what they were up against. Whites were angry because after years of the whites trying to keep decent jobs to themselves in the trade unions, blacks were being offered the same opportunity through a court order. The whites felt the blacks were taking their jobs and at the same time making too much money. So on these jobs the blacks got most of the manual labor, harassment, and intimidation. So much of this had happened, it forced the blacks to stand together to find a way to solve this problem. But at times it seemed as though there was no hope of blacks and whites getting along with one another.

Clinton went into the room where the electricians were having their discussions. Earl went into the room where the ironworkers were having their discussions. Clinton and Earl's associates went into the rooms where other trade representatives had their discussions.

There were six electricians attending the meeting Clinton attended. One electrician brought his complaint to the committee, identifying himself as Alvin Minor, a resident of the south end of town. Alvin's complaint was as follows: He was working on an eight-foot ladder splicing wires in a four-by-four-by-two-and-a-half-inch junction box on a ceiling when two Caucasian ironworkers deliberately knocked his ladder over. Alvin sprained his ankle and skinned his elbows trying to break his fall on the concrete. Alvin spoke to the shop steward about the incident, and he said there was nothing he could do. The next morning when Alvin came to work, he was sent back upstairs to finish what he had left from the day before. Work started at 7:30 A.M. Around 9:00 the same two ironworkers came back upstairs where Alvin was working on the fifth floor. But this time when Alvin saw them coming, he climbed down off his ladder and stood beside it. As the two ironworkers came walking past him, one of the ironworkers elbowed Alvin in the abdomen. Alvin doubled over. But when he straightened up he had a two-by-four in his hands. When the ironworker tried to hit Alvin, he drew back and let the two-by-four land across the ironworker's head. As the ironworker was going down, he tried to block another attempt with his forearm. It was broken. Seeing his friend was hurt, the other ironworker quickly headed for the exit stairs. But when he got to the exit door he felt a two-by-four-by-twelve-inch block hit the back of his head. But instead of slowing the ironworker's speed down, it only increased it. When the word got back to the foreman and the shop steward about the incident, Alvin was fired. So Alvin brought his complaint to CAMP because he felt he shouldn't be the only person victimized by this incident. After learning about the complaint, Clinton told Alvin he would bring up this grievance at the next NLRB meeting.

In the ironworkers' room, Earl told of a different sort of problem. A black named Bill Moony and his friend Jason had gone to a bar after work with two Caucasian ironworkers to have a drink. One of the white's name was Bob Shelby. The other one's name was Fred Kocks. They went to a tavern called It'll Do. The tavern was only a few blocks from the job in Georgetown, South Seattle.

In the tavern Bill and Fred were drinking pretty heavy and bragging about how much steel they laid. Bill compared the amount of steel he laid to the amount laid by Kocks. One word led to another. Soon both men began to argue. Jason and Bob tried to calm the two ironworkers down. But it started getting worse. Bill and Fred started arguing over who was tougher. The bartender came over to the table as the two were getting loud and told them if they were going to start fighting, they'd have to take it outside.

It was getting late and both men agreed to wait until the others were ready to leave. It was around eleven o'clock when the four men left the tavern. Bill and Fred had done quite a bit of drinking and were pretty well intoxicated and only had part of their senses remaining. Jason and Bob hadn't had as much to drink and were aware of what was going on. Heading back to the parking lot that was just across the street from the job site, Fred bumped into Bill, knocking him onto a car parked on the street.

"You did that on purpose!" shouted Bill. Then he took a swing at Fred. As Bill made the attempt, he stumbled into Fred, and both men fell to the ground. Jason and Bob helped Bill and Fred to their cars as they were still arguing. They got in their cars and drove out of the parking lot.

The next day at work, Jason and Bob thought all was forgotten, until Fred came to work with a small cut on his lower lip. He was angry. "That nigger hit me when I was drunk," he said to another ironworker. "I'm going to get me a couple of niggers."

The rumor spread among the Caucasian workers. Jason and Bill were unaware of the conspiracy being plotted against them. On this particular job there were only four blacks on the job: Bill, Jason, an apprentice electrician, and an apprentice carpenter. Bill and Jason were working high up on a beam laying steel when they ran out of beam bolts. Jason volunteered to go down and get more beam bolts out of the supply shack, located on the other side of the job site, not far from where Bob, Fred, and the other white workers were working.

The beam bolts were inside a Crockett sack sitting in a far corner from the doorway. Jason went into the supply shack and filled his pockets with the bolts to take back to Bill. But when Jason got outside the shack, he saw Fred and seven other white workers waiting outside for him. Trying to blow it off, he said, "What's up?"

Fred was holding a tow chain in his hand and twirling it around. "You and Moony jumped me last night, and I'm going to get you for it," he said, smirking. Then he took a swing at Jason.

Jason blocked the blow with his forearm. "Man! You know I never touched you," he shouted.

"Yes, you did, nigga," said Fred as he took another swack at Jason. "You and Moony tried to beat me up when I was drunk."

Once again Jason blocked the attempt with his forearm. The pain was increasing rapidly. "I didn't!" shouted Jason repeatedly. "Why don't you tell what really happened? You try to hit me again with that chain," and he picked up a two-by-four, "I'm going to bust your head open."

The other ironworkers who were standing by grabbed their hammers, picked up two-by-fours and pipes lying around, and began to advance slowly toward Jason, who drew his board back, as he tried to ease himself away from the shack to get in the open so he could have some room to swing. The ironworker with the pipe came at Jason, but Jason warded him off with the board. Seeing that Jason was highly serious, Fred and the others began to advance very cautiously.

While this was going on, it started attracting the attention of the other workers. They ran over and broke the fight up. As Jason was backing away from the incident, Fred kept threatening, "We'll get you before the day is out." Jason felt he had better get back to Bill and tell him what to expect. When Jason got back to Bill, he told him what had happened; then they both left the job site. The next day they went to the NLRB and reported the incident. The NLRB told them unless there was proof, there was nothing they could do.

After hearing the testimonies from the tradesmen including

the complaints from Bellevue, and their experiences, Clinton and Earl and their associates resumed their meeting in the auditorium. Their staff took the front of the auditorium. Then Clinton began to explain the steps they were going to take to see if they could stop the intimidation and the harassment from the whites. For months the Urban League had fought these incidents, but they had obtained unsuccessful results through the NLRB and the court orders. Clinton was going to call a demonstration march starting from Fourteenth and Yesler and going to Third and James, where the municipal building stood. This was the place where trials were held. The march was supposed to start at nine o'clock the following morning.

While Clinton and his staff were making speeches, there were two new faces in the auditorium, unknown to the trade workers. They sat in the middle row of seats next to the electricians. The strangers were two attractive females, one Caucasian and the other a high-toned (light-complected) black. Clinton noticed the two women sitting in the auditorium. At all the meetings he had attended he had never seen them before. But he felt it was good if he meetings could bring in more people. *This way, it'll help the Urban League achieve its purpose,* he thought.

The two women were policewomen, working out of the detective bureau. Maraisha Thomas, the black woman, about five feet, five inches tall, weighed about 110-120 pounds. Her hair was shining silky black, as though she was part-Indian. The other policewoman's name was Sharon Talliver. She was a sunny yellow blonde. Her weight and height were about the same as Maraisha's. The women were dressed as though they were in the trades also.

Maraisha and Sharon had been sent to get inside the tradesmen's meetings and find out what they were up to, then report back to the detective bureau so the department could get ready in case any violence broke out. There were coffee and doughnuts for the workers during breaks. Maraisha and Sharon found time to question a few of the workers. The workers had nothing to hide. All everyone was going to do was march to City Hall's doorstep and demand the courts have the trade unions give black workers an opportunity to work. This the two women understood. For the rest of the meeting Maraisha concentrated on Earl and Clinton, because they were the heads of the meeting.

Around eleven-thirty the meeting terminated. Some of the workers left right away, because they had to go to work the next morning. A few stayed around to congregate with others who were going to march in the morning. But parked down the street about a half a block was a green '65 Dodge Volare. Three police officers were sitting in the Dodge, waiting. At night the car seemed black. It was specially equipped with a CB unit and a police radio.

Maraisha and Sharon came out of the building, walked down the street, and got into the car. About half an hour later, Clinton, Earl, and a few others came out of the building. They had a few more discussions before going to their cars. Moments later the parking lot was empty except for Clinton's and Earl's cars. As the two brothers talked, Maraisha said, "That's the one you want to talk to," and pointed at Clinton. As the two brothers pulled out of the parking lot, the green sedan followed them. They headed northbound.

When the two cars came to the intersection of Twenty-third and Union they separated. The green sedan followed Clinton until they came to Twenty-third and Madison. At a red light the other police let Maraisha and Sharon out of the car. About two blocks down the hill on Madison, the police caught up with Clinton and put their lights on him. When Clinton saw the red light he pulled over to the curb. *Now what did I do?* he asked himself.

The green sedan pulled up behind Clinton. The driver got

out of the sedan and approached Clinton. "May I see your driver's license?" he said.

"What did I do?" asked Clinton as he reached into his back pocket and pulled out his wallet and handed the police officer his driver's license. "I know I wasn't speeding. What did I do?" he repeated.

The police officer took Clinton's license back to his car. When the officer was on the way back to Clinton's car, his passenger was with him. Clinton saw them coming through his rearview mirror. *What should I do now? I can't run. If I do, every cop in Seattle will be after me,* he thought. But Clinton thought for a moment. *What do I have to be afraid of? I didn't do anything wrong. They're probably after me because of what I'm doing with the trades. I'll just wait and see what these pigs want.*

This time the police approached Clinton from both sides of his car. What was going on? Both doors on his car opened. The officer who opened the door on Clinton's side said, "Will you get out please?" Although Clinton got out of the car, he didn't like the way the officer spoke. The two police officers led Clinton back to the squad car. When Clinton got to the police car, there was a man sitting in the backseat. He cuffed Clinton's hands behind his back, placed a blindfold across his face, and laid him on the floor in the backseat.

"What's this for?" Clinton asked nervously.

The police officers were silent as the car pulled away. The night was windy. Clinton tried to figure out the direction he was going. The car started eastbound for about three blocks, until it got down to the bottom of the hill. Then it made a right turn. *Where are they taking me,* he wondered. The car headed southbound for about five blocks before it came to another stop. It stopped for a few seconds, then continued. When the car pulled away, under his breath Clinton started counting.

The ride was smooth. Estimated speed was between thirty and forty-five miles an hour. Clinton could tell that the car was moving through town because of the stopping for traffic lights. When Clinton's count got to 630, the car came to another stop. Again Clinton wondered where he was, but the stop told him he was at another signal light. He heard tires slushing through water. *It must be raining again,* he felt. When his count got to 640, the traffic stopped. The car continued straight. But this time the car picked up speed.

The car traveled from the CD (Central District) to the south end of Seattle. It stayed on Empire Way, which ran from the CD to South Seattle and on toward Skyway. From Skyway, Empire Way ran into Renton. It turned into Rainier Avenue, which ended when it came to the freeway entrance. The freeway ran out of Renton, past Kent, and to Auburn, where it ended and Interstate 18 began.

By the time the count was up to 2,800, the car stopped again, but this time for a train. Clinton heard the sounds of rail wheels rolling, the horn blowing as it was crossing a street, the roaring engine thundering. It sounded as though it was a switch engine. Clinton estimated the wait. It was about two minutes. When the sounds of the train faded away, the car started rolling again. *We're no longer in Seattle,* Clinton felt.

Digging back into his early years as he was growing up, Clinton remembered what his father told him and his brothers as they were watching a racial movie on television. Everyone was gathered around in the living room. "There were times when blacks were picked up from their homes by the police and went on rides with no return. They were found dead later." Clinton felt this could happen to him but remained calm.

Every so often the officer sitting in the backseat made a few sarcastic remarks about Clinton not showing his fear. "Just wait till we get you to the warehouse and see how cool you are," he said.

The signal bells of the train had stopped. The street was wet. It had been raining, but not as hard the day before. There was the sound of slushing tires. The car was moving with the flow of traffic. But the traffic was thin. Soon the car turned off the street and onto a bumpy, rocky road. The car went a mile or so, then stopped. Clinton had counted up to 3,031. The police officers in the front seat got out of the car. Then they helped the police officer in the backseat escort Clinton into a warehouse he had been unaware of. His hands were still cuffed behind his back. The blindfold covered his eyes as he was led through the warehouse into an office and placed on a chair.

The office was cold; the only sounds were footsteps. Then a dog came up and sniffed Clinton from his feet to his waist. He was scared. The thoughts never left his mind: *What's on their minds? What do they want with me? No one knows I'm here. They can't let me go, because I saw one of them. Any wrong move I made may give them a reason for a quick kill. They're probably afraid I might file a kidnapping charge against the police department. They might just kill me to keep me quiet. But what good would that do? I know I don't have anything they want. But when does a white cop need a reason to kill a black? They've been doing that for years.*

Clinton felt a grip on his coat collar. A voice said, "You're going to tell us what you niggers are up to."

Clinton remained silent.

"A smart-ass, huh! We're going to teach you niggers how to respect the law and our society." Then Clinton felt a backhand across his face, which caused him to fall over out of the chair. Then he was kicked in the stomach. As Clinton moaned a little, footsteps from outside the office were just coming through the door. At first he felt they were going to beat him up badly. But as the footsteps approached him, two sets of footsteps moved away in the opposite direction. They went to the far side of the office and stopped. There was whispering going on. Then Clinton felt another set of hands picking him up off the floor and placing him back into the chair.

The footsteps came back to Clinton. *Oh! Oh!* he felt. *Now they're really gonna work me over.* But when the footsteps stopped in front of him, a grip raised him up out of his chair. He was led back through the warehouse and placed in the backseat of the sedan. *Now what's going on?* Moments later, the same two police officers came and got in the car. It pulled away from the area.

Clinton heard the sound of a switch-engine train moving past them. When they got back on the pavement, there was the sound of a work whistle. He counted four sets of tracks and a dip in the street before coming to a stop. The car made a left turn. This route told Clinton the police were going back the way they came. He tried to recognize the route; it came to a blank. Finally the police took him back to his car. When the police pulled up near Clinton's car, the driver got out, took Clinton out of the backseat, and led him to his car. Then he removed the blindfold and uncuffed his hands from behind his back. "Just get in your car and go home," he said. He drove away.

During Clinton's absence, Joan had been resting her head on Wyatt's shoulder while sitting on the couch watching television. Quiet was sitting next to them. The telephone rang. It was sitting next to Quiet on the couch. He answered, "Hello!"

Before Quiet could say anything else, Margaret asked worriedly, "Have you seen Clint?"

A strange expression came over Quiet's face. "No!" he said curiously. He paused for a moment. "I thought he and Earl went to a meeting."

"I just talked to Earl. He said the meeting was over at least three hours ago. Clint should've been home by now."

Wyatt noticed the odd expression on Quiet's face. He rose from the couch. "What's the matter?" he said hesitantly.

Quiet rose from the couch also, his eyes trained on the floor.

"Okay!" he said. "I'll be right over." Then he put the phone back on the couch.

Joan, although listening to the conversation, had never seen the brothers in action together. She remembered the fight they had had with five other boys at a party. But since then they had never been in any serious altercations. For fear of Wyatt getting hurt, she wanted to try to talk him out of finding out why his brother hadn't come home yet. But she understood how they felt toward one another. These were strong feelings. So she left the house with them.

When Quiet, Wyatt, and Joan got to Margaret's, they saw Earl sitting on the couch in the living room, trying to keep Margaret from worrying. Quiet was afraid to say what he was thinking. Maybe a car accident. But there was no police report of an accident. Hospitals had no record of admittance. Clinton wasn't in jail. It was too late to visit any friends. The mental block in the back of Quiet's mind was kidnapping. Why? He didn't know. The thought of kidnapping came to his mind. There wasn't anything anyone could do but wait for the word. So everyone waited patiently.

About an hour later, as everyone was sitting in the living room in silence, they heard a key turn in the front door lock. The front door slowly opened. It was Clinton poking his head through the doorway. At the sight of Clinton all tensions were relieved. Margaret jumped to her feet and ran into his arms and smothered him with kisses.

Earl got up from the couch casually. "Say, Bro! Where have you been? We all were worried about you."

Clinton explained what had happened: the kidnapping, the ride, and the sounds he tried to use to pick up where he was taken. But as he was blindfolded, Clinton couldn't tell. For some reason, after he had been kidnapped, the police brought him back.

When Clinton was finished explaining, Quiet, sitting on the

couch, suggested that since Clinton was back, everyone could go home and get some sleep.

The night was fading. Gray clouds were moving the darkness out of view. It looked as though it was starting to rain. The streets were deserted of vehicles, a few night owls walking up and down the streets. In a black district, police cars were patrolling the streets.

Wyatt and Quiet drove Joan home. Then they went home. When they got home, they went straight to bed. While lying in bed, Quiet couldn't sleep. He lay back staring up at the ceiling. Anger filled his thoughts. But why did they want Clint? Why did they kidnap him and turn him loose? "It'll never happen again," he mumbled. Then he turned over and went to sleep.

It was two o'clock Saturday afternoon when Quiet was wakened by the chirping sparrows. So he got up and took a stretch while looking out the window. Although the rain had stopped, there were still signs it had been raining. The sun was trying to peek through the clouds. It seemed it would be a warm day. But in Seattle nothing could be promised.

Quiet went to the end of the bed, where he had laid out his clothes, and started putting them on. "They're not going to keep messing with my family," he mumbled. When he finished dressing, he went downstairs into the kitchen and began cooking himself some breakfast. While the breakfast was cooking he went into the bathroom to wash up. Later, while eating his breakfast, Quiet was scanning the newspaper and saw an article about a black youth found dead in some bushes by some schoolkids in Kent. He was a youth believed to be in his middle teens. He had been beaten to death. The police said they would treat the case as a homicide. No arrest was made. The case was under investigation by the Kent Police Department.

Seeing the word "police" in the newspaper brought a hateful expression over Quiet's face. But the expression soon went away when he came to the classified section. While scanning through the miscellaneous section, he saw ads for different types of guns. "I never want to hold another weapon, but cops have them," he mumbled.

When Quiet finished his breakfast, he went outside, got in his car, and headed north, toward town. He took the same route the cab that had brought him home had taken. Cruising down Jackson Street, he saw the usual blacks at their old hangouts. And, also as usual, cops were in the area, two or three squad cars at a time. There were no fewer than two officers in a car and no more than four. It seemed as though Chinatown was owned by the blacks and Chinese. When whites drove through Chinatown, they didn't stop but kept going.

Driving through the downtown area, traffic was heavy, but it moved. It was a nice day for shopping, especially for women. Sunny days were nice days for shopping. Few of the women were escorted by a man. Quiet pulled near a curb in front of a meter sitting outside Tall's Camera Shop. He got out, put the money in the meter, and started walking. The foot traffic was thick also. Many stores had business that day, because it was getting close to summer. A few clothing stores where Quiet used to shop had been replaced by other stores. He saw a few groups of black youths, ages ranging from fourteen to seventeen, going in and out of department stores throughout the downtown area.

Jewelry stores, shoe stores, and clothing stores had some of their sale items displayed in their windows. Quiet went from store to store doing a lot of window-shopping, not knowing what he was looking for. The prices on some of the items were too high, he felt. They were nowhere near the price a person would pay in Saigon or Tokyo. Over there prices were much cheaper. The Seattle downtown area, in spite of the few businesses, still looked the same.

Quiet window-shopped his way from the business section to the public market, located about in the heart of town. This was a place where a few farmers who lived just outside the city limits brought their vegetables and fruits to sell. Two years ago, the prices here were more reasonable than those in a grocery store. Quiet remembered how when he was a small boy, his mother used to bring him or one of his brothers to the public market and do some shopping. That was when three dollars would buy a week's groceries. But now three dollars wouldn't buy a decent meal at a restaurant.

The public market wasn't only a place where poor people came to buy groceries. It also had other participants, like hoboes and tramps, prostitutes, pimps, and young thieves. To a hobo, the public market was a paradise, like few other places, where he could get a free meal and a place to live. But most of the hoboes who lived around the public market area slept on steps of nearby hotels and along the alleys.

The public market also had other business. Prostitutes had plenty of business. A few had turned tricks for undercover police officers and been arrested. But they spent no more than an hour in jail. They were bailed out by their pimps. Women during the day, ladies of the night.

The public market also was a place where young thugs hung out when they had noplace to go and/or nothing to do. Just their appearance made the people who rented the stands nervous. At first sight of the kids, they would call the police, who would come and chase the kids away. The kids were known for running through the public market snatching a few items off the food stands.

Down the streets from the public market to Pioneer Square were camera shops, pawnshops, and jewelry stores, plus other types of stores on almost every block. Walking down the street, Quiet came to a gun store. He went inside and looked at a few weapons. On the shelves and hanging on the walls were crossbows, rifles of different brands, pistols, and knives. "But I told myself I never wanted to hold another weapon in my hand," he repeated. But the thought of Wyatt getting beaten up by the police and Clinton being kidnapped by the police made Quiet want to buy a weapon. Still, he felt the prices were too high. He left the store and continued walking on down the street.

On First Avenue some of the hoboes were walking around like zombies. Quiet wanted so much to help them as he observed them. *There must be a place they can go to get help,* he thought. After seeing some of the Vietnamese, he had understood. When people lose their homes, self-respect, and property, and begin the life of tramps or hoboes, they're known to human society as outcasts. So they get no help from the public, nothing but ignorance. No one knows why a person becomes a tramp. Only a handful cared, some old people. Others didn't want anything to do with the hoboes.

Farther down the street Quiet noticed a particular hobo about halfway down the block on the other side of the street, panhandling a few people as they were walking by. He was asking for money to buy a bowl of soup or a bottle of wine. But the people just kept on walking. Something was familiar about this hobo. *I think I know him,* thought Quiet. So he walked to the end of the block, waited for the green light, crossed the street, then advanced toward the hobo.

As Quiet approached the hobo, he said, "Dino," uncertainly. "Is that you?" Quiet took a closer look as the hobo wondered who was calling his name. "That *is* you. What are you doing down here?"

Dino was about Quiet's size and had been one of Quiet's running buddies during junior high and high school days. But after high school, each went his separate way. Dino got married when he was eighteen. He was married for four years; then his wife got a divorce. They had bought a house and owned it for two years before Dino lost it to his wife. They had two late-model cars, which Dino lost, though he was forced by the court to pay them off. Then Dino was served a restraining order by the court, told to leave the premises with only the clothes he had on his back. Up to last year Dino couldn't hold a job. He had gotten three jobs over the last two years and lost them through a habit of being drunk on the job.

Dino was drunk when Quiet called out his name. "Yeah!" said Dino as he tried to stand up straight. "Who called my name?"

"It's me," said Quiet. "Jones," he added as he placed his hand upon Dino's shoulders.

Dino took a closer look. "Hey, man!" he said joyously. "How you been? Jonesy, right?"

Quiet nodded.

"I heard you went in the war. When did you get back?"

"It's me all right! But what happened with you?"

Dino sobbed a little. "It's a long story."

Dino cried on Quiet's shoulder; then the two men started walking down the street. Quiet led Dino to a nearby restaurant and bought him a cup of coffee and a bowl of soup. In a booth, the conversation started by remembering old times. They laughed and joked about the tricks they had pulled on other boys, the girls they used to go steady with, parties they had gone to, and other friends they used to run around with. Then Dino began to explain some of his problems, why he ended up where he was. Quiet understood. So he offered to buy Dino a pair of trousers and a shirt and help him get back up on his feet. Dino refused Quiet's offer, but Quiet insisted. After Quiet had bought the clothes for Dino, he offered to take Dino home with him. Dino cried like a baby. They went to Quiet's car and left the downtown area.

When Quiet and Dino came walking through the front door, they saw Wyatt sitting on the couch staring up at the ceiling, leaning his head back. Wyatt seemed disgusted.

"What's the matter, Bro?" said Quiet sympathetically. Without getting up, Wyatt pointed to a piece of paper lying on the table.

Quiet walked to the table and picked up the paper. "A traffic ticket. When did you get this?"

"On the way home after dropping Joan off at her mother's," said Wyatt grumpily. "It was the same two cops who arrested me. One of them said they were going to stop me each time they saw me."

"What did you do?" asked Quiet curiously.

"Nothing, Bro!" said Wyatt seriously.

Dino was standing just to the side of Quiet. When Wyatt saw the hobo, he asked, "Who's he?"

"Don't you remember him? It's Dino."

Wyatt took a closer look at Dino. "Yea-ah! Now I remember. You two guys used to be running buddies. It's been a long time."

Quiet explained to Wyatt that Dino would be living with them for a while, at least until he got back on his feet. So Quiet, Wyatt, and Dino stayed at the house for the rest of the day playing cards while watching television. Later that evening they went to a house party across town. At the party, they met a few of their acquaintances from yesteryear. They mingled for a while and danced to the music. Around 4:00 A.M. the party terminated. Leaving the party, Quiet, Dino, and Wyatt drove to Earl's house and woke him up. Wyatt told him about the ticket. Earl got dressed in moments, and they went to Clinton's house. They woke him up also.

Later that morning, around eleven o'clock, Quiet was still lying in bed, but awake. He was lying there staring up at the ceiling. His mind was very active. *What should I do?* There were many questions filling his mind, but there were no answers. *The police are harassing my brothers. I don't want to fight them, because they are too strong. I remember once Dad said the whites tried to make blacks fight them when only a handful owned weapons. But this is the police. What do they have against my brothers? I want them to stop before there is trouble between us. I'm not afraid. I'll fight if I have to. But if we try to fight them, they'll kill us all. Somehow I've got to make them understand we want to be left alone. Some blacks were killed by the police for owing traffic fines. If the officers' lives were in jeopardy I could understand, but to kill someone for owing a traffic fine, there is no excuse. There was no reason to come after my brother. I've got to talk to them. I know I'm bitter. Maybe I'd better wait till I cool off. I'll go to Clinton and Earl's craftsmen meeting. Maybe I can see what this is all about. The meeting starts at twelve o'clock. That gives me an hour to get dressed.*

So Quiet got up and went through the motions as he did every morning, putting his clothes on. Quiet went to the meeting. Around seven o'clock the meeting was terminated. During the meeting Quiet couldn't see anything unusual. It was just craftsmen and -women discussing the problems they had encountered on certain jobs and ways they might get around these problems.

The weekend went by fast. Before Quiet realized it, it was time to go back to work. Every day work started at 7:00 in the morning. So he left home around 6:00, to have enough time to go to the cafeteria and have a cup of coffee. The streets were crowded with cars of people going to work. The traffic looked like traffic at the 4:30 P.M. rush hour. Before the Boeing entrance gate vehicles were backed up at least four blocks. But still the traffic moved slowly.

After Quiet parked his car, he went through the entrance gate and stopped by the cafeteria on his way to his work area. About twenty minutes after work had started, Mr. Scofield came into the work area. He approached Quiet. "Can I see you in my office for a moment?"

Curiosity showed all over Quiet's face. "Yes," he answered.

He followed Mr. Scofield to his office and closed the door after they entered. "What's up?" he asked.

"Have a seat," said Mr. Scofield as he gracefully walked around to his desk.

Quiet sat down.

"I heard you have a brother who works here. An employee of Boeing. I also heard he's been having some problems with his work and with his boss."

"He's on suspension," interrupted Quiet.

"My boss is lifting that suspension and wants your brother to come back to work. My boss is assigning your brother to be under my supervision. I wonder, can you keep him out of trouble?"

"I don't understand," said Quiet cautiously.

"You don't have to," said Mr. Scofield, getting up out of his chair and sitting back down on top of his desk. "Your brother can start tomorrow."

A big question mark showed on Quiet's face as he got up out of his chair. *What's the reason for this?* he thought. "Thanks!" he said. Without another word he left the office and went back to his work area. *I know they don't expect me to watch my brother and report to them when he does something he's not supposed to. What are they after? I've run into a lot of mess since I've been back. Where is it going to lead? I don't like what I've seen so far,* Quiet thought.

All day long Quiet felt uneasy as he worked. Slowly but surely things were beginning to fall into place. It was not only what his brothers had warned him of, but what his friends had said, too. Then Quiet came to realize it wasn't Wyatt or him the whites were after. It was Clinton and Earl, or people like them, for doing what they are doing for blacks. Why should the whites try to stop such men? They did no more than the whites had done when they wanted to create trade unions in the early 1900s.

The police kidnapping Clinton and then turning him loose was a mystery. Wyatt getting beaten up by two police officers who had taken him into custody was only to be expected, because police had beaten and killed blacks for no apparent reason for years. The story always had been one-sided, in the police's favor. But Quiet never knew there was so much of this while he was away from home. The things his father had told him made Quiet feel Mr. Jones must have gone through a lot of hell while growing up. Quiet thought, *The whites speak so much of peace, but in their own way they make war. Where will it stop?* Thoughts troubled Quiet's mind. The feeling of fighting again was entering his system. First he had to serve in Vietnam and fight a war no one understood. Thought that fight was behind him, he had to come home and fight again, because the police were harassing his brothers. If this continued, sooner or later someone was going to get hurt or killed. *I'll go downtown after work to see if I can put a stop to this before it goes any further,* he decided.

Come 3:30 P.M., it was time for Quiet to get off work. When the whistle blew, all the employees turned in all the company tools, cleaned up their work area, and waited for the final whistle. When employees were leaving the Boeing plant, its traffic was the worst in Seattle. People always rushed to get home only to get ready for work the next day.

When Quiet got to the parking lot, the Boeing traffic was thick. It took him from fifteen minutes to a half hour to get clear of the Boeing traffic. The cars were almost bumper-to-bumper as he was leaving the exit gate. But instead of going home, Quiet headed straight for downtown by catching the freeway. Although he wouldn't get out of the rush-hour traffic, this would at least get him out of the bumper-to-bumper traffic. When Quiet got downtown he ran into more traffic, but not as thick as Boeing's. The traffic was just building up. He knew he had to be out of the downtown area at least by 4:30 P.M because that was when a lot of people would be getting off work and he might have to spend a lot of time just getting out of stop-and-go traffic.

When Quiet pulled into the downtown area, there was a heavy flow of traffic. A rally was being held at the municipal building. Police officers stood in front of the building with their equipment, waiting for something to happen. Quiet looked around for Clinton as he drove by. Although he didn't see Clinton he knew his brother was there somewhere. Within a block of the municipal building Quiet pulled near the curb in front of a parking meter. He got out, put his coins in the meter, and walked toward the building. The rally was being held near the entrance to the building on Third Avenue. Quiet entered through the back entrance on Fourth Avenue. He went to the directory in the lobby. The building was patrolled by uniformed police officers. The detectives' office was on the fifth floor. Quiet entered the building and caught an elevator to the fifth floor. When he got to the fifth floor, he made a left turn and started walking down the hallway. Arrows in the hallways pointed to certain rooms on that floor. While walking down the hallways, Quiet saw something he had never noticed before. A camera was mounted at each end of the hallway on the ceiling, and two cameras in between. "They never had this before," he mumbled.

Just behind the camera was a door leading to the detectives' office. It read: "Detective Bureau." Underneath, underlined, was: "Homicide and investigations." Quiet approached the door and entered the office. A secretary's desk was sitting just to the side of the door as he opened it.

"Can I help you?" she said as Quiet stood in front of her desk. The secretary was brunette and appeared to be in her early forties. Her clothes were sexy.

Quiet counted seven detectives sitting and standing around the office. As they stared at him, Quiet said coldly, "Yes. I want to see your boss."

"You must mean Lieutenant Miller. Hang on for a second.

I'll buzz his office," she said as she swung her chair around and pushed a button. A voice answered through a squawk box on the secretary's desk. The secretary said, "Someone out here wants to see you."

Miller came out of his office wearing a white shirt open at the top, a blue tie dangling around his neck, and wrinkled gray suit pants. He was about in his midfifties and a little on the chubby side. "What's your problem?" he said when he saw the black standing next to the secretary's desk.

"I want to ask you a favor," said Quiet casually.

"Are you part of that outside?" asked Miller.

"In what way?"

"Demonstrating!"

"No!"

"Then what's your favor?"

"I want you to call your dogs off. Leave us alone."

Another detective, sitting on the other side of the office, got up from his desk and walked over to them. "That's strong talk for someone who's by himself when there's quite a few of us," he said sarcastically.

Quiet just looked at him and the rest of the detectives. As he was walking way, the second detective said, "If we don't, what does it mean to you?"

Quiet was about in the hallway as he turned around to face the detective. "Your life or mine." Then he continued walking.

The detective's name was Lawrence Shatter. He looked to be in his late thirties or early forties. Watching Quiet walk down the hallway, the detective thought, *Must think he's a bad nigger.* Six feet tall, Shatter had graying hair and weighed about 230 pounds.

Listening to the way Quiet spoke, the detectives didn't know whether or not he was serious. Miller watched until Quiet turned the corner. "When a dude like him says something, you'd better listen. He's the type don't talk much, just do," he said.

"What can a nigga like him do? We'll blow him away," said Shatter angrily.

Miller sighed disgustedly for Shatter's benefit. "Don't you think he knows that? It's not us against him I'm worried about. It's him against us. How many of us do you think he'd get before we got him?"

"None, because he won't stand a chance. He won't know when we're coming. A person like him, we'll catch him when he's sleeping."

"You put him on guard; he won't sleep. He'll be hitting from all directions before we know what hit us." Miller slowly headed back to his office. "But I would like to know what he was talking about."

4

The few days Dino spent with Quiet and Wyatt went by quickly. Dino and Quiet picked up where they had left off before going their separate ways: running the streets. Dino started cleaning himself up more often and began to look as he had in his early years. Dino and Quiet spent a lot of time with Wyatt and Joan, especially on the weekends. Dino wasn't much of a partygoer, but on weekends there was always a party somewhere. One of Wyatt's or Joan's friends almost every weekend had some type of house party. Like old times, Dino and Quiet went to the parties to meet single women. Dino was beginning to feel more like himself, again. A few times he went with Quiet to Clinton and Earl's craftsmen's meetings. Other times Dino would drop Quiet off at the meetings, borrow his car, and pick him up later.

Many times Quiet attended the craftsmen's meetings. At one particular meeting he was sitting among carpenters. As he had attended quite a few meetings, a few of the craftsmen had come to know him as Clinton and Earl's younger brother. Every now and then they would have some type of discussion about the meetings. Two women came to the meeting about an hour late. Quiet noticed them as the black woman went and sat in the electricians' section. Clinton was on the platform talking to the craftsmen about steps they should take toward unity. Whenever the craftsmen shouted and cheered at his statements, the women shouted also. The white woman went and sat among the ironworkers. Although the women were dressed like the tradesmen, for some strange reason Quiet felt they didn't belong there. Constantly Quiet watched the two women. Now and then the black woman caught Quiet's eye but ignored it.

It was around 11:30 P.M. when the meeting terminated. Everyone else was leaving while Quiet, Dino, Clinton, and Earl, along with a few others, stayed behind to discuss matters further.

The black woman was one of the people who had left the meeting. When she got outside she was joined by the white woman. They walked around the block and got in a green Dodge. They sat in the backseat. The same three police officers who had kidnapped Clinton were waiting for them.

"How did it go?" asked the driver. His name was John Maulder and he was a young man in his late twenties with blond hair, blue eyes, and a small goatee. He was about six feet, four inches tall and weighed about 240 pounds. He was a kung-fu expert.

"That brother of theirs gave me a scare. I thought he'd never take his eyes off me," said Maraisha.

"I know what you mean," said the police officer who was sitting in the backseat. His name was Jack Marty, and he had a dark complexion, black hair, and brown eyes. About six feet tall, he weighed 240 pounds. He also was a young man in his late twenties.

"Don't worry about him," said a police officer sitting on the passenger side. His name was Mike Schmidt. Mike Schmidt was in his middle to late fifties. His hair was silver white, and he had a few wrinkles around his cheeks. Old-age fat made him look to be about 260 pounds. He was about six feet, three inches tall. He always wore a gray suit and tie.

Maraisha and Sharon told the officers what they wanted to know about the meeting, then got out of the car and went and got in theirs, which was a block ahead parked near the curb. Maraisha drove the car to the end of the block, where she could keep an eye on the front door of the building. Parked in the shadows she watched a few of the tradesmen still straggling out of the building. Then about a half an hour later the lights in the building went out. Moments later Quiet, Clinton, Earl, and Dino walked outside. Clinton's and Earl's cars were parked in the parking lot. Quiet's car was parked on the street across from the building.

Dino and the three brothers stood in front of the building. They were the only ones left. Maraisha kept a close eye on Quiet. She watched every move he made while Dino went and sat in the car. He kept up his part of the conversation from a rolled-down window, while the car was running to keep the motor warm. When the conversation was over Quiet went and got in his car. Clinton and Earl did the same, but more alertly. Unaware, Quiet drove past Maraisha and Sharon.

"Why don't we follow them?" said Sharon.

"I'm not sure I want to after the way that one looked at us at the meeting," said Maraisha. She glanced down at her watch. "We'd better head in. It's late." Sharon agreed as the two women drove away from the area.

Around nine o'clock Monday morning, Dino had an appointment to meet Earl at his office. Quiet and Wyatt had already gone to work, and Wyatt had left Dino his car. Earl had found a job opening in the pipefitters and plumbers' trade union. The union was down on the percentage of hiring a certain amount of minorities and had to hire at least five more minority members to fill the requirement of the state's equal-opportunity-to-work code.

Dino drove the car into the parking lot, locked it, and went into the office building. Earl was sitting behind the desk talking on the telephone when Dino entered. When Earl got off the phone, the two men talked for a few moments, then left the office. Since Dino didn't have a valid driver's license, Earl suggested they use his car.

The pipefitters and plumbers' union was Local 32. It was located on First and Cedar Street in downtown Seattle. At this union hall members of Local 32 and out-of-town pipefitters and plumbers met every morning, five days a week, to bid on jobs available. But to get in the union the member would have to go to school for four to five years and serve as an apprentice to learn the trade. School was two nights a week, Wednesday and Thursday, three hours a night. During the day, students had on-the-job training. On jobs all trade unions have certain duties to perform. Each union has great respect for the others. This attitude keeps a good relationship among the workers.

Earl had come to Fifth and Mercer when a motorcycle police officer put his red light on. Then the sound of the siren forced Earl to the curb. "What did I do now?" he mumbled to himself. Earl just sat in his car as he watched the police officer get off his motorcycle, pull out his ticket book, and approach them.

"You went through a red light back there," the officer pointed out. "May I see your driver's license?" he asked.

"You're a liar," said Earl as he handed the officer his license. Hatred and anger suffused the officer's red face. It gave Earl a good feeling when he saw the officer's expression as he gave Earl the ticket and then continued on his way.

Earl pulled up near the curb in front of the Labor Temple on First and Cedar. He and Dino got out of the car and went into the building. The Labor Temple was open to quite a few trades. Each door identified the trade: carpenters and sheet metal, sheet rock, taper, boatland, and iron, as well as pipefitters and plumbers, etc. Every morning the Labor Temple was packed with men who were trying to get out and go to work. The white craftsmen hated to see the blacks show up for job calls. They felt the blacks were taking away their jobs. Earl led Dino into the plumbers' room, where he could get his name on the out-of-work sheet and become an apprentice at the same time. The next day Dino was scheduled to fill out an application and take an aptitude test. After spending a little over two hours in the examination room, Dino finished the test. Patiently he waited in the hallway until the examiner was done grading his paper. Moments later the examiner came out into the hallway and told Dino he had passed. Relieved, he felt this was the ideal time to become a plumber, for at least he'd have a solid background if he wanted to try something else. Two days later, after the paperwork was done, Dino was sent to a job in East Kent. It was a remodeling job in a shopping center.

On this job Dino worked with a journeyman. Dino felt he was learning a lot about the trade. Days turned into weeks. Weeks turned into a few months. There were good times, and there were bad times. There were good days, and there were bad days. But the weather always seemed the same: rainy and wet. If it wasn't raining, then cold filled the air. In the Jones house it seemed as though Dino was more of a brother than a friend. There were no more mortgage payments 'cause the house was paid off. All the furniture and everything else in the house was paid for as were the cars. So Dino just helped buy groceries and made a few payments on the utility bills. Quiet and Wyatt tried to talk him out of it, but Dino insisted.

In the few months that had passed, the tensions between the blacks and the police had gotten worse. But it wasn't only the blacks being intimidated by the police. The whites were getting their share also. The whites usually took sides against the blacks when white police officers arrested blacks on misdemeanor or felony charges and were railroaded into jail or prison by an incompetent lawyer. But when a white was arrested, that person had to be proven guilty in court. The uprising blacks had settled down and gave the police little or no reason to harass them. Very few blacks had committed crimes and were sent to jail or prison, because they knew no matter what the crime, they would serve the maximum, even if a white would get probation for the same crime.

Quiet and Wyatt were at their machines one morning when one of Boeing's employees came to work with bitterness in his voice. His name was Calvin Lassinger. Around thirty, he was a Caucasian who weighed about 160 pounds. Five feet, eight inches tall, he had a red face today. Angrily Lassinger paced back and forth in his work area, next to Quiet and Wyatt's. When Wyatt heard Lassinger huffing and puffing he asked what was wrong.

"I was driving down Twenty-third Avenue on my way to work when I saw these people in the crosswalk, crossing the street. On Twenty-third and Atlantic I slowed down until the people were almost on the other side of the street. Then I drove on. When I got about halfway down the street, a cop sitting on a side street came out and pulled me over. He said I refused to yield the right-of-way to the pedestrians. Them people were about to step onto the curb before I sped up. I'm going to take this to court. That bastard gave me a ticket," explained Lassinger.

Other employees saw the distress on Lassinger's face. Quiet knew exactly what Lassinger was talking about. He went back into his memory bank to when the Bellevue police had pulled him and Wyatt over, right after he bought his car. When he heard the word "police" pierce his ears, a chill of hatred ran through his body. When Quiet was twelve years old he had had his first bad experience with the police.

One day Quiet's mother sent him and Wyatt to the store to pick up a few items she had forgotten earlier. The store was located a few blocks down the hill from the house on Rainier Avenue. She was unaware that earlier that day a few kids had intimidated an old man whose house was on the corner of Eighteenth and Atlantic in another neighborhood Quiet and Wyatt had to walk through to get to the store. The kids had made the old man angry, and he had started shooting at everyone

95

passing his house. His eyesight was poor, which caused him to miss. The old man was about in his midseventies. His shots were wild and high. Whenever the old man took a shot, his victims disappeared.

What made the old man angry was the kids in the neighborhood had been throwing rocks and sticks at his house. The old man warned the kids that if they didn't stop, they were going to get shot. But the kids kept intimidating the old man until he grabbed his pistol and started shooting. Like a burst of smoke, the kids scattered. This was about the time Quiet and Wyatt were on their way to the store.

While walking down the hill, Quiet and Wyatt ran into Dino and Louie, who were running up the hill. "Whatcha guys running from?" asked Quiet curiously.

Dino and Louie were exhausted from running up the hill. They were breathing hard, huffing and puffing with each step. But when they approached Quiet and Wyatt, Dino said, exhaustedly, "Don't go down there! The old man is crazy. He's shooting at everyone who walks past his house."

Wyatt asked about it and Dino told the brothers some kids had been bothering the old man. Wyatt explained that he and Quiet had to go to the store for their mother but since they had been warned about the old man's shooting, they would circle the block and not pass the old man's house to get to the store.

In fear of her younger kids getting shot by the old man, a woman called the police, who came and confiscated the old man's pistol. When the old man explained to the police about the kids throwing rocks and sticks at his house, the police began to patrol the neighborhoods looking for the kids. The kids were described as "niggers."

Quiet and Wyatt were about two blocks from the store when the police car pulled up beside them. "Where are you kids going?" said the driver.

The sarcastic sound of the officer's voice made Quiet a little angry. But Wyatt answered, "We're going to the store for our mother."

"Where do you kids live?"

"Up the street," Wyatt pointed.

"Do you kids know anything about an old man shooting at kids?"

"No," answered Wyatt.

"I heard some black kids were throwing sticks at the old man's house. You wouldn't happen to know anything about that, would you?"

"No," answered Wyatt.

The officer sitting on the passenger side said, "That one acts like he can't speak. He looks like the type would do something like that," referring to Quiet. "Let me see your hands."

Quiet opened his hands and showed them to the officer. They were clean.

"Whatcha do? Go home and wash them?"

"No!" answered Wyatt quickly.

"Hush, boy!" interrupted the officer. "I'm talking to him."

Quiet answered, "No," disgustedly. "We just came from home and are going to the store for our mother."

"Well, you kids better get on to the store, then get your asses back home. If I catch you down here again, you both are going to the youth center," said the driver.

When the police car pulled away, Quiet and Wyatt continued on to the store, got what their mother wanted, and headed back home. When they got back home, Wyatt told his father what had happened. Mr. Jones became angry. . . .

From a distance Quiet heard someone calling him. When he came out of his thoughts, Wyatt asked, "Are you all right, Bro? Looks like you were in dreamland."

"I was." Quiet smiled. "Let's get to work," he said as he walked around his workbench, picked up his tools, and started grinding material. The woman who reminded Quiet of Mrs.

Jones gave him many thanks when she came into his area to clean up. Ever since the incident that first day, the woman's supervisors just told her what they wanted cleaned up, then went about their way. With Quiet's appearances in the area it seemed as though all the supervisors tried to avoid the woman as much as possible.

At 3:25 P.M. the time-to-quit whistle blew. Quiet and Wyatt, along with the other employees, turned their company tools in to the toolroom. They went through the same routine of punching their time cards out, then walked to the parking lot, got in their car, and drove home and went inside. Quiet felt that someone had been there. Although it seemed as if nothing had been disturbed, curiosity got the best of him. Thoroughly Quiet went through each room to see if anything was missing. He searched the clothes closet and the dresser drawers. Nothing had been touched. Although Quiet didn't find any clue, the thought of the police entered his mind. *But what do they want here?* he asked himself. *Maybe it's just my imagination. Maybe no one's been here. But until I'm proven wrong, I'm going to believe someone was here. Maybe Dino came home early. I'll just have to wait and see.*

Wyatt noticed the expression on Quiet's face as he also went through the house slowly. He asked Quiet, "Why?" Quiet didn't know any explanation. After this long a period of time, he felt that all should have been forgotten. But the feeling of his family being tampered with by the police came back to his thoughts. Even then, Quiet didn't know the reason why. About an hour later Dino came home and Quiet asked if he had been home earlier. Dino answered that he was at work all day.

Quiet went upstairs, alone. He felt he had to get somewhere alone and do some thinking. *What should I do?* he wondered. He felt depressed. So he got up off the couch and went outside and got back in his car. He started his car up and drove away from the house. Wyatt and Dino had noticed Quiet was troubled. When one of them was troubled, the others were troubled also.

For some reason Quiet headed back south, the same way he came home from work. Driving down Rainier Avenue, he noticed a few sights he never noticed before. The store Quiet used to go to when he was growing up was now an electrical shop. The ice-cream parlor was boarded up, with a BUSINESS FOR SALE sign on the door. Farther down the avenue, he saw Dag's Drive-In where the high school students usually went at lunchtime when they didn't go to the school lunchroom to eat had been torn down and replaced by an overpass. Next door a Church's chicken drive-in had been added. Farther down the avenue were added strip malls and banks, on through Columbia City to Rainier Beach.

Quiet's drive took him through Renton and to the Kent city limits. Within the last two months there had been four black bodies discovered by some unidentified passersby near some railroad tracks in the Kent area. The killings were unsolved. Quiet believed that for some reason Clinton, when he was kidnapped, had been brought out here. But where? That was another question Quiet couldn't answer.

As long as Quiet had lived in Seattle he had never stopped in Kent. He always drove straight through when he was on his way to either Auburn or Tacoma or just somewhere south. Quiet didn't know why he drove to Kent now. But since his travels took him there, he drove around and through the Kent area until he came upon an area where a black male had been found. The location had been noted in a newspaper.

The Kent area covered a lot of territory. Quiet could see why Kent was a dumping ground for bodies. Once a person got out of the downtown and residential areas, Kent was covered with trees and open cow pastures. Then there were houses scattered at great distances off the roads. To hear a woman scream at the next house, a person would have to almost turn

99

the TV set off. A dead body would take months to find if stashed in the right place. And there were many "right places" around. In the last few weeks, all the dead bodies found had been those of craftsmen. Railroad tracks passed all through Kent in every direction. It would be hard for anyone to pinpoint certain areas to recover bodies off the road, unless that person was very lucky.

Quiet pulled about a hundred feet off the road into an area ideal for dumping off a dead body. Uncertain of the area, Quiet got out of his car and looked around. It was quiet, no breeze in the air, and cold. From a distance he heard the sound of a train going toward town. Soon the sound faded away. Quiet walked away from his car and headed for the woods, only a short distance away. For about fifty feet he walked over stumps, fallen trees, and snake holes before coming to a grassy field. The field was about twenty-two acres. *It's pretty,* he thought, *a place where someone could raise livestock and poultry.* He found a stump and sat down, then admired the area for a few moments. *It is really pretty,* he thought again. But his mind became full of other thoughts, including the reason he had come to a place like this: the police.

While sitting here Quiet began to realize that over the years he had lost quite a few casual acquaintances to the police. Larry Taylor, someone who used to run around with Quiet and Dino, wasn't a close friend, just an acquaintance. He was a victim of a police officer's bullet. During high school, Taylor used to push marijuana among his associates, until he sold marijuana to a narcotics agent. Taylor spent eighteen months in Walla Walla State Penitentiary. When Larry got out he got a job working for a Coca-Cola trucking company out of Bellevue. He got married a year later and had a three-year-old daughter at the time of his death. While he was sitting up one night watching a movie on television, his wife and daughter were in bed asleep. The telephone rang about 1:00 A.M. A friend named Johnny Roberts called. Among his friends, Roberts was known as a TIP (turn-in pusher). He wasn't to be trusted. Roberts used to sell marijuana and cocaine until he, too, got caught selling dope to a narcotics agent. But instead of serving any time, he accepted an offer to set up as many dope pushers as he could for the narcotics agents. And a fee was paid for each pusher prosecuted and sent to prison. This was how Roberts began to make his living.

The wind was blowing really hard that night. Rain poured by the bucketful. It was stormy. Whenever a breeze went past the windows, it left them rattling. Whistling wind through the trees drowned out the other sounds from the outside. There was very little traffic. The streets seemed deserted. It was so cold, even the barking dogs in the neighborhood had to take a night off.

When Taylor answered the telephone, Roberts responded. He told Taylor he had just come in on a Greyhound bus from California and needed a ride home. Taylor agreed and put his jacket on. Usually before leaving the house Taylor would let his wife know. But at this hour she and his daughter were sleeping. So he decided not to wake his wife. He just casually went outside, got in his car, and drove away.

Although Taylor had stopped selling dope, he managed to keep a little on hand for himself, either in his dresser at the house or in his glove compartment in his car. On the way to the bus depot he reached into his glove compartment and pulled out his stash and rolled himself a joint. When Taylor got to the downtown area, traffic began to build up. But still, the streets were deserted. It was 2:00 A.M. when Taylor pulled in front of the bus depot to the passenger loading zone. He saw Roberts standing in front of the doorway of the depot with a newspaper, using it as an umbrella.

Roberts greeted Taylor as he was getting out of his car, "Do you have some smoke? I need something to get me straight."

Taylor and Roberts used to be the closest of friends. Without thinking anything of it, Taylor reached in his pocket and pulled out two joints and handed them to Roberts. Roberts suspiciously took the marijuana and slowly started backing away.

"What's the matter, man?" asked Taylor suspiciously. Then he cautiously looked around.

As Taylor started to get back in his car, a voice hollered, "Halt!" It seemed to come from across the street. Taylor was almost surrounded before he realized what was happening. There were four detectives coming across the street, six uniformed police officers running down the street, and three more uniformed officers coming up the street. When Taylor raised his hands a hail of bullets came flying his way. It seemed as though he was hit with hand grenade fragments. He was dead within moments. He fell facedown, with his head leaning over the curb.

When the shooting started, Roberts fell to the ground. When it was over, he gradually got up and walked away. The people in the bus depot when they heard the shooting came out to see what the commotion was about. But when they saw Taylor's body lying in the rain, they began to mumble, "What happened?" The police dispersed the crowd, as they slowly moved away. About six months later Roberts was found in Kent Valley near the railroad tracks, with four bullet holes in the back of his head. The case was unsolved. It was still under investigation, supposedly.

The day was getting gray. Night was trying to fall. Time had slipped away, and it was time to head back home. Quiet got up off the stump, headed back to his car, and drove away. It was about six-thirty when Quiet pulled near the curb in front of the house. When he got inside the house, Wyatt asked with concern, "Where have you been?" Quiet explained. Then he and Dino got ready to go to the craftsmen's meeting. It was nearing seven o'clock.

At the meeting, Quiet sat in his usual seat, in the visitors' section, which was for people who weren't in the trade unions but came to hear what the meetings were about. The doors were open to everyone. Maraisha was at the meeting also, but this time sitting in the pipefitters/plumbers' section. *What is she doing here? She's not a trade worker. For some reason or another they don't belong,* thought Quiet. Curiosity got the best of him as he casually got up from his chair and walked toward the rest room through the corridors, down the hallway. Beyond the rest rooms was an exit door that led to the back of the building. Instead of going to the rest room, Quiet went through the exit door and on outside. Outside in the shadows near the building he crept toward the front. As he neared the sidewalk, two men were standing in front of the entrance talking and laughing. Quiet hid in some bushes and carefully looked around. All he saw up and down the street were parked vehicles. But as he was about to turn and go back the way he came he noticed a manlike figure about three-quarters of the way down the block get out of a car. Two men were changing places behind the steering wheel. "That's why Clint was kidnapped," Quiet mumbled. "Cops! They're watching the building." *Better get back inside,* he thought. So Quiet headed back to the exit.

When Quiet got back into the auditorium, Maraisha's eyes followed him back to his seat. Intentionally Quiet caught her eye, then turned toward the platform. The meeting was nearing adjournment. Quite a few tradesmen had already left the CAMP building. It was around eleven o'clock. Only a handful stayed behind, as usual, to mingle.

Seeing the police made Quiet stay behind also. He had become suspicious of the two women and the police. Many questions ran through his mind unanswered.

When Clinton and Earl were ready to leave, Quiet looked for Dino but found him nowhere inside the building. So Quiet decided to wait for him in the car. But when Quiet got outside he saw Dino standing on the sidewalk between the building and the parking lot, talking to Sharon. Maraisha was standing farther down the sidewalk, waiting. Without disturbing them, Quiet went on to the car. Maraisha never took her eyes off him. But when Dino saw Quiet, he cut his conversation short and went to the waiting car. After Clinton and Earl got in their cars and drove away, Quiet did also.

Through the week Dino and Sharon began to talk a lot to one another on the telephone. Came weekends Dino would ask Quiet for his car. Without asking any questions, Quiet would give Dino his car keys. Quiet wanted so much to share his secret with Dino and his brothers, to tell them the two women were police officers and he believed the trade union work was why Clinton was singled out to be kidnapped. But how could he tell Dino? Ever since they were kids, Quiet and Dino had been friends. He didn't want to take a chance on their friendship by exposing Sharon. If she was any kind of woman or had any feelings for Dino, she would tell him what she was doing, although it might cause the end of their relationship. For lying to a man was one of the worst things a woman could do, 'cause what feelings he had for her would slowly or rapidly fade away.

Clinton and Earl had grown fond of the two women. *How would they react if I told them what I suspected about the two women? I know they would feel I was jealous. Through the years we have shared many secrets among ourselves. But this type of secret is different. I wouldn't feel right telling them about Sharon and Maraisha. I would feel guilty if they found out I knew but didn't tell them. I don't know what to do,* Quiet thought. *I'll just keep this to myself and wait for an appropriate time, I guess.*

Dino tried to get Quiet to go with him a couple of times to Maraisha and Sharon's apartment. But Quiet always refused. He found something else to substitute. Through the weeks and on weekends Dino and Sharon were seeing a lot of each other. Dino was using Quiet's car as though he owned it. But it seemed as though Quiet didn't mind.

Maraisha and Sharon were renting in the Beacon Hill Valley View Apartments. Their apartment number was 415. It overlooked all of Rainier Valley as far as the eyes could see and a good portion of Mount Baker Hill District, which was about a mile across the valley on another hill, and the viaduct bridge that led to the Floating Bridge and the tunnel. Quiet's house was in perfect view of the apartment.

One weekend in the apartment, early evening, Sharon was in the bedroom getting dressed to go out with Dino who was coming over later. "Maraisha!" she called. Maraisha was sitting on her bed watching television. Sharon continued, "Do you feel what we are doing is right? I mean the brothers have no intention of breaking the law. Why do John and the others want us to watch those guys?"

"I don't know," said Maraisha exhaustedly as she got up off the bed. Then she left the bedroom and headed for the kitchen. Sharon followed. "Our orders, continued Maraisha, "are to watch them and report back to the men." She started making a pot of coffee.

Sharon walked into the kitchen and sat down at the table. "Doesn't it seem strange that John wants us to report to him and the others and not to headquarters about Earl and Clinton?"

"What about Dino and Quiet?" added Maraisha.

"I don't think they're in this. They're just their brother and his buddy."

Maraisha walked over to the table and sat down. "What's the matter? You falling in love or something?" she asked.

"I don't know," answered Sharon sorrowfully. "But I don't feel it's right spying on them for no reason. What are we looking for? If they're doing something illegal, then why don't we arrest them?"

"Our job is not to ask any questions, just do what we're told," said Maraisha as she got up from the table to check the coffee. It was ready. So she went to the cupboard and pulled out two teacups and poured them each a cup of coffee. Then she went back to the table and sat across from Sharon. Sharon drank her coffee black. Maraisha drowned hers with cream and sugar. "Don't get hung up on this guy. We have a job to do."

"I haven't been to bed with him yet. But all he has to do is ask. I'm afraid I may not be able to help myself. I've thought about it a lot. It seems a losing battle." As Sharon looked at Maraisha seriously, she asked, "Why don't you go out with the other one and we'll make it a double date? It'll be easier on me."

"No!" said Maraisha, disturbed. She got up from the table and went back to the bedroom and sat down on the bed in front of the television. Moments later, Sharon came and stood in the doorway of the bedroom with sorrow in her eyes. When Maraisha saw the hurt look on her face, she apologized. "I'm sorry. I didn't mean to snap. It's just that his eyes give me the creeps. He makes me nervous whenever he looks at me."

"I know the feeling," said Sharon. Just then the doorbell rang. "That must be Dino." Sharon went and answered the door. She lightly kissed Dino on the lips as he stood in the doorway. Then he entered. When Maraisha came out of the bedroom, Sharon said, "CAMP is having a dance next weekend to raise money for unskilled workers to start a craftsmanship class. We want you to come."

"Yes! I'll be there," answered Maraisha as she watched Sharon and Dino leave the apartment.

Came next weekend Quiet was dressed in a black polyester bell-bottom suit for the dance. Wyatt was wearing the same style, but his suit was gray. They left the house to go by and pick up Joan. Joan was dressed in a white gown. Dino borrowed Quiet's car to pick up Sharon and Maraisha and bring them to the dance. He was wearing a yellow jacket and black slacks. Clinton and Earl were dressed in their everyday suits as they brought their wives to the dance. A fourteen-year-old baby-sitter from next door sat with Clinton's daughter. Moments later Mitchell and his Caucasian date came walking through the entrance/exit door.

When Quiet saw him, he got up from his chair, walked over to them, and led them back to his table.

The dance was well under way. Sitting with his brothers and their dates close to the bandstand, Quiet noticed Maraisha, Dino, and Sharon come walking through the entrance/exit door. Sharon was dressed in a long red gown that brushed the floor where she walked. Maraisha was wearing a black silk ankle-length gown with gold threads running through it. It was V-shaped from the shoulders to her breasts. *Sexy,* he thought. Her measurements looked as though they were 40-24-38. *Without them work clothes on, she looks like a real woman. Very pretty,* he thought. As the women and Dino stood in the doorway looking around, Wyatt stood up from his chair and motioned them over to where he and the others were sitting.

When Dino brought the two women to the table he introduced them to Mitchell and his date. Then purposely Dino, like a gentleman, seated Maraisha next to Quiet, who had no expression on his face. Dino and Sharon sat next to Wyatt and Joan. When a slow song played, everyone at the table got up and danced.

Quiet and Maraisha sat in silence next to one another while other people danced. Quiet noticed the scent of Maraisha's perfume. It was the same faded scent he had smelled that day when he and Wyatt came home from work. *Now that she finally really met us, what does she want?* he wondered. Digging back in time again, Quiet remembered what Mr. Jones had said while in the living room watching a movie on racism. "Through the years, the whites used our women and kids to get at the black man. Runaway slaves were captured and put to death, by hanging, firing squad, and torture. Back in them days it was much easier to use a woman than it is now."

When that song was over, another song played right after, but with more rhythm to it. A few couples walked off the dance floor while the rest stayed. When Dino got back to his chair, he said joyously, "Hey, you guys! You're not just going to sit there. Let's party!"

Still without any expression, Quiet looked at Maraisha. "You want to dance?" he asked, his voice soft yet firm.

A chill flowed through Maraisha's body. Then fear came. "Yes," she said nervously. Slowly Maraisha got up from her seat and Quiet led her by the arm onto the dance floor.

On the dance floor, although Quiet had the rhythmic movement, he just didn't feel like dancing. There was a time when Quiet would take the whole dance floor and a crowd would gather around and watch him dance. Maraisha felt pretty much the same, except she was a little livelier. When the dance was nearing an end, Quiet suggested they go back to their table and sit down. Maraisha agreed and they walked off the dance floor.

Two-thirty A.M. rolled around. Sunday morning. The dance was nearing an end. Dino suggested they leave and go to an all-night restaurant. Before leaving Quiet asked Clinton and Earl if they wanted to come with them. But the two had to stay behind and watch how the dance went. Wyatt and Mitchell waited behind also.

Dino had parked the car in the parking lot. Quiet got behind the wheel, and Maraisha sat beside him. Dino and Sharon sat in the backseat.

The night was clear. The stars were bright, and the moon lighted up the night The air was fresh. It was warm. *Today,* Quiet thought, *is going to be a warm spring day.*

Around 3:00 A.M. Quiet pulled into the House of Pancakes parking lot on Tenth and Union. Usually on this side of town when the parties and dances were over, the Pancake House was a weekend meeting place, where everyone went before going home. They got out of the car and went on inside. Quiet and Dino each ordered a steak and potato dinner. Maraisha and

Sharon each ordered a hamburger and fries, plus coffee. Moments later their orders came.

Sitting at a table in a booth, for the first time Quiet got a good look at Maraisha and Sharon. Both women looked like beauty queens. They were quite attractive. But the fact that he believed they were policewomen never left his mind, although they *were* cute. Bitter words came out of Quiet's mouth whenever he spoke. Without knowing the reason why, Dino would interrupt to change the subject. He felt he might have made a mistake in trying to get Quiet and Maraisha together.

So finally Quiet got up from his seat, grabbed the bill, paid the cashier, and went to the car. Dino and the two women stayed to finish their orders. When they were finished, they went to get in the car also. Quiet started up the engine, pulled out of the parking lot, and headed on home.

When they got to the house, Quiet got out. Dino got behind the wheel and drove the women to their apartment. When he pulled into the parking lot, before he came to a complete stop Maraisha jumped out of the car and ran to the building.

As Sharon watched Maraisha go inside the apartment building, she said, "I wonder what's wrong with her? It seemed as though she was going to cry. Think maybe she and Quiet had some kind of fight?"

A curious expression was on Dino's face. "I've known Quiet ever since we were kids. I've never seen him act this way unless he was ready to do battle," he said disgustedly. "Something is wrong."

"Why don't you come in and let's talk to her?" said Sharon.

"No!" said Dino. "I'd better head in and see what's the matter."

"Please!" begged Sharon.

When Dino saw the love-hungry look in her eyes, he said, "All right," and they got out of the car and headed for the building. By the time Sharon and Dino entered the apartment, Maraisha was already in bed. Her bedroom door was closed.

Later on that morning around seven, when Quiet got up, he dressed in his outdoorsman outfit, then went downstairs and washed up and made himself a cup of coffee. After loading his car with cooking utensils and a sleeping bag, Quiet went and checked on Dino and Wyatt. They were still asleep. So Quiet went and sat down on the couch to finish his coffee. He leaned his head back and closed his eyes but couldn't sleep. Maraisha filled his mind. As long as she was there, other thoughts couldn't enter. Feeling he had to get somewhere and think, Quiet got up off the couch and headed for the front door. When he got outside, he saw Maraisha, to his surprise, standing at the bottom of the stairs, as though she was waiting. She was wearing a brown corduroy above-the-knee skirt and a brown leather jacket. On her feet she was wearing hiking boots. As he continued to his car, Quiet let her know he noticed her attractiveness.

When Quiet got in the car, Maraisha got in also. "I want to talk with you," she said. Quiet never said a word as he pulled away from the curb. He headed east.

Quiet drove across the viaduct and on toward and through the tunnel. Crossing the Floating Bridge, he noticed many sailboats floating in the water. It was a good morning for boating and fishing. Already the sun was burning the few remaining clouds away. The temperature was in the upper sixties. It looked like a warm, sunny day. Quiet continued on across the bridge and to Mercer Island, where he saw early-bird kids playing around in the business parking lots with their go-carts and bicycles. Driving across the East Channel Bridge, they didn't see as many boats floating around in the water. They were marooned at the marina.

After they had left the city limits, all that was in view was trees, farmlands, and distant scattered houses. Beyond the sky were a few remaining stars fading away. He drove past the

Bellevue turn-off and on toward Issaquah. Issaquah was just to the right of the freeway. It looked like a ghost town. Beyond there, Quiet had an open highway to himself. Few cars were going west. So far his was the only car heading east.

After about forty minutes of driving, Quiet pulled into a hick town called North Bend, about thirty miles out of Seattle. It was still early, and there was not a sign of life, except for a twenty-four-hour gas station. So Quiet pulled into the station and filled his car up. Then he continued down the road for about two miles and turned off, heading for the back streets, which led to a country road that ran into roads that led to the forest. There were no more houses in sight as Quiet followed the country road for about twenty miles, then turned off onto a trail. Driving among the trees in the forest, Quiet felt he needed a truck.

The road went for about seven miles off the country road and ended about thirty feet away from a running river. The river was about fifty feet wide and unquestionably deep. It ran from Mount Si to Lake Sammamish and on to Lake Washington, which led to the Sound.

All the while Quiet was driving, Maraisha, instead of trying to hold a conversation, wondered where he was taking her. Neither one spoke a word. When Quiet stopped the car, once again their eyes met. All Maraisha could see in Quiet's eyes was evil. Then his eyes turned toward the running river. He got out of the car and walked toward the water. From the bank he jumped on one rock after another until he came to about the middle of the river.

When Quiet sat down on a rock, Maraisha got out of the car also and walked toward the river. She came and sat down beside him. Many questions came from his eyes, but no words came from his lips, no sound from his voice. Together they sat in silence.

Once Quiet's eyes fell upon the river, although the rapids were speeding, the sun cast its glare. Water splashed against the rocks. Very little breeze passed by. The trees on both sides of the river were sitting still as they followed the river around the bend. Above the mountaintops, a few lingering clouds glided across the sky. Across the river a raccoon came down from the forest to get a drink of water. It ignored Quiet and Maraisha as they watched. When the coon got its fill, it looked at the couple for a short moment, then went back into the woods. Farther down the river a female deer and a spotted fawn came out of the forest to the river to get a drink also. At first sight of Quiet and Maraisha, the doe became leery of coming down to the river, but something told her she was in no danger. A moment later a buck came out of the woods to join them. When they got their fill they, too, went back into the woods.

"How'd you find this place? It's very pretty," said Maraisha in admiration.

"Many times when I was a small boy my father used to bring me here," said Quiet grumpily. He got up from the rock and started jumping back the way he had come. Maraisha followed right behind him. When he got back onto the riverbank, slowly he started walking. As Maraisha walked beside him, he asked, "What do you want with us?" in a soft, but demanding tone of voice.

Maraisha felt the seriousness in his voice. She took a breath of fresh air. "What do you mean?" she pretended.

Quiet stopped in his tracks and turned to face her. "You know damn well what I mean," he said as he grabbed her by the shoulders, shook her around, then pushed her to the ground, which was covered with grains of sand and scattered clumps of grass. "First you caused my brother to be kidnapped. Then you broke into our house. What do you want?"

Quickly Maraisha got up off the ground. "I didn't know your brother was kidnapped!" she cried. As Quiet paused for a moment, Maraisha quickly threw her arms around his neck. "I want you," she whispered as she tried to smother his mouth with

112

her lips. Quiet wrestled her arms from around his neck and threw her back to the ground. With tears rolling down her face, she stated, "I love you!"

"You're a cop!" he shouted angrily. "A cop doesn't know what love is. You just keep away from me and my family."

As Quiet turned to walk away, like a tackle Maraisha got up off the ground, ran, and grabbed him by the waist. While they were wrestling on the ground, she said, "You're not going to stop me from doing what I want to do to." She kept her arms tight around his waist. "Hurt me. I don't care." When she managed to get on top, Maraisha tried to find his lips with her tongue.

When Quiet finally managed to get her mouth away from his lips, he said softly, "You're a cop. What do you want?"

Slowly Maraisha pressed her lips against his. "I want you. Just you. I want you to want me," she whispered.

"But you're a cop," he said as he gently ran his hands through her hair.

"I'm a woman," she wept.

Sensitively Quiet wiped the tears away from her eyes, put his arms around her body, and pressed it against his, as he smothered her mouth with his. He pulled up her skirt and pulled off her panties. On the ground they made love.

Near the bank, the water was shallow. When Quiet and Maraisha were finished, they took off their clothes and went into the water nude, playing and swimming. The water was cold but soothing. The morning had gotten warm. The sun began to burn the moisture out of the sand. When they came out of the water, Maraisha went to the car and pulled out the sleeping bag and the cooking utensils. The sleeping bag she spread on the ground. Then she and Quiet lay on top of it. The heat from the sun dried the wetness from their bodies. Again, after wrapping themselves in the sleeping bag, they made love. Exhaustion from the exertion forced them to take a nap.

The morning slipped by and ran into early afternoon. Quiet

113

slowly woke up. He glanced at Maraisha. She was still asleep. He rose up and trained his eyes on the flow of the running river. This caused him to once again go back into his past. It was on a bright sunny day in Vietnam, when he and two other men were resting on a riverbank after a long march through the jungle. Raymond Jacobs, from New York, and Frank Richards, from Los Angeles, were two blacks Quiet had become friends with when he came to Vietnam. Quiet was in his fourteenth month and had a little less than two months to serve. Raymond was scheduled to leave on a morning flight back to the States. His duty was up. Frank was to leave two days after. While sitting on the bank of the river, Frank suggested that when they got back to the compound they change and go down to one of the villages and celebrate the short time they had left to serve in Vietnam. The village was about a half a mile away from the army compound.

Frank had a Vietnamese girlfriend in the village whom he had met about two weeks after coming to Vietnam. He talked Quiet and Raymond into going down into the village with him. But it didn't take too much persuasion, as leaving the compound was a pleasure.

Frank's girlfriend's name was Mai. She lived in a Vietnamese hut with two other women. They were prostitutes. That was how they made their living. Quiet, Frank, and Raymond were sitting in the living room on a straw couch drinking beer. There were four other GIs in the living room sitting round a table drinking beer also. The Vietnamese hut had two rooms, one a bedroom, the other room a dining room, living room, and kitchen combined.

They had been there all that afternoon and a good portion of the evening. It was getting dark. By this time Quiet, Frank, and Raymond were a little tipsy. The beer had gotten to them, but they managed to keep their senses about them. While sitting on the couch, Frank saw Mai in the other room, nude. She was standing a step from the doorway, motioning for him to come forward. There were strands of material in the doorway that separated the living room from the other room. The doorway was about six feet high, three feet wide. Frank stumbled to his feet and advanced toward the doorway. Quiet and Raymond laughed as they watched.

When Frank got to the doorway he grabbed his neck, as though something had bit him. When he grabbed his neck something bit him on his arm. Then Frank started screaming as he started grabbing all over his body.

"Snakes!" shouted Quiet.

"I'm gonna kill that bitch!" shouted Raymond as he and Quiet grabbed their weapons and headed back out the front door. But by the time they got outside and around to the back, the four GIs who had been in the hut were already around back pumping lead into the three women's bodies. They were bloody. There was nothing Quiet could do, so he decided to go back into the hut and see how Frank was doing. He was dead. Quiet pulled Frank's body away from the snakes and carried him outside. The snakes that hung like material were still once again. Quiet grabbed a torch and set the hut in flames. Within minutes, the hut and all its contents were in ashes. . . .

Maraisha moaned, tossed, and turned to her side, bringing Quiet back to the present. When she opened her eyes, Quiet was staring at the running river. There was a doubt expressed on his face. "What's the matter?" she asked as she slowly rose and leaned her head on his shoulder.

"Nothing!" said Quiet grumpily as he grabbed a handful of sand and threw it at the water.

He was still angry, she felt, maybe because she had pointed Clinton out to John and the others. "Okay," said Maraisha sorrowfully as she got to her feet. "Maybe you do have a reason to stay mad at me. But I was only dong what I was told. They told me they wanted us to point out the person who chairs the meeting. How was I to know Clinton was your brother? John told me they just wanted to talk with him—"

"Why?" Quiet interrupted.

"I don't know," she continued. "I was only following orders."

Maraisha got up out of the sleeping bag and started to head back to the car. But Quiet quickly got up and grabbed her by the arm and pulled her into him. "What about breaking into my house?" he asked as he held her arms behind her back.

"I couldn't go on seeing bits and pieces of you," she said sadly. "I wanted to see you once and for all. I had to get you out of my mind. I was tired of tossing and turning at night trying to get to sleep. Ever since I saw you, I became frightened. That day when I broke into your house, I waited till the last second, when I saw you and Wyatt drive up. I got scared and ran. This morning, after last night, my nerves built up, again. But if—"

Quiet placed his hands behind her head and pressed his mouth against hers and smothered her words. When he released her, he said, "Whatcha gonna do now? Your secret is out in the open."

"I don't know!" she cried. "Those guys are crazy."

"Don't worry about it," Quiet said understandingly. "I know who I can see about them. Let's go for a hike."

They put their clothes back on. Quiet got his fishing net, and they followed a trail that led to a shallow stream that ran into the river. There he saw a few trout swimming around.

"That's illegal," Maraisha smiled. But she suggested she go upstream and chase them down to where Quiet would be waiting with the net. Quiet netted eleven trout and took them back to where he and Maraisha had made camp and cooked them. For the rest of the day they walked through the woods, admiring what nature brought, a wilderness so full of life and joy. Maraisha felt really intent about nature. She had never seen anything so beautiful except on television, never experiencing it firsthand before. She and Quiet played a little hide-and-seek but mostly acted like lovers. She felt safe and warm when he held her in his arms. He could see that there was no way Maraisha wanted to leave this paradise. She would stay here forever, if it was possible. But her job would interfere.

Later that afternoon, on discovering Maraisha was gone, Sharon, like a frightened hen worried about her chick, began to question her own thoughts. *Where could Maraisha be? I know she's not with Quiet. There's no way those two would ever get together.* So Sharon got on the telephone and called Jack Marty, John Maulder, and William Ross, her police friends.

About an hour later, coming from the north end of town, the three policemen pulled up near the curb in front of the apartment building in their green police car. They got out and went into the building. When they got to the apartment, John knocked on the door. Sharon answered. The three men walked in and sat down on the couch. Sharon sat on a chair across a coffee table in front of the men. Then she began to explain how she had looked for Maraisha and found her gone.

"Maybe there's nothing to worry about," said John.

"I don't know," said Sharon doubtfully. "She has never done this before."

"We'll check on it," said John. "But I don't think there's anything to worry about."

The men stayed for a few moments, drinking some coffee. Then they left the apartment.

When John, Jack, and William left the apartment, Sharon got dressed, went downstairs to the garage underneath the apartments where she parked her car, got in, and drove away. She headed down and around the hill to Quiet's home. Dino and Wyatt were still in bed when the doorbell rang. Dino got up, put on his robe, and went to answer it. When the door opened, to his surprise, Sharon and Joan were standing on the front porch.

Joan had driven up with a friend who dropped her off in front of Quiet's house just as Sharon drove up, then drove away. As the two women walked into the house and sat down on the couch, Sharon began to explain to Dino how when she awoke Maraisha wasn't anywhere in the apartment and she became worried.

Dino grabbed a seat on the armchair. "Maybe she's with Quiet. He's gone also."

When Dino told Sharon Quiet was gone, on second thoughts, she realized Quiet and Maraisha might be together. But by the way they acted last night, one wouldn't suspect it. *Oh, oh. I messed up,* she thought. *I called John and the others. They might cause trouble for Quiet.*

Hearing the loud talking in the living room, Wyatt came out of the bedroom. "What's all the fuss about?" he asked grumpily.

"Quiet and Maraisha are gone," explained Sharon.

"Is that all?" said Wyatt with unconcern. "Tell me something that's new."

"Whatcha going to do about it?" said Sharon.

Wyatt turned around. "Go back in the bedroom and watch some television." Then he closed the door behind him. Moments later, after talking to Dino and Sharon, Joan went into the bedroom also.

Later that evening around eight o'clock, Quiet and Maraisha pulled up near the curb in front of the house. There was still some daylight left. When they got inside the house and upstairs, Dino was sitting up on the couch, resting his head on the back, with his feet resting on the coffee table, Sharon resting her head across his chest. Quiet smiled as he walked over and shook Dino. "Hey, man! Wake up," he said.

Drowsily Dino opened his eyes. Everything was blurred for a short minute. When he got up, Sharon woke up also. "Hey, man!" he said joyously. "Where have you two been?" But when he saw Maraisha, he said, "Your girlfriend has been looking all

118

over for you." As he looked back at Quiet, he remarked, "I thought you two would never get together."

The three couples stayed up till about twelve o'clock playing rise and fly bidwhiz, a card game similar to the popular card game bridge. Then they went to bed. Once again Maraisha and Quiet made love.

Came the next morning, Quiet and Wyatt got up, dressed, had their breakfast, then went to work. The women were still in bed when they left.

Around noon, after both women finished their breakfast, they were sitting at the dining room table. Maraisha noticed Sharon had a strange look on her face. "What's the matter?" she asked.

"I did something stupid," said Sharon sorrowfully.

"What's that?" asked Maraisha curiously.

"When I found you gone, I got worried, so I called John. He brought Jack and William over to the apartment with him. I'm afraid I did wrong."

"Oh, no!" said Maraisha sadly. A worried expression came over her face. "He'll fight back if they mess with him. I don't want John and the other guys messing with Quiet," she said. "He's not just some black the police can push around without a fight."

"He knows how to handle himself. Although I've never seen it," Sharon said with confidence.

"What can he do against a police force?" said Maraisha. "That's all the reason they need to kill him. I'm not going to let John, Jack, or any of the other guys mess with them. They've already kidnapped Clinton for some reason and brought him back home. That's not going to happen with Quiet."

Sharon sympathized with Maraisha, for she was stunned for a moment when Maraisha mentioned about Clinton being kidnapped by John and his crew. But when the name Quiet came back to her, she wondered aloud, "That's an unusual name, Quiet. How'd he get a name like that?"

"When we were in the mountains I teased him about his name. After he was born he didn't make a sound until he was about three months old. His father always called him the quiet one. Even now he's quiet."

"I know," agreed Sharon.

As Maraisha took a sip of her coffee, she caught Sharon. "Why are you looking at me that way?"

"I'm sorry," Sharon apologized. But curiosity got the best of her. "Did you tell Quiet you're a cop?"

"I didn't have to," answered Maraisha. "Somehow he already knew. What about you? Did you tell Dino?"

"No!" answered Sharon. "I'm afraid to. I might lose him."

"You'll lose him if you don't. One way or another, he'll find out."

"You think Quiet will tell him I'm a cop?"

"If he hasn't told him by this time, he won't."

"I'll tell him," said Sharon uncertainly. "As soon as he gets home."

"Look at us," laughed Maraisha. "Two undercover cops falling in love with guys we're supposed to keep an eye on. What are the guys gonna say when they find out? Are we a couple of fools?"

"If we are a couple of fools, I like the idea," said Sharon as she was cleaning up the dishes from the table. She went into the kitchen. Maraisha went upstairs, turned the television on, and sat back on the couch.

Come noon, it was lunch break. The sun was bright and the day was warm. Quiet and Wyatt decided to have their lunch outside and were joined by a few other workers, four blacks and three Caucasians, whom Quiet knew from the plant. They were sitting near the fence when Quiet noticed a black German shepherd on the other side of the parking lot playing alongside the railroad tracks with some kids. The dog reminded Quiet so much of Shep, 'cause it looked so much like him.

Shep had belonged to Mr. Jones. Usually wherever Mr. Jones went, Shep went also. Outside of Mr. Jones, Quiet was the only one in the family Shep would listen to. Many times they had walked back and forth across town, visiting friends or whatever. Then Quiet remembered some of the places they had gone: the Woodland Park Zoo to look at some of the wild animals and to the woods in the neighborhood to pretend they were in forest. With these few thoughts, Quiet became lonely for a dog. After work he planned on going down to the animal shelter and finding himself a dog.

After work Quiet pulled up in front of his house. Wyatt got out, then Quiet continued on toward town. This time of day the traffic was thin. Quiet felt he'd better rush to the Humane Society before traffic got heavy. He took the usual route on down to the waterfront. The Western Avenue route ran into Elliott Avenue, the same avenue where the Humane Society was located.

The Humane Society kept dogs, cats, and other small domestic animals. It was a small building but large enough to hold the animals brought in. Year-round, the Humane Society officers drove through neighborhoods collecting stray dogs roaming the area. But some dogs in the shelter were not strays. Dogs living in certain neighborhoods got caught because they were not on a chain or fenced in, but roaming up and down the streets. In some of these neighborhoods, neighbors called the Humane Society to pick up their dogs because they either didn't want them anymore or just couldn't afford to take care of them. Dogs of almost all breeds were taken to the Humane Society. The dogs the Humane Society collected they tried to sell and the dogs they didn't or couldn't sell were put to sleep, mainly the old dogs.

Quiet pulled into the Humane Society parking lot. But as

121

he got out and was on his way to the building, he saw Mitchell dragging a dog across the parking lot by his leash. The dog looked to be about nine months old, a light-colored German shepherd.

"Hey, man! What's happening? Quiet laughed. "Whatcha gonna do with him?"

The dog jumped each time Mitchell jerked the leash. "I'm going to get rid of this bastard," he said angrily.

As Quiet looked at the dog, he said, "He looks like a pretty nice dog. If you don't want him, I'll take him."

"Well, you can have him," said Mitchell as he handed Quiet the leash. "What are you doing down here?"

"Looking for a dog." Quiet took the dog and led him to the backseat of his car. Then he and Mitchell stood by the car and talked for a moment before going into the building.

As they entered the building, an office was in front. A door separated the office from the cages where the dogs were kept in an area behind the office. When Quiet and Mitchell got to where the dogs were kept, they walked among the cages looking at one dog after another. In each cage there were about five dogs. There were twenty cages in all, containing Doberman pinschers, German shepherds, Labradors, collies, and other breeds. Quiet couldn't make up his mind which one he wanted. So he decided to keep the one Mitchell had given him. On his way out Quiet walked by the cages where the puppies were kept. He saw a little three-month-old black shepherd he wanted. The attendant opened the cage and handed the puppy to Quiet. He examined the puppy. It was a female. He took the puppy to the front desk to get a license for it. Then he put the puppy in the backseat of his car. He and Mitchell said farewell in the parking lot and drove away.

In the meanwhile at the house, Dino had just pulled the car up to the curb. He got out and went into the house. Maraisha and Sharon were sitting on the couch when he entered. Wyatt was sitting at the dining room table. Instinct told Dino that something was wrong by the expressions he saw on their faces. But he acted like he never noticed as he walked over to Sharon and lightly kissed her on the cheek. "How you doing, baby?"

"Fine," she answered.

"Going to take a shower. Be right back," he continued joyously.

As Dino started to walk away, Sharon said, "Wait!" and got up off the couch. "I have something to say."

"I'd better leave," said Wyatt as he got up from the table. "This sounds like it may be serious."

"I want you to hear this also." Sharon turned toward Dino. "I love you," she said softly. "Do you love me?"

"Of course," he said curiously. "But what does that have to do with what you have to say?"

With guilt spread over her face, she dropped her head and paused for a moment. "I'm ashamed I haven't told you something before. I was afraid you'd send me away. But you would have found out sooner or later. I'm a cop. And so is Maraisha."

"What!" said Dino, shocked. "A cop!" Then he became silent.

Wyatt was stunned also. "Cops," he said jokingly, then laughed.

Sharon came from around the coffee table and stood near the front door. She hunched her shoulders as she opened it. "If you don't want me here, I'll leave," she said sadly. Tears rolled down her face.

Dino walked over to Sharon and pulled her into his arms and held her tight. "You don't have to leave." He looked at Maraisha. "That's why Quiet kept snapping at you the night of the dance?"

Maraisha nodded.

Just then Quiet walked through the front door. "Uh-oh!" he said when he saw the gloomy expressions on everyone's faces. "I think I walked in on something. Maybe I should go and come back later."

Dino looked at Quiet, then at Maraisha. "Did you know those two were cops?"

"I knew," answered Quiet disgustedly. "I suspected them after Clint was kidnapped by their friends. They were waiting for him down the street after the meeting."

"We never hid anything from one another before. Why didn't you tell us?"

"Would you have really wanted me to?"

"No!" Dino paused. "I guess not."

When everyone was back to normal, Quiet said, "Wait till you see what I have." He went back outside, got the dogs, and brought them into the house. "This one is yours," he said as he handed the puppy to Wyatt. With the other hand he held the other dog by his leash. The dog was scared. "This one I'm going to train."

"Wish you luck," said Wyatt. "That one seems like he'll run from his own shadow. Where'd you get him from?"

"Mitch," answered Quiet. "I ran into him down at the Humane Society shelter. Remember Dad's dog, Shep?" Wyatt nodded. "That's what I'm going to call him."

This Shep didn't look anything like Mr. Jones's Shep. He was slim, as though he was underfed, and white where his chest was supposed to be, with black and tan over his body. His ears stood straight up, but his tail drooped, as though he was always in fear.

Wyatt held the puppy up. "I'll name her Mitzie."

Meanwhile, at Maulder's house on the north side, just beyond the Seattle city limits, there was a meeting going on, but a different type of meeting. All these men were working out of the detective bureau. There was Sidney Davis, in his forties. Gray streaked hair on the side of his head. He weighed about 250 pounds and was about six feet, two inches tall. Lawrence Tanner, forty, was present also. He weighed about 240 pounds, and was six feet tall. Everyone called him Larry. Tanner's partner, Jack Marty, was twenty-eight. Six feet tall, he weighed about 200 pounds. Whenever Tanner or Davis wanted to be up on any information Marty would get it to them. William Ross, twenty-nine, was working undercover out of the bureau. He weighed about 195 pounds and was six feet tall. He was Maulder's partner. Vince Morrison, Bill Marcy, Bob Bishop, Josh Randall, Richard Munson, and Mack Daniels were all uniformed officers working together with the special police officers. Each one of these officers was in his twenties. All were Caucasian. These men were sitting around the living room chatting. Maulder owned a Doberman pinscher named Spike. Whenever he had company, Spike would either be in the back bedroom or outside in his kennel in the backyard.

It was a large four-bedroom house. The living room was in the front, facing north. Through the living room to the west was the dining room. Then a hallway separated the dining room from the bedrooms. Directly behind the living room was the kitchen, south of the living room. The couch was sitting in front of the big window that covered the whole side of the house. The living room was about twenty by twenty.

Maulder looked as though he just got out of bed. His leg was cocked up, resting over the arm of his armchair, sitting next to a fireplace. "What are we going to do about this nigga?" he said sarcastically. "That brother who got out of the army?"

"You mean the one called Quiet?" answered Tanner. "He's no threat. But if he gets in our way, leave him to me. I'll take care of him. Like we did the others." He was sitting in the armchair on the other side of the fireplace.

"Larry wants us to lay off of him anyway," added Davis, who was sitting at the dining room table. "He has special plans for him. But the others are fair game. You three," he referred to Maulder, Marty, and Ross, "watch them meetings. Make sure them dumb bitches stay on their jobs, to keep us well informed of what goes on. I want to know every move them blacks make."

"Right!" agreed Maulder.

"We could've found out what we wanted to know when we had one of their leaders," said Ross as he came into the conversation. He was sitting on the couch. "If we put a scare on him, the rest will back off."

"That's what they said about Martin Luther King," interrupted Tanner. "But he never stopped. We'll have to get something on him other than calling union meetings. But we have other problems to worry about." He paused. "What we have done forced blacks to come together. There's an unknown group going on a cop-killing spree. If any of them black union men know anything about it, I want to know. We'll bypass headquarters and take care of them ourselves."

"Like the old days, huh!" agreed Morrison, who was sitting at the dining room table also.

"I have a report on these blacks who've been ambushing and sniping uniformed officers," continued Tanner. "No doubt some of them blacks know something about it. We'll have Sharon and Maraisha get in good with them, so they can find out who they are."

"We have them working on that right now," said Maulder. "They'll be at the meeting tonight. And so will we."

"Don't let them get too good inside," said Davis, coming back into the conversation. "I heard Maraisha spent a day with Quiet. We want someone we can trust."

"We can trust them," assured Maulder.

5

Every Monday the tradesmen's meeting started around 7:00 P.M. but usually terminated between 9:30 and 10:00 P.M. When the tradesmen had a particularly interesting discussion, the meeting might go to 1:00 or 2:00 A.M. Jim Boner, a friend of Clinton and Earl, about thirty, with a light complexion, weighed about 150 pounds. His height was five feet, eight inches. He also worked at the Urban League. Around 9:30 P.M., the meeting still in session, Boner decided to leave. He told Clinton, Earl, and a few other staff members he had something personal to take care of and that he'd be back at work the next day.

That night on his way home Boner was stopped by Maulder, Marty, and Marcy on Twenty-third and Yesler. They went through the same routine with him as they did with Clinton. Maulder pulled Boner out of his car, cuffed his hands behind his back, placed him in the backseat of the police car, and drove out to Kent, to the same warehouse where they had taken Clinton. Boner also was placed in a chair in the back office, with a dim light hanging overhead. He could hear mumbling voices from the other room up front. Then footsteps came back into the back office. Fear ran through Boner's body, but he tried to hide it.

"What do you want with me?" asked Boner, frightened. There was no answer but footsteps moving back and forth in front of him. Then a backhand smacked across his face. Boner

127

fell out of his chair. A pair of hands helped him back into the chair.

A voice spoke. "We want the names of the members of the militant group that's been going around having open season on police officers. Give us the names and we'll let you go free."

"I don't know what you're talking about."

"We can do it the easy way or we can do it the hard way. The choice is yours. So why don't you cooperate?"

Whenever the officers questioned Boner about the militant group, he gave the same answer: he didn't know who they were. But each time Boner denied knowing the militants, he got a punch in his face or a foot in his stomach when he was on the floor. Each time he fell on the floor, he was helped back into his chair. This went on practically all night until Boner died. Then Boner's body was taken away from the warehouse and dumped in some bushes about a mile south of the warehouse. Later that morning on their way to school, some kids found Boner's body. They went home and told their parents, who called the police. Two older boys took the police to where Boner's body was.

When Clinton came to work, he looked for Boner. Boner didn't show up. Clinton wondered if he felt that his personal affair was more important than work. But later that afternoon after Clinton read the newspaper, he called Quiet and Wyatt at home and asked them to come up to the office. Earl was next door. Quiet and Wyatt had just gotten home when the telephone rang. It was around 4:00 P.M. when Wyatt pulled into the parking lot, got out of the car, and went into the building. When they got into the office, Clinton showed Quiet and Wyatt the newspaper. He pointed out the article on Jim Boner.

"He was at the meeting last night," said Clinton sadly. "He had to leave early to pick his kids up from his mother's. Margaret is still in Saint Louis visiting her relatives. It's going to be hard on her when she finds out Jim's dead. The paper says Jim was found in Kent this morning by some kids. Jim was beaten to death, police said."

"How in the hell did he get from here out to Kent?" asked Wyatt curiously and angrily.

"Kidnapped," said Quiet coldly. "There's no end. The police seem to think they can get anyone they want."

"Yes," agreed Clinton. "I wonder why they let me go?"

While Clinton continued, Quiet remembered his father saying there were times, when he was growing up in the South, that kids on their way to schools or stores or just visiting a neighborhood friend down the road aways came up missing. A few of the bodies were found miles away from home. No one knew how they got there.

In fear of one of his brothers getting kidnapped or harassed by the police again, the next day after work Quiet went downtown. He parked his car in the public market area, then went to one pawnshop after another looking at different types of weapons. He was at the far south end of downtown when he came to a pawnshop, the Emerson, where he found what he was looking for: a .357 Magnum single-action revolver, Smith and Wesson cowboy-style holster, 30-30 Winchester rifle, .32 automatic pistol, and .20-gauge shotgun with a three-round clip.

Two days after Boner's death, in the CD a blue-and-white squad car answered a call to an address in the valley. The complaint was about a dispute between a man and a woman going on at a certain house. The man had threatened the woman with a weapon. Two uniformed officers answered the call. But when they got up on the porch, they found the house was deserted. It seemed as though no one resided at this address at any time. When the police realized they had been set up, four blacks with automatic weapons fired a hail of bullets at them as they came from around both sides of the house. Then the snipers fled. The two officers had died instantly.

The following night a speeding motorist, doing about sev-

129

enty miles an hour in a thirty-five-mile-an-hour zone, drove down Empire Way southbound. Two officers were sitting off on a side street when the motorist came speeding by. They saw the motorist and went in hot pursuit. The chase lasted a few miles before going onto a back street, Chesty Street, a countrylike road behind Rainier Vista on the south end, in an isolated area. Chesty Street ran about three miles from Empire Way to Beacon Hill Avenue. Between those two streets were trees and a few scattered houses.

When the motorist saw the squad car come up behind him, he pulled to the side of the road and stopped. The driver of the squad car got out and approached the motorist. When the officer got between the motorist and the squad car, from around the trees and bushes four blacks, again with automatic weapons, fired a hail of bullets at the two officers, killing them instantly.

There was an incident of a car being reported as having been stolen. It was late afternoon when two police officers found a '65 Lincoln Continental abandoned on a side street near Lake Washington Boulevard South. It was off a path that led to an isolated area. There had been a few dead bodies found in the area, and the cases were still open for investigation. The area looked too suspicious. With all the incidents that had occurred lately, the two officers were cautious as they approached the car. First the driver reported his position and asked for a backup unit. Then he got out of the police car and cautiously approached the vehicle, while his partner stayed near the police car with a shotgun, ready to fire. When the driver came near the vehicle, once again, a hail of bullets came at the two officers from out of nowhere. The passenger managed to get off a couple of rounds in their general direction but fell to the ground. He was in critical condition going to the hospital. The driver died instantly. By the time the backup unit arrived, the ambushers had vanished. The police swore vengeance but had no clues.

Every day after work Quiet would take Shep underneath

the viaduct and work with him. Underneath the viaduct looked more like a park than a way for arterial streets. Years ago Quiet and a few of the neighborhood kids used to play ball under the viaduct when they couldn't play in the street in front of their houses.

When Quiet first brought Shep home, he had a lot of puppy play and fear in him. But in a few weeks Quiet taught him discipline and to obey. Shep began to mature quickly. Maraisha would sit on a bank and watch. He became more used to being around Quiet and Maraisha than the others. A few things Quiet taught Shep: to come when he called his name or whistled, attack on command, go away, sit down, and, at the snap of a finger, bite. The training ran into months. Shep seemed serious in his work. Another thing Quiet wanted Shep to learn was not to be afraid of weapons.

Six months passed. Quiet and Maraisha took Shep to the woods with them. It was around winter. There was snow on the ground. Quiet had with him his 30-30 Winchester rifle and his .357 Magnum pistol. He remembered his father telling him many times never to go into the woods without a rifle and a pistol for a backup, in case he should meet something danger-ous. It was cold that morning, very little wind. The clouds showed signs of a snowstorm approaching.

Walking up a narrow trail admiring the view overlooking the lowlands, Quiet noticed Shep quickly dashing off at a movement just up ahead. When Shep caught up with what had moved, he grabbed it and started swinging it around. By the time Quiet and Maraisha got to Shep, he was eating a rabbit. "First time I ever saw him kill anything," said Quiet. "Dad told me once a dog tastes blood, he'll always kill whatever he gets in his mouth." Maraisha was quiet. It made her sick watching Shep finish the rabbit. They continued up the trail until they came to the top of the ridge. Quiet remembered this place well. It was where he was almost attacked by a cougar, a long time ago. Shep, Mr. Jones's dog, came to the rescue.

Quiet pointed out certain sights: the clouds gliding across the sky, the distant mountains higher than the clouds, and the river flowing beyond where the eyes could see. The river was shady green and icy. Evergreen trees grew on both sides of the river. Water flowed around rocks as big as houses. The air was still but yet fresh. Instead of flying south, a few birds remained, flying around in the air. The sun was barely peeking through the clouds. But it had nothing to do with the temperature. Below was a valley of meadows. A few deer were grazing in it.

Many times Quiet's father had brought him there, when he wanted to get away from it all, because this was more of his way of life. Maraisha felt she had been living near paradise all the time but didn't know it. This was about the first time Maraisha got a chance to look at and admire nature. The closest she'd been to nature had been at a public park. But to her this was the real outdoors, nature itself. If she were to make a home for herself, this would be the place. When the day was gone, Quiet and Maraisha headed back to the lighted city.

Since the killing of Jim Boner, Maulder and his two associates had eased off on harassing blacks. They started stalking certain blacks, who they felt might be a threat to the white power structure. Other meetings of blacks had been watched by the police, but Clinton and Earl's were at the top of their list. But since Clinton's abduction and release, they had been untouched. If anything should happen to any one of the Jones brothers it might ignite an uprising among the black construction workers against the police. This would cause the National Guard to step in and bring martial law to the city. *A lot of blood would be shed on both sides before that happened,* thought Maulder and his superiors. Then there would be an investigation that might cause the undercover plots to be uncovered. The police would wait till tensions cooled off.

In spite of Maulder and his superiors' warning to ease off, Mack Daniels and Bill Marcy, in their uniforms, sat in a squad car parked about halfway down the street from Quiet's apartment building. It was around 10:00 P.M. when Quiet drove past them. He pulled his car underneath the apartment building. Shep gave a little growl as Quiet drove by. The warning put him on the alert. When they got out of the car, Shep gave a couple of barks.

"What's wrong with him?" asked Maraisha suspiciously. "I never saw him act that way before."

"Cops," said Quiet coldly. "I passed them down the street. They were parked."

As they were heading for the entrance door, she said, "I'm a cop, too."

"I know. That's what bothers me," he answered with no expression. "Someday you'll have to make a choice."

Quiet was walking in front of Maraisha. She pulled him by the arm. As Quiet stopped and turned around, she wrapped her arms around his waist, then eased her lips against his. "I love you," she whispered. When she released him, there was evil in his eyes. He uttered not even a whisper. Fear flowed through her body. Her nerves began to jump uncontrollably. "I want so much for you to trust me," she said softly.

Quiet wrapped his arms around her. "Let's go inside," he said grumpily.

When they got inside the apartment, Quiet went to the front window and eased back the curtains. He looked up and down the street. The police car was too far away to see.

"Can you see them?" asked Maraisha.

"No," he said. "But I know they're still out there."

Shep whined for a moment, then went and lay down in front of the couch, between Maraisha's legs. Quiet walked over and sat down beside her.

"Want some coffee?"

"Yes," he answered.

So Maraisha got up off the couch and went into the kitchen. Later, when she came back with the coffee, cream, and sugar on a tray, Quiet was standing at the rear window admiring the view.

The first thing Quiet noticed was his parents' house. From the front street to the backyard and on to the alleyway that led to the house from the rear the view was very clear. The streetlights from the Mount Baker Hill District on to Twenty-third and Rainier made it seem as if one could reach out and touch the house. A few cars drove across the viaduct and went through the tunnel. When he turned his back on his home, suspicions filled his mind.

"Coffee is ready," said Maraisha as she set the tray down on the coffee table.

As Quiet turned and faced her, he demanded, "How long have you been watching my house?"

For a moment Maraisha was silent, as she saw the cold evil in his narrowed eyes. She shrugged her shoulders. "I haven't lied to you," she said humbly. "I don't know what to say. For the first time, all I know is I'm scared. I didn't know that was your house until one morning I saw you and Wyatt going to work. Sharon and I didn't know why they put us up here."

"They!" he repeated. "Who's 'they'?"

"The police. The guys I work with," she continued as Quiet walked over and sat beside her. He drank his coffee. "Stay with me tonight," she begged in a lovesick voice.

"Whether or not I *want* to stay, I have to go," he replied as he finished his coffee.

Troubled fear ran through Maraisha's body as Quiet got up from the couch.

Maraisha got up and walked into his arms. "Please, don't go," she whispered. "At least for the night."

"I have to," he repeated, walking toward the door. He

134

lightly kissed her on the lips, then left the apartment, after telling Shep to stay there.

After getting in his car and driving down the street, Quiet saw the police car pull away from where it had been parked and start following him. *I wonder what they want?* he thought. But as the police car was gaining, another set of headlights, from out of nowhere, was gaining fast on them. When the headlights came up beside the police car, a hail of bullets flew into it. At the sound of bullets Marcy and Daniels ducked down in the front seat. The police car ran up on a neighbor's front law. A '65 red Corvette, with two young blacks driving, zoomed past Quiet. *I wonder who they are?* he thought. *Maybe those are the militants I heard so much about.* He just drove on home.

Come early next morning, while Quiet was in the bathroom washing up, Dino walked in. He spoke with joy in his voice. Quiet returned the greeting. But as Quiet stood looking in the mirror, Dino could see there was something on his mind. "What's the matter, man?" he asked curiously. "Is something wrong?"

Quiet looked at Dino, then turned away. "I don't know," he said indecisively. He paused for a moment. "Did you see any cops or a red Corvette last night when you dropped Sharon off?"

Wondering why Quiet had asked that question, Dino answered, "No! Why?"

Quiet explained. When he got through, Dino said, "Oh, I see. Sharon dropped me off, anyway." As Quiet was leaving the bathroom Dino asked, "What are we going to do if they come our way?"

"I don't know," he said grumpily. "See you after work."

Later that afternoon, after going home and changing their clothes, Quiet and Wyatt drove up to Clinton's office. When they got there unexpectedly, Clinton greeted them. "What brings you two by?" he asked.

Putting formalities aside, Quiet said seriously, "The black

135

killings I believe were done by the police." At the accusation Clinton and Wyatt were stunned. Just then Earl came into Clinton's office. It was nearing quitting time.

Quiet continued, "In the last year, or so, them blacks who were killed all had something to do with trade unions. Whatever reason, I don't know, the police were always there. Someone had to point them out. Just like with you, Brother Clint. Sharon and Maraisha gave you away to the police. I don't think they understood what was happening. Do you think you can find that place where they took you?"

"I don't think so," said Clinton curiously. "Why?"

"I believe that was the blacks' first stop. From there, they ended up in a ditch or just somewhere they could be found. But away from Seattle."

"Where'd you come up with this theory?" asked Earl.

"Last night when I left Maraisha at the apartment," continued Quiet, "two cops followed me. But I believe when they were about to make their move a Corvette with two blacks blasted them. The blacks saved me from killing two cops. I believe Maraisha knew they were going to try to pick me up. That was why she wanted me to stay at the apartment last night."

"Does Dino know about this?" asked Earl.

"No! I don't think so," said Quiet. "I don't know if I'm right. It's just a theory. But if I am right, we've got police trouble."

"The worst kind," Wyatt whistled.

"Now what do we do?" asked Earl.

"Nothing we can do, for right now anyway," said Quiet. "Except, go home and do some homework."

When Quiet and Wyatt walked through the front door, Dino and Sharon were sitting on the couch. The lights were dim. Soft music was playing on the radio. Maraisha and Joan came out of the kitchen when they heard the front door close. They were cooking a chicken dinner with rice. The two women approached their men. Maraisha held Quiet firmly. He could

136

feel the trembling chill running through her body as they touched. He led her upstairs.

When they got upstairs Quiet walked over and turned the television on, then went to the couch and sat. He leaned back while resting his feet on the coffee table. Maraisha walked over and leaned over and slowly rolled her lips around his. When she released him, he showed no expression, as though there was no feeling. His eyes of death made her nerves lose control and begin to jump. She leaned over and kissed him again. But this time she slowly rolled her mouth around his, trying to find his tongue with hers. Quiet began to press her body against his, as he started rubbing his hands gently up and down her body.

Her body was warm and soft. It's hard for any man to resist the caresses of a woman. Quiet loosened Maraisha's blouse with one hand and unsnapped her skirt with the other. He slid her brassiere and slip straps over her shoulders, down to her waist, while the same instant Maraisha was loosening his clothes. When they both were nude Quiet picked her up and carried her to the back bedroom. They got under the covers and made love.

The next morning Quiet, Wyatt, and Dino went to work. Maraisha and Sharon stayed behind and cleaned up the house. When they finished, they went back to their apartment. Sharon went into the kitchen to make a pot of coffee. Maraisha was sitting in the living room with the television on, reading a magazine. Shep was lying on the floor, between Maraisha's legs. He gave a growl; just then the doorbell rang. "Quiet," she said as she got up to answer it. Shep was silent.

John, Jack, and William were standing at the door. Shep got up with a couple of barks when Maraisha invited the men in. John headed for the couch but hesitated when he saw Shep in his way. "Nice dog," he said admiringly. "Where'd you get him?" As John slowly tried to pat Shep, the dog showed him his pearly white fangs. John backed away. "Not too friendly, is he?"

"No!" answered Maraisha as she went and sat down on the couch. "What brings you guys by?"

Just then, Sharon came into the living room with a tray of coffee, cream, and sugar. "Hi, guys!" she said happily, but surprised, as she set the tray on the coffee table. "Want some coffee?" she offered.

"Yes! Please!" said John, and Sharon went back into the kitchen.

"Maraisha," John began, then paused. "We haven't heard from you two in quite a while. What's been happening? Shatter wants us to crack down on them black construction workers. Maybe a few of them could give us a line on them militants. They're constantly terrorizing the police department. We want them bad."

"Most of them construction workers have homes and families to go to," said Maraisha defensively. "They haven't got time to go around terrorizing the police department. Why do—"

"Whoa! Whoa! Hold on a minute!" interrupted Jack as he came into the conversation. "We just want the ones who might know something about the cop killers. You and Sharon can help with that."

"No!" answered Maraisha quickly. "No more construction workers. I gave you one, their leader, and you guys didn't take him downtown for questioning. You took him somewhere out of town. I'm not—"

"Where'd you learn this from? Your boyfriend?" interrupted William sarcastically.

Maraisha was stunned at the accusation, and anger filled her eyes.

"Now if you girls don't want to work with us, I'll just tell Detective Smith and he'll put you back in uniform."

Sharon was sitting between John and Maraisha. "If we felt any of them construction workers were part of the militant group, we'd arrest them ourselves."

"Bill and Mack were fired upon the other night down the street from here," said John. "We believe your boyfriend may know something about it. Mack said you two girls have been seeing a lot of these two guys. Shatter is beginning to worry whose side you're on."

"You want them, don't you? What better way of watching than getting close?" said Maraisha.

"Or vice versa," added William.

John continued, "We want you two to stay close to them meetings, so you can get us some leads. Those militants are setting up too many ambushes."

"Okay," said Maraisha doubtfully. "But I still feel you're making a mistake. I don't believe the construction workers have anything to do with it."

John finished his coffee and got up off the couch. "That's a nice shepherd," he said, adding before going out the door, "We'll be in touch." The door closed behind the men.

When the men left, Sharon got up off the couch and went to the front window. "What are we going to do?" she said worriedly. "If they start messing with Quiet and his brothers, he may try to find a way to stop them. Sooner or later, they'll have to meet. And John has the whole police force behind him. Quiet and his brothers and Dino won't stand a chance."

"I know," moaned Maraisha.

"Are you going to tell Quiet about John and the others?" asked Sharon curiously.

"Yes," said Maraisha as she got up off the couch. "I never lied to him. I want him to trust me. Although he doesn't trust me all the way, I don't want to ruin any trust he has for me." She carried the tray of empty coffeepot and cups back into the kitchen.

Sharon followed. "What about John, Jack, and William? Are you going to report Quiet, Dino, and his three brothers to them?"

"Not on your life I'm not," said Maraisha as she put the

dishes into the sink. "He said someday I'll have to make a choice. And my decision is very simple. Quiet is my man. I'll never turn against him, for anyone. You'll have to make a choice also."

"Thanks!" a relieved Sharon stated as she exhaled. "I feel the same way." Then she left the kitchen.

Later that afternoon when Quiet came home from work, he washed up and changed his clothes, then went to the girls' apartment. When he got up there, he knocked on the door. There was no answer, except a couple of barks. So Quiet unlocked the door with a key he got from Maraisha and let himself in. When the door opened, Shep jumped up against Quiet's chest, glad to see him. Quiet played with Shep for a short while, then went into Maraisha's bedroom. Maraisha was asleep. So Quiet took off his clothes and got in bed beside her. He went to sleep also, while Shep stayed outside the bedroom door.

The long day ran into night. When Maraisha awakened, to her surprise, she found Quiet lying beside her. She rolled on top of him, and he woke up. As they lay in bed she told him of her visit and explained. Quiet showed no expression, as though he didn't care. He pulled her lips down to his until they touched. While they were kissing, Maraisha was puzzled by Quiet's moods. They were unpredictable. He was a dead serious man without any emotions, it seemed. He rolled Maraisha on her back, and they made love. It seemed as though Quiet was trying to make up for lost time, 'cause for hours they stayed in bed making love, taking breaks in between.

As the days went by, every day after work Quiet took Shep and his weapons to the woods for target practice. As for Shep, Quiet made him more aggressive in his attacks. If an enemy had a dog, Shep might have to defend himself. The thought of Aaron Mitchell came to Quiet. Aaron lived in the CD. He trained dogs to fight. *Maybe he can train Shep to fight also,* Quiet thought. *But his dogs are pit dogs. They fight for money or till one kills the other.*

The following weekend Quiet took Shep to Aaron's house. At first glance, Mitchell was surprised to see how well Shep was put together. He looked strong, physically and in his spirit.

"Is this the same dog I gave you?" Aaron admired the animal.

"The same one," said Quiet as he went to the couch and sat down. Shep sat down beside him.

"He would make a good fighter."

"That's what I brought him by for. Could you teach me to teach him how to fight?"

"He'll learn how to defend himself without any help. You made him into a good dog. Look at the way he stays beside you. He's your protector."

"How'd you teach your dogs how to fight?"

"I didn't have to teach them. If they can't fight when I get 'em, then they die. Follow me. I want to show you something," said Aaron, then to the kitchen and on downstairs into the basement. The basement was a place where Mitchell entertained his guests. Below that was a subbasement, where he kept his dogs in cages. When they got downstairs into the subbasement, Aaron showed Quiet his dogs as the men walked among the cages.

There was Blimp, a four-year-old, Aaron's favorite. He usually spent most of his time upstairs in the living room when there wasn't any company. He was a black Doberman pinscher. Next to his cage was another Doberman pinscher. His name was Blizzard. He and Blimp were brothers, but Blizzard was black and brown.

On to the next cages, where there were two German shepherds. One was white, and Aaron called him Snow. The other dog was a black Aaron had named Midnight. They were five-year-olds.

Beside their cages was three other cages occupied by three

collies. They were Duke, a five-year-old; Ringo, a three-year-old; and Pat, a four-year-old.

On the other side of these cages were two Labradors four years old. Their names were Blackie and Darton.

Next to their cages were three bull terriers, Pacer, Dancer, and Destroyer, three-year-olds. They were also brothers. They were the strongest of all the dogs.

At the far end of the cages were two purebred shepherds: Desert, a six-year-old, and Sands, a four-year-old. All these dogs were pit dogs.

Then there was a pet bulldog Aaron kept upstairs at all times. Her name was Pip Squeak. Aaron went to the cage with his dog leash and brought out Blimp. He led Blimp to the fight pit. "This is where my dogs earn their living."

Quiet walked to the edge of the fighting pit. Then he looked at Blimp. The scars he wore showed he'd been in many fights. What if he lost? It was a cruel way of life, but he was surviving. The fighting pit was about eight foot square. The subbasement was large. After Aaron had shown Quiet around in the subbasement, they headed back upstairs.

In fear of Shep encountering the pit fighters, Quiet, before going downstairs, commanded the dog to stay upstairs. But when Shep heard the sounds of other dogs' feet he gave a couple of barks, knowing the challenger he was. Hearing the couple of barks, Blimp pulled the leash out of Mitchell's hands and rushed upstairs. The basement door was cracked open. Blimp had no trouble opening the door to attack Shep.

Aaron was holding the leash loosely, but when it jerked out of his hands he tried to catch it. But Blimp was too fast. So Aaron and Quiet hurried upstairs. By the time they got upstairs, Shep and Blimp were already fighting. Quiet wanted to stop the fight, but Aaron talked him into letting the two dogs continue. So as the dogs fought in the kitchen Aaron opened the back door, hopeful they'd take their fight outside.

When Blimp got upstairs, in no time he was all over Shep. Shep, surprised, put his tail between his legs and started running around the kitchen. Blimp never let up, staying right behind him. Realizing there was no place to go, Shep turned to defend himself. The two dogs got up on their hind legs and started snapping at one another. Pitting strength against strength, Blimp began to push Shep backward. They battled; then Shep twisted his body like a wolf, causing Blimp to land on all fours and then lose his balance. But quickly Blimp got back on his hind legs before Shep could take advantage. Again the two dogs fought and snapped at one another.

Shep bit Blimp across the bridge of his nose. Blimp nipped Shep on his ear. Around and around the two dogs went until they found themselves in an alleyway outside. The fight became more of a brutal battle. The nicks and scratches became cuts and gashes. Blimp got a piece of Shep's fur around his neck. Shep twisted and turned, then spun around, causing Blimp to release his grip. Blood flowed. Then Blimp maneuvered to the other side and hooked his fangs into Shep's side as he was coming around. He left a chunk of meat hanging as Shep turned to face him.

Shep had fought dogs around the neighborhood a few times, when the other dog had the advantage. But this dog was different. Shep knew this dog was a killer. It wasn't like two dogs getting in a fight and calling it a draw. Only one could win, and that was by death. Realizing what he was up against, Shep like a wild beast charged into Blimp, forcing him back until he landed on the ground. The fight had attracted the attention of other dogs in the area, and they came and watched it. A few acted as though they wanted to get into the fight.

Quiet, after seeing the blood, wanted to stop the fight. Aaron knew this was Blimp's way of living, like a wild animal, kill or be killed. But it was a new experience for Shep. This fight, if Shep pulled through, would make him "graduate" into a new status as a killer. It took the average neighborhood dog six years to "graduate." But the fight had gone too far. It was just a question of time, now, which one would live. Both dogs now were killers.

Shep held Blimp down by his ear. Blimp struggled and wrestled his way back up to his feet but lost part of his ear in the process. Blimp came at Shep, after he forced Shep to let his ear go, and bit him across the forehead. Shep, like a coyote, started from Blimp's shoulder and hooked his fangs into his neck when he dropped his head. Blimp twisted and turned as he tried to break Shep's hold. But the grip was much too tight. The more Blimp struggled, the deeper Shep dug his fangs into his enemy's neck. Blimp's eyes began to glaze. He was slowing down. In his business, seeing many dogs killed, Aaron knew it would be over in just a matter of moments. Soon Blimp lay still. This time he didn't try to get up. When Shep eased his fangs out of Blimp's neck, he was dead. Shep just dropped with exhaustion. Gently, Quiet picked him up and carried him to his car and laid him down in the backseat.

Aaron came down the stairs as Quiet was getting in his car. "How much would you sell your dog for? Just name your price. I can give you 50,000 in cash, right now."

Without hesitation, Quiet said humbly, "I appreciate what you've done for me, but I wouldn't sell Shep for anything."

"I am the one who should appreciate you. But I understand." Aaron looked at Shep. "His kind is hard to come by. And to think I had him all the time and didn't know it." The car started up. "I'll see you." When the car drove away, Aaron went back into the house.

It was already late in the afternoon when Quiet took Shep to the veterinarian, located on Twenty-third and Rainier where they crossed. When Quiet brought Shep into the veterinarian's office, he said, "This dog is chewed up pretty bad. What happened?"

Tears rolls down Quiet's face. "He was in a fight!" he cried. "Think you can patch him up?"

"Yes," said the vet. "It'll take quite a few stitches, but we'll get him back to new. Would you mind leaving him overnight?" Seeing the doubtful look on Quiet's face, he said, "I'll tell you what. I'll patch him up and you can take him home with you. I'll give you some medication. He'll have to rest easy for about two or three weeks for his wounds to heal. Then give him plenty of exercise." Quiet agreed and the veterinarian went to work on Shep.

It was later that evening, around seven-thirty, when the veterinarian brought Shep back to Quiet, who was waiting in the reception area. "Here you are, sir. He'll be good as new in about from four to six weeks."

Quiet gently took Shep and carried him back to his car. The veterinarian came outside just as Quiet was about to drive away. "Hey, Mr. Jones!" he called. "I'm curious. What about the other dog? Can you bring him in so I can have a look at him?"

"He's dead," said Quiet.

The two men looked at one another; then Quiet drove off.

Maraisha was sitting at the dining room table, playing rummy with Sharon, when Quiet came in the house carrying Shep in his arms. "What happened?" she asked, astonished as she got up from the table and came over to Quiet. Shep was wrapped up like a mummy. When Quiet laid Shep down in front of the couch, Maraisha gently rubbed her hands up and down his body. Tears followed. "What happened?" she sniffed.

Dino and Wyatt, upstairs when they heard Quiet come in, came downstairs. Wyatt had Mitzie in his arms. He put her down on the floor. Mitzie immediately ran over to Shep and tried to play with him. But Shep gave Mitzie a couple of snaps, making her back off. "You took him by Mitchell's house!" Wyatt exclaimed.

"Yes," said Quiet disgustedly. "I wanted him to teach me

how to teach Shep to fight. But he already could handle himself."
Then Quiet turned and walked out of the house.

It was dark as he stood on the front porch, head hanging down, and Maraisha came outside. As they faced one another, no words were spoken. She could see the hurt look on his face. She felt he knew he had hurt something he loved but dared not question it.

"It's pretty at night," said Maraisha. "I mean Seattle." She wrapped her arm around Quiet's waist.

Quiet looked up and around, at the sky, the clouds, the moon, and the stars. "I was dumb. I almost cost him his life. Never again will I play a stupid role. I'll let nature take care of its own. Whatever falls in place, I'll have to accept it."

Maraisha reached around and kissed him on the lips. "You understand so much," she whispered. "I was brought up in a lost world. I had no brothers or sisters, just a mother. I don't know when my father deserted us. I never knew him. My mother never talked about him. You guys are lucky. You can compare your ideas together. I let many people tell me what to do, even to becoming a police officer. In a way, I'm glad I'm a cop. In another way, I'm not. But it's my job."

"It's not the cop that makes a name for himself. It's the person behind the badge. Some let their authority go to their heads, and that makes it bad for the good ones. You can't judge a book by its cover or a person by his uniform. It's how one expresses himself."

"Thanks!" she said. "I needed that." She kissed him on the lips repeatedly.

"Let's go back inside," suggested Quiet.

While they were upstairs in the recreation room, Maraisha asked, "Do you know anything about them militants? John said two police officers were fired upon by them."

"Them police officers tried to pick me up that night I left the apartment. Them so-called militants may have saved my life.

146

But I don't know who they are, if that's what you want," said Quiet.

"I won't ask again," she whispered as she walked into his arms. "I don't want to lose you, no way."

As a few days passed, Shep's wounds rapidly healed. They were almost unnoticeable. The days had run into weeks. Quiet started giving Shep plenty of exercise, taking him under the viaduct and going back to his training, although Shep's wounds at times bothered him. He had a lot of heart. At times Shep, working on his man attacks, got a little careless. He felt that Quiet wouldn't hurt him. When Quiet, holding a stick in his hand, commanded Shep to attack, Shep disregarded the stick. Quiet let him feel the stick across his shoulder. Shep yelped, confusion on his face as to why his master had hit him. Shep moved back. Quiet hit Shep hard enough to let him know a man with a stick was not to be taken lightly. The second time Quiet ordered Shep to attack, he attacked, but with more caution. Whenever Shep attacked, he dodged the stick, moving from side to side. When Quiet would take a swing, Shep quickly moved back. Maraisha would just sit on the bank and watch. Her expression showed fear for Shep, almost as though she felt his pains. But Shep seemed to enjoy it. Quiet would practice with Shep until the day was gone. Then they would go back home.

The days had already started getting long. The nights were getting warmer, a sign summer was coming nearer. The following weekend Quiet and Maraisha went back to the woods. Shep went with them. But this time, Quiet took them to the north Cascades, about 270 miles from Seattle, twenty miles below the Canadian border, inside Washington State. Quiet had just turned thirteen the last time he came here up with his father. Mr. Jones didn't come here that often, only when he wanted to spend a few extra days hunting and fishing. The camping area was about twenty miles off the highway, in an isolated area. Very few campers ever came this far off the highway.

In this area there had been quite a few black bear attacks on campers and their supplies. Bears were known to raid a garbage can and ruin locked trailers. Bears also zeroed in on food left out by campers when they took a hike through the woods. Bears had been known to make picnic grounds look like a garbage dump.

Quiet pulled into the designated area early Saturday morning, around seven. He and Maraisha put their tent up, locked the food in the trunk of the car, then went for a stroll toward the river. Walking along the riverbank, Quiet noticed three sets of bear tracks, of two cubs and a mother. He became a little leery of going any farther. The tracks continued a little up the bank, then went into the forest. Shep began to whine. Maraisha noticed the hesitation written on Quiet's face and began to look around. There were no signs of any bears around. Quiet felt it was best to go back to camp. Without any questions, Maraisha went, also.

Quiet and Maraisha were about twenty feet from camp when they saw a black bear cub come dashing out of the tent. Shep took off after it. The cub led Shep into the woods. Moments later there was a growl, a couple of barks, then Shep came running out of the woods. The mother bear was chasing him. Shep was leading the bear toward Quiet and Maraisha. When Quiet saw this, he drew his pistol and fired a couple of shots just over the bear's head. The bear turned and ran back into the woods at the sound of gunfire. Shep came and stood by Quiet's side. When Quiet and Maraisha reached camp, they pulled out the cooking utensils to prepare breakfast.

Maraisha carried a few of the utensils back down to the river to rinse them out. The river was about fifty feet from camp through the woods. A narrow trail led to a clearing about twenty feet from the river. This part of the river was shallow. While rinsing out the few utensils, Maraisha heard a twig crack. She turned around but didn't see anything. So she hunched her shoulders, as though nothing were there. There was another crackling sound. A strange feeling came over her, as though something was watching. She turned her head around again. But still she didn't see anything. The thought of the bear still being in the area frightened her.

While at camp, Quiet was still setting up. He had a trailer hitched to the car he had rented. Shep began to whine a little as he paced back and forth between the camp and the woods. At first, Quiet felt something was wrong when Shep gave a couple of barks, then dashed toward the river. But on second thought, he figured Shep might still be excited scenting that mother bear. Unless wounded and panicked, a bear wants no part of a firearm. She was probably long gone by now. Everything seemed all right, so he went about getting set up for cooking. As Quiet started making a camp fire, he heard Maraisha scream, then the sounds of Shep fighting. "No! No!" Quiet shouted with fear as he dashed off toward the river. "I should have followed Shep." When he got there, Shep was entangled with a cougar.

The cougar struck repeatedly at Shep with his claws. Shep dodged the claws, the way he dodged the stick, and put a scratch mark on the big cat. The cougar charged. Shep got ahold of the cougar's ear but released the grip when the cougar dug his claws into the dog's shoulder. Shep yelped. At the sight of blood, Shep became like a mad dog, like when he fought Blimp. Shep had a killer instinct.

Quiet was concerned about Shep's wounds that weren't completely healed. But judging by the way Shep was fighting, the wounds didn't seem to bother him. Shep barked and snapped as he kept circling the cougar. The cougar stayed mostly on his back, fighting off the dog. Surprisingly, to the cougar, Shep was fast. He didn't care what part of the cougar he got, when given a chance, the tail, a back leg, or a hip. Whenever the cougar spun to face Shep, he quickly got away from the cat's claws.

149

After a few rallies, Shep could see that fighting this cat was much different from fighting an alley cat. The cougar was bigger, stronger, faster, and more aggressive than any cat Shep had faced. The cougar drew blood from Shep's nose, cutting his forehead and wounding his shoulder. At each attack Shep was becoming bolder. He took a few scratches to get in one or two bites. But they weren't deep enough to do any damage. After getting a few scratches across his face, Shep began to protect himself by keeping his body between the cougar's claws and his head.

At first sight of the cougar, Quiet had drawn his pistol. He tried to get a shot off, but Shep kept circling and Quiet was afraid of hitting him. When Shep finally got clear of the cougar, Quiet put three shots down at the cougar's feet. The cougar got up and took off running. Shep started to chase after him, but Quiet called him back.

After the excitement, Quiet helped Maraisha finish rinsing out the cooking utensils; then they headed back to the camp area. When they got back, Quiet continued building a camp fire. Maraisha, still feeling uneasy about the incident, started preparing the food. Quiet noticed her tension as he walked over, so he placed his hand on her shoulder, trying to soothe her. "I'm okay," she said. Shep was lying down in front of the tent. Maraisha walked over and knelt down and hugged him, as she gave him many thanks for saving her from the cougar.

When they were finished eating, washing the dishes, and putting everything away, Quiet took Maraisha on a hike. They went along the riverbank until they came to a high waterfall, which seemed as though it were coming out of the clouds. A small trail led about a mile farther up to the top of the waterfall. When they got to the top, exhaustion forced them to rest. Quiet had made a few sandwiches before leaving camp, and he carried them in his backpack.

It was early afternoon. The sun was high, not a cloud in the sky for miles. The day was warm. A few hawks in the distance flew around. Other birds stayed hidden among the trees. The only other visible wild animals were chipmunks and squirrels, and not too many of those. Below, where the water fell, a river ran an indeterminate number of miles into a valley. Like the sky, the river seemed to have had no beginning and no end. The valley was green. Trees almost reached the clouds when visible. God's country, it was a paradise of peace and quiet. But although nature offers beautiful sights, its way of life is cruel.

Quiet was very aware of nature. Maraisha was learning. She admired nature for its beauty and for what it brought: life and happy feelings. Quiet, looking at Maraisha, noticed she was full of love. Why would someone like her want to be a police officer? On the way back to camp, in late afternoon, Shep led the way. That night it rained. Quiet and Maraisha made love.

The next morning around seven-thirty, there was a knock on Aaron's door. For a long period of time, Maulder had had a few uniformed officers keep Mitchell's house under surveillance. Bishop, Randall, Munson, and Morrison. Sleepy, Mitchell, wearing his pajamas, slid on a robe and went to answer it. "Yeah! What is it?" he yawned.

"Say, Brother! What's happening?" the leader of the police said joyously. "My name is John Maulder. A friend of mine named Jones said you had a dog to match mine. I got fifty dollars says mine can whip yours."

Mitchell looked at Spike, a well-muscled Doberman pinscher, that looked strong. In the car Ross and Marty were sitting parked in front on the street. Right off Mitchell felt Maulder was lying. Quiet would never send a stranger to his house. "I don't know anyone named Jones," he said doubtfully. "You must have the wrong address."

As Mitchell tried to close the door, Maulder put his foot in the doorway and forced it open, then pushed Mitchell backward. Maintaining his balance, Mitchell turned and headed downstairs through the kitchen. Going downstairs, he heard Maulder shout, "Spike!" Then there was a bark as Mitchell heard Spike coming after him. When Mitchell got into the subbasement he quickly released Snow from his cage and went out the back door and started running through the alley going past a police officer hiding in some nearby bushes.

The police officer stood up with a .12-gauge pump shotgun. "Halt!" he hollered. Then there were gunshots. The first buckshot hit Mitchell in the leg. It only slowed him down. But as Mitchell was going past another police officer farther down the alley, the officer rose and put some buckshots in Mitchell's back. Instantly Mitchell fell to the ground. When Maulder and the other police officers approached Mitchell, he raised his head. "Bastards!" he shouted. Then he died.

When Mitchell released Snow, he had stopped Spike on the basement stairs. They started fighting, going from the stairs down into the basement, and ended up in the middle of the fighting pit. Both dogs squared off on their hind legs, snapping at one another, trying to get a fatal grip. Snow used his strength as he tried to force Spike off balance. But Spike quickly twisted his body and forced Snow to land on all fours, then spun around to face Spike as he tried to come down on Snow's neck with his fangs.

The two dogs wrestled around the fighting pit. The fight quickly became a bloody battle. Snow got ahold of Spike's ear and drew blood. Spike broke the grip by going for Snow's leg. Snow tried to sink his fangs into the back of Spike's neck. But Spike took his leg and pushed Snow back to all fours. As Snow tried to retrieve his balance, Spike saw an opportunity to hook his fangs in the back of Snow's neck. The grip was fatal. The more Snow struggled, the deeper Spike's fangs went into his neck. A chunk of flesh came out of Snow's neck. Blood flowed as in a bloodbath. Moments later, Snow was dead.

During the chase, residents of the neighborhood who had heard the shooting opened their curtains and drapes. A few windows were raised and doors opened as people tried to see what the commotion was about. A couple of neighbors who saw a few police officers in their backyards got their weapons and ordered them out.

In the CD news traveled fast. Neighbors got on their telephones and called their friends and relatives and spread news of the incident. Clinton was sitting on the couch in the living room reading a newspaper at about eight-thirty that morning when he got a call from Earl. There was excitement in his voice as he told Clinton of Aaron's death and Aaron's dogs being impounded. A Humane Society van came and transported them.

Clinton was stunned, hearing about Aaron's death. In his bathrobe, Clinton got up off the couch. He got dressed, hurried to his car, and went to pick up Earl. When Clinton picked up Earl, they headed for Aaron's house. The incident was over. The police had drawn a crowd, but by the time Clinton and Earl drove up, the police had already left and most of the crowd had dispersed. Only a few neighbors stayed behind for more discussion. Clinton and Earl got out of the car and asked a few neighbors about the incident. They got several different stories before investigating the inside of the house. It was undisturbed. When they left the area, they headed for Quiet's home.

Wyatt and Joan were partners in dominoes playing Dino and Sharon in the dining room when Clinton and Earl drove up. Wyatt let them in when he heard the doorbell ring. Wyatt noticed his two brothers seemed disturbed as they came into the house and sat down on the couch. "What's the matter, Bros?"

"Aaron Mitchell is dead," explained Clinton. He paused for a moment. "Where's Quiet?"

"He and Maraisha went camping yesterday morning,"

answered Wyatt. There was sorrow on his face. "What about . . .?" His head drooped. "Nothing," he said sadly. Then Wyatt walked toward the kitchen. Seeing the look on his face, Joan got up from her chair and followed him. When Joan came into the kitchen, Wyatt was standing at the back window. She came up behind him and wrapped her arms around his waist. Wyatt turned to face her. They hugged. Joan could feel that Wyatt was saddened by Aaron's death. *A woman's touch can soothe any man's feelings,* she thought.

Later that afternoon after Sharon left Quiet's home, she was about two blocks away and around the corner before she was pulled over by an unmarked police car. A plainclothes detective got out of the car. Sharon recognized him right away. It was Detective Mike Schmidt. He was wearing a baggy gray suit that needed pressing. "When are you going to buy another suit?" joked Sharon. "What brings you out here?"

There was a fearful expression on his face. "I have to talk to you and Maraisha," said Detective Schmidt. His voice sounded worried. "Where's Maraisha?"

Sharon became frightened. "Is something wrong?" she asked curiously. She stared at him for a moment, as she felt something was bothering him. "Can I help?"

"I have to talk to you and Maraisha," he stated nervously. "There may be trouble for us."

"What do you mean?" A curious look came over Sharon's face. "Don't scare me."

"We can't talk here," he said as he started for his car. "Follow me. I have something to give you." He got in his car and drove away.

Sharon followed. Schmidt circled two blocks and got on Seventeenth Avenue. He drove one block, made a right turn, and headed across the Floating Bridge. He took the second exit off the freeway on Mercer Island, then made a right turn and drove east on a countrylike road. After about ten miles of twisting and turning, Schmidt pulled into a driveway near Lake Washington. Sharon pulled up behind him.

When they got out of their cars, Sharon ran over to him. "What's this all about?"

"Come inside. I'll show you."

They went into the house. Schmidt went to a safe behind a picture of George Washington in the living room. He opened the safe and pulled out a large envelope. "Our lives may be in danger," he said, frightened. "In case anything should happen to me, I want you to give this to Lieutenant Miller." He handed Sharon the envelope.

"I'm afraid. What are you talking about?" she asked, also frightened.

"That envelope will explain everything. Lieutenant Miller will understand. Now take it and get out of here. If I'm right, they'll be coming after me. You just don't know who to trust. Some of our people on the force are no good. They've committed major crimes. Now get out of here."

Frightened, Sharon took the envelope and walked out of the house, got in her car, then drove away. While driving back across the Floating Bridge, she glanced down at the envelope on the front seat beside her. Her thoughts began to play tricks on her. *What was Mike talking about? He said our lives may be in danger. Who was he waiting for? I could tell John and the others. Maybe they can help. I'll take this envelope to Maraisha. Maybe she will understand what Mike meant. But she's with Quiet. No telling when they'll be back.* She continued driving until she pulled near the curb in front of Quiet's home. She parked, got out, and headed back toward the house.

When Sharon got inside, Dino said curiously, "I thought you were going back to the apartment to wait until I picked you up." But as Dino saw the strange expression on her face, he asked, "What's the matter, baby? Something wrong?" and sat down beside her on the couch.

With love and fear in her eyes, Sharon looked at Dino for a moment, then jumped up and threw her arms around his neck. "I don't know!" she cried. "I ran into one of my bosses as I was leaving the house. A few things he said didn't make any sense," she explained.

"Tell me about it," said Dino. While Sharon began to explain, Wyatt and Joan came out of the kitchen and sat down on the other side of Dino. Mitzie lay down in the center of the living room floor.

When Sharon got through explaining, Dino said, "There's nothing we can do. Why didn't he call for help from some of his police buddies?"

"I thought of that, too. But he didn't know who he could trust."

"He trusts you," relied Dino.

Meanwhile three unmarked cars were parked down the street from Detective Schmidt's house. Maulder, Marty, and Ross sat with Spike in one car. Daniels and Marcy were in the second car, and Davis, Morrison, and Munson were in the third car.

When the cars pulled up to the curb, Maulder and Davis got out of their cars and walked up the street toward Schmidt's house. When they got on the porch, Maulder rang the doorbell. The door opened. Schmidt invited them in.

"What brings you guys here?" he said as he led them into the living room.

The men sat down on the couch. A moment later Schmidt's wife brought in a tray of coffee, cream, and sugar. She placed the tray on the coffee table in front of the couch, then left the living room.

"I heard you have names of some cops who conspired to kill blacks. I wonder if you could show them to us," said Maulder as he was fixing himself a cup of coffee.

"No one knew of that but Tanner. I told him I was going to give it to Lieutenant Miller," said Schmidt.

"Tanner sent us to bring him the list of names," said Davis. "I don't have it here."

"Does he have it? We'll get it from him," said Maulder.

"It's too late. It's already on its way to Detective Smith's office."

"Smith is on vacation. He won't get the document until he gets back," Maulder replied. "Why don't you let us hold it for him?"

"Are our names on the list?" asked Davis suspiciously.

Schmidt paused for a moment. "What you guys did was murder, and I'm going to turn you in for it."

"Where's your evidence? It's just your word against ours," said Davis.

"I have proof. When Miller gets the list of names, you'll lose your badges and go to jail, where you belong."

Maulder stood up from the couch. "Spike!" he called. Spike's ears stood straight up. A snarl came from his mouth. His pearly white fangs were showing. Spike looked at Schmidt. "Now!" continued Maulder. "I want you to give us that document or I'll have Spike rip you to pieces." Schmidt got up from the couch as though he were going for the document, then tried to get his pistol which was hanging on the living room wall. "Spike! Get him."

Just as Schmidt got to his pistol, Spike was all over him. "Get him off me!" the man hollered as he wrestled Spike. But Spike was too strong and fast for the middle-aged man. The dog was chewing on Schmidt's arm as he tried to protect his face. Schmidt got bitten on his arm and cheekbone as he screamed, "Get him off!" But Maulder refused to call Spike off.

Schmidt's wife was in the kitchen when she heard the screaming and fighting. She came running. When she saw her husband getting chewed up, she went for Schmidt's pistol. But Maulder drew his pistol and put four slugs in her back. She died instantly. Then Schmidt let out a final scream. Spike had bitten his throat. "We'd better make it look like them militants did this," said Maulder.

"Right!" Davis agreed as he started pumping lead into both bodies. "We'd better find that document before someone else gets their hands on it." Both men thoroughly searched the house. Maulder went upstairs, while Davis looked downstairs. They went through every room, crack, and opening in the house. But still they couldn't find the envelope. When they met back in the living room, Davis suggested, "If we make ashes of this place, the evidence will go up in flames with it. Then we'll have nothing to worry about."

In his search through the house for the document, Davis had seen a five-gallon can of gasoline in the basement. He went downstairs, got the gas, and spread it through the house. When Davis put a match to the gas, it burst into flames. When Maulder and Davis got back to the others, they explained what had happened; then everyone got in their cars and drove away.

6

Early Sunday evening around six, Quiet and Maraisha came back to Seattle. There were signs of it having rained. The streets were still wet. Clouds slowly were gliding across the sky. Not many people were walking on the streets. Quiet drove straight to Maraisha's apartment building, parked the car underneath it, then went up to the apartment. It was empty. "I wonder where Sharon is," said Maraisha as they entered the apartment. They went through both bedrooms and the kitchen and the bathroom.

Maraisha went into the kitchen and made a pot of coffee. Then she went to the bathroom to take a shower. Quiet waited on the couch, reading a newspaper. Shep was lying down in front of him underneath the coffee table. There was a crackling sound in the hallway outside the apartment, like footsteps. Shep's ears rose.

"What is it, fella?" Quiet said. "Someone out there?"

Shep just whined. So Quiet got up and went to the door. He looked up and down the hallway. It was empty. Feeling that someone was out there, Quiet closed the door and went back to the couch, took a pistol out, and placed it under a pillow near where he was sitting. Then he went to the kitchen, got a cup of coffee, and took it back into the living room and sat back down. He began to sip. When Shep's tensions eased off, the feeling of someone still being in the hallway went away. After both Quiet and Maraisha got cleaned up, they went to a movie.

It was about 1:00 A.M., after the movie, when Quiet pulled the car back underneath the apartment building. Dino and Sharon were sitting on the couch watching television when Quiet and Maraisha entered the apartment.

"It's about time," said Sharon as she glanced at her watch. "We've been waiting for you two." Sharon paused for a moment as Quiet and Maraisha were about to get comfortable. "I have something to tell you." She caught their attention. "Something happened while you guys were gone."

"What is it?" Quiet asked calmly.

With a strange and indecisive expression, Sharon began to recount Aaron's death, mentioning the information she had received from Clinton and Earl, and Detective Schmidt's strange actions. "Cops conspired to kill blacks, and our lives may be in danger. He said some of our people can't be trusted. I couldn't make much sense out of it, but the way he acted put a scare in me."

"Why would they want to kill Aaron Mitchell?" said Quiet as he paced back and forth across the floor. "Think you can find Detective Schmidt's house?"

"Sure!" said Sharon. "Maraisha and I have been there a couple of times. He said he was expecting someone when I left, if that means anything."

"I want you to take me there," said Quiet.

"I don't know why, but I'll take you. He might get mad at us for waking him up," said Sharon.

"If it's what I think, he won't be sleeping; he'll be dead. And so will be anybody else who might be in the house." Quiet motioned for Shep to stay as Dino and Sharon got up off the couch and headed for the door. Everyone went downstairs and got in Quiet's car. Sharon sat in the front seat next to Quiet to give directions, while Maraisha and Dino sat in the back.

It was raining heavily when Quiet pulled away from the apartment building. The raindrops were as large as ice cubes. Sharon's vision was impaired. After they came off the Floating Bridge, she caused Quiet to make a couple of wrong turns, as though she had forgotten where Detective Schmidt lived. Maraisha had to assist her. Finally they pulled up in front of Schmidt's house. It was in a shambles, a total loss. All that was left of the house, besides rubble, were the cement stairs that had led up to the house and the stairs that had led to the basement. Sharon became scared for the first few moments as she looked where a house used to be. Quiet got out of the car and walked among the rubble with a flashlight. Very few items could be identified of what used to be there. The rest was beyond recognition. "This was why we passed them fire trucks on our way back to Seattle," he mumbled. "Whoever did this made it thorough." He went and got back in his car.

On the way back to Seattle, Quiet said, "Detective Schmidt must have known something more important than just cops conspiring to kill blacks."

"What do you mean?" asked Sharon.

"A person don't burn down his home unless he expects to collect insurance money."

"I don't understand," said Sharon.

"I mean Detective Schmidt left something behind, and someone tried to find it. They didn't find it, so they felt it was still in the house somewhere, and the best way to destroy evidence is by fire."

"What now?" asked Maraisha.

"Back to the apartment, I guess. There's nothing we can do. It's up to the police."

The next day at work Quiet couldn't help but listen to some of the gossip going around after the morning news on the radio. Everywhere he went, almost everyone was talking about how Detective Michael Schmidt had died. The gossip was that the black militants had killed Schmidt and burned his house down. Nothing was said of Schmidt's wife. But ever since Clinton's kidnapping, a few things had begun to bother Quiet: the killing of Boner, Mitchell, and other blacks. Some things seemed strange. *What is the reason behind all this?* he thought.

Meanwhile, Sharon drove downtown to the municipal building to have a talk with Lieutenant Miller. But when she arrived, Lieutenant Miller was out of town. Detective Lawrence Tanner's secretary suggested Sharon talk to him as he was second in command. When Sharon entered Tanner's office, she explained, "I saw Detective Schmidt yesterday. He gave me an envelope to give to Lieutenant Miller in case something should happen to him."

"Do you know what's in the envelope?" asked Tanner.

"No."

"Do you have it with you?"

"No. I left it at the apartment."

"Why don't you get it and bring it in? I want to have a look at it."

"Mike said I should give it to Lieutenant Miller."

"I'll see that he gets it."

"I don't know—" she began doubtfully.

"If you have any evidence about Mike Schmidt's murder, I want it, or I'll have to charge you with withholding evidence," interrupted Tanner.

"Okay. I'll get it," said Sharon as she slowly got up from her chair, then walked out of the office. When Sharon got back to the apartment, Maraisha, in her bathrobe, was sitting on the couch reading a magazine. A cup of coffee was sitting on the coffee table. Shep, as usual, was resting underneath the coffee table. Sharon walked in and flopped down at the other end of the couch.

Maraisha noticed the disturbed expression on Sharon's face

and placed the magazine down on the coffee table, picked up her cup of coffee, and took a sip. "What's the matter?" she asked.

"I don't know. Everything is starting to happen at once," Sharon said disgustedly.

"Like what?"

"It's hard to explain. Detective Schmidt, for instance. The department believes it was the militants who killed Mike and his wife and burned his house down. Quiet believes it was someone else. What do you think?"

"I don't," sighed Maraisha as she got up off the couch. "It's a mystery to me, too." She went to the kitchen to get a refill.

At the same time, down at the Jones house, Mitzie was lying down on the floor in the center of the living room when she felt she heard something outside. At times Quiet had taken Mitzie underneath the viaduct with Shep and trained her to obey. But Mitzie had become more of a pet than a watchdog. Around the house she became territorial around other dogs, all except Shep. The dogs she couldn't handle Shep would run off. When Mitzie heard a noise, which seemed to come from the back, she got up and went to the kitchen. She trained her ears toward the back door. There was no sound. She went and looked out the window. No sign of anything. But she knew something was outside. She went back to the living room and lay back down.

There was another sound. Again Mitzie's ears stood straight up. The sound again, seemed to come from the back. So Mitzie got up and went back into the kitchen. But this time when Mitzie trained her ears on the door, she heard the sound of another dog whimpering. Mitzie gave a couple of barks. The whimpering stopped. But she knew the dog was still out there. So she ran back and forth from the kitchen to the living room, barking. The second time Mitzie went into the living room, there was a crash at the back door. When Mitzie heard the crash, she hurried back toward the kitchen. But when she got between the kitchen and living room in the hallway, yelping and barking, she ran into Spike.

Shepherds have an instinctive suspicion of strangers. When Mitzie first saw the three Caucasian strangers and a dog, she became afraid of being harmed. Instinctively Mitzie attacked.

Both dogs got up on their hind legs and started snapping at one another. Mitzie tried to match her strength against Spike's, but it was no contest. Spike was stronger, faster, and more experienced. He forced Mitzie backward and she landed on all fours. Then she spun to face him, again. But, before Mitzie had time to fully regain her balance, Spike was all over her. The dogs fought from the hallway on into the living room.

Mitzie finally managed to get away from Spike's pressure as they got back up on their hind legs again. Growling, barking, and snapping, Spike used his strength to force Mitzie back up against the front door. She fought her way off the door and they got in the middle of the living room floor. Spike forced Mitzie off balance, which gave him an opportunity to grip a vulnerable spot on her neck. Mitzie struggled to get free. But each time she struggled, the grip got tighter. Rapidly Mitzie began to weaken. Her pulse was slowing. Moments later the struggle was over. Mitzie lay dead.

When the fight was over, Maulder, Marty, and Ross went through the house and searched it thoroughly, looking for the envelope. Maulder searched the three rooms upstairs. Ross searched through the downstairs bedrooms. Marty went through the kitchen, the bathroom, the living room, and the dining room. When they didn't find the envelope, the three men left.

It was around two-thirty that afternoon and Sharon was looking out the living room window. Maulder, Marty and Ross had just come walking out of the house, through the back door. "Oh, no!" she said in a low frightened voice. A big lump clogged her throat. Trembling fear ran through her body as she dashed out of the apartment, ran downstairs to the parking area, got in her car, and drove away. Sharon headed for Quiet's home through the back alleyway, so she wouldn't be seen by Maulder or his associates if they should come her way by the street route. The alley ran six blocks before ending up behind Quiet's home, then continuing on toward the entrance. Sharon pulled her car into the back driveway and parked.

The back door was cracked open. Sharon hurried toward the house. She drew her pistol from her purse, pushed the door open wider, and cautiously entered the house. After moving through the kitchen slowly, she crept into the living room. Carefully she looked around. The room was empty. Then she saw Mitzie lying on the floor in front of the door. A big chunk of meat had been taken from her neck. "Oh, no!" Sharon cried as tears rolled down her cheeks. She walked over to Mitzie and gently rubbed her hand up and down Mitzie's fur. "Why you?" sobbed Sharon. "Quiet is going to be angry." She moved Mitzie away from the door and placed her in the center of the living room. Then she straightened out the house and went and sat down on the couch when she was finished. *What will Quiet do? He, Wyatt, and Dino loved that dog,* she thought.

Maraisha was in the bathtub when she heard the door slam. "Sharon! Sharon!" she called. There was no answer. So Maraisha got up out of the tub, put her robe on, then walked into the living room. "Sharon! Sharon, where are you?" Still there was no answer. She went through the apartment and to her bedroom. "Where could she have gone?" she asked herself. "Oh, well." She went back into the bathroom.

Around four o'clock Dino came home early. He had been working under a house in a residential area when a pipeline had burst. His clothes got wet, so he decided to go home for the rest of the day. But when he saw Mitzie lying on the floor and Sharon sitting on the couch, he demanded, "What the hell happened?" Sharon was silent as Dino went over and examined Mitzie. He saw the wound on her neck. "Quiet is going to be angry. She's been in a fight. There's bites all over her body. Someone has to answer for this." Still Sharon was silent. Her tears never stopped flowing.

Just then Quiet and Wyatt walked into the house. When Quiet saw Mitzie lying on the floor he froze. "Mitzie," he said in a low voice as he walked over to her and examined the wounds. "Killed by another dog." He glanced around the room. A few things were broken. He could see that someone had straightened the house back up. When Quiet looked at Sharon, coldness was in his eyes. "What happened?" he demanded. Sharon just cried. "Who was here? Some of your friends?"

Sharon didn't say a word as she got up from the couch, looked at Quiet and then at Dino for a moment, then took off running through the kitchen and out the back door. She got in her car and drove away. Dino started to follow, but Quiet grabbed him by the arm. "Come with me. She's going back to the apartment," he said.

Maraisha, still in her bathrobe, was sitting on the couch, resting her feet on the coffee table, reading a magazine when Sharon came rushing through the door. There was a sad look on her face. She was crying as she ran into her bedroom. "Sharon! Sharon, wait!" called Maraisha as she got up off the couch and tried to follow. But the door slammed in her face.

As Maraisha started to enter the bedroom, she heard a key turn in the front door. It opened. Quiet and Dino came walking through the door. Shep was sitting up when he saw Quiet. He jumped up, ran over to Quiet, and jumped in against his chest, playing. Not in a playful mood, Quiet commanded Shep to sit down.

"Where's Sharon?" he said. Quiet patted Shep, but there was an angry look on his face. "In the bedroom," answered Maraisha. Although Quiet looked angry, he didn't seem angry, just puzzled.

Dino looked at Quiet. "I'll get her," he said, then headed for the bedroom.

Quiet walked over to Maraisha and led her away from the door to the couch. A few moments later Sharon and Dino came out of the bedroom with his arm around her waist. They stood before Quiet.

"I'm sorry about Mitzie—" Sharon began.

"What about Mitzie?" Maraisha interrupted.

"She's dead," answered Quiet.

Maraisha was saddened as Sharon continued, "It was John's dog that killed Mitzie. I saw John, Jack, and William leaving your house, from our window."

"What were they doing at my house?" Quiet asked curiously. Sharon was silent. "Your boss, Mike, did he tell you or give you anything? 'Cause those guys were looking for something. Whatever it was, they didn't destroy it in the fire like they thought. What brought them to my house?"

"Maybe they were looking for that envelope Mike gave me," said Sharon.

Maraisha got up off the couch. "Are you serious? Those are cops," she added doubtfully. "They wouldn't do something like this. There must be some mistake."

"Yes," agreed Quiet. "And they made it, *plus.*"

Maraisha still found the accusations Quiet had brought against her associates hard to believe. She was trying to find excuses for what the police were doing, but Quiet didn't see any good reasons for their actions. So Quiet got up off the couch and walked to the window. He looked down at his house, then at the distant clouds. It showed signs of rain. He placed his hands in his front pocket. "Where's the envelope?" he asked.

"I hid it under the hood of my car," said Sharon. "I'll get it." She left the apartment. Shep followed. When she got downstairs in the parking area, Shep gave a snarl, and whimpered as he circled around Sharon. "What is it, boy?" She became cautious

167

as she looked around, but she didn't see anything. Daniels and Marcy made their appearance, coming from the direction of her car. "What a relief. I'm glad to see you guys," she said when she saw the two men. Shep showed his fangs. Then Sharon became a little suspicious but tried to hide it. "What are you guys doing down here?"

"We're just on our way up to see you and Maraisha," said Marcy.

"I'll just be a minute. I got to get something out of my car. Be right with you." Sharon continued to her car. *They were probably looking for that envelope,* she thought. When Sharon got to her car, she pulled her pistol out of the glove compartment, put it in her purse, and went back toward the men. "I forgot this," she said as she showed them her pistol. "Come on up."

When they got into the hallway on the first floor, Daniels said, "Well, you go on up. There's a couple of things we have to check on. We'll see you later." The men left.

When Sharon got back upstairs, she told Dino, Quiet, and Maraisha that she had met Marcy and Daniels in the garage. Quiet told Shep to stay in the apartment. Then he, Dino and Sharon went back downstairs. When they got in the garage, Sharon went to the car, raised the hood, and pulled out the envelope. She gave it to Quiet.

They went back upstairs; then Quiet opened the envelope. "This document could send some quite important guys to prison," he remarked as he scanned the document.

"Mike wanted me to give this to Detective Miller," added Sharon. "But he's been out of town since last week. At least, that's what Larry said."

"Who's Larry?" asked Quiet.

"Lawrence Tanner," she answered. "He's the head of Internal Affairs."

"It may be a shock to you, but his name is on this list, too." Quiet looked at Sharon. "Did you tell him about the envelope?"

"Yes." She paused for a moment. "Why?"

"That's why my house was ransacked and Mike Schmidt's house got burned down. They'll be after us now."

The expression on Quiet's face told Maraisha many rapid thoughts were going through his mind. "Whatcha gonna do now?" she asked.

Resting his chin on his thumb and index finger, pacing from one side of the living room to the other, he said indecisively, "I don't know, yet." As he walked near the door, he called, "Come, Shep!" Shep gave a couple of barks as he followed Quiet out the door. Maraisha ran behind them. About halfway down the alleyway she caught up with Quiet. He turned around. "Go back," he demanded, "and put some clothes on."

"Not until you come back with me," Maraisha demanded. "You're going to get yourself killed."

Quiet saw the fear for him in her eyes. "You can't come, baby. I have some thinking to do."

As Maraisha walked into his arms, she said softly, "I'm a cop. I work with those guys. I know now what they're doing is wrong. But what can you do against the whole police force? You may get a few before they kill you, but what would that accomplish?"

"Nothing! But I'm not going to stand by and watch them keep bothering my family. They've ransacked my home, kidnapped one brother, beaten up another one, and killed one of my dogs. It's got to stop somewhere, whether or not someone gets hurt."

"I'll talk to them. Maybe they'll leave us alone."

"It's too late for talk. You heard what Sharon said. Your life and hers may be in danger. It's best you let me handle this. And don't let your friends know that you suspect what they're doing is against the law." When Quiet saw the worried look on Maraisha's face, he said, "Look! I'm nobody's fool. No way I'm going to pick a fight with the police force. They're too strong.

169

Now! Go get some clothes on. I'm going over to Clinton's. Be back in about an hour." He handed her the envelope. "Put this in a safe place."

Maraisha watched as Quiet disappeared through the exit door. Then she and Shep went back to the apartment.

About two blocks away from the apartment, a patrol car put its lights on Quiet. He pulled over to the curb. The driver got out and approached him. "Get out, please, sir," he said.

"Did I do something wrong, Officer?"

"Get out and get in the backseat of my car," demanded Randall, the officer, while Bishop waited.

This must be how they grabbed Clinton, Quiet thought as he got out of his car and went and sat in the backseat of the police car.

"Put your hands behind your back," said Bishop as he put handcuffs on Quiet's wrists. Then he placed a blindfold over his eyes and ordered him to lie down on the floor. Then Randall drove away.

Quiet wanted to resist the fact of handcuffs being put on his wrists. But what could he do against the police, alone, his hands cuffed behind his back? He was angry. *What are they going to do with me? What do they want? I know these are some of the police officers that have been going around killing blacks. Are they going to kill me, too? I can recognize them if they have me in court. They wouldn't want to take that chance,* he thought.

The car drove on one back street after another. Quiet didn't hear much traffic. At times there wasn't any. He knew they were near water, 'cause he could hear water splashing up against a shore. *Lake Washington,* he thought. *It's sure not the route they took Clint. They must have something special planned for me. At least until they find that document. Maybe I'm safe till then.*

Randall picked up the mike. He called his time in for the day. Then Randall used another mike to let his partners know they had the man they wanted and would meet them at an isolated residence. Quiet was taken through a back alley to a vacant house. He was escorted by Bishop and Randall to the basement and placed in a chair in the center of a room. It was cold. Then the blindfold was removed.

Randall crossed in front of Quiet. "You have something we want," he said.

"I don't know what you're talking about," said Quiet coldly.

"That's okay," said Randall as he grabbed Quiet by his chin. "When the other guys get here you're going to sing like a chatterbox."

When Quiet was apprehended, Maulder and Ross drove up behind Quiet's car and gave it a search for the envelope. They came up empty. So they proceeded to where they were supposed to meet Randall, Bishop and the others, at the same time unaware that an apple-red '65 Corvette followed the police car that held Quiet at a safe distance. Two young blacks in their early twenties, Michael Taylor, a younger brother of the slain Larry Taylor, and a close friend, Leroy Young, were in the sports car. It had a high-performance 427-cubic-centimeter engine made for racing. Following the Corvette was a '66 navy-blue Ford Cobra containing Ted and Calvin Renfro, two brothers in their early twenties, cousins of Leroy Young. The Cobra had a 428-cubic-centimeter high-performance engine. It, too, was designed for racing.

When the police pulled into the driveway, the four blacks waited at the entrance of the alley to where Quiet was being taken. Then they parked their cars one block up the street around the next corner. They got out of their cars and made their way to the house, through the back alleys. The alleys ran for about a mile.

When they got to the house, first Michael circled one side of it while Young went around the other side. They checked the windows and the doors as they went along. The house was locked. It was a three-story house, with a basement. Calvin and

Leroy watched over them from the back. The two blacks met in the back of the house. Seeing that everything was locked, Michael pulled out his pocketknife and jimmied the lock on the kitchen window. He raised the window and the four blacks crawled through it.

Crawling over the kitchen counter, they saw no one seemed to have lived in the house for months. Almost everything they touched was dusty. They drew their weapons and quietly searched the first floor thoroughly. Ted went to the bottom of the stairs and trained his ears on upstairs. Nothing. Calvin went to the basement door and trained his ears toward the basement. He heard low mumbling voices. He motioned for the others to come and listen. Quietly Michael opened the basement door and they silently crept down the stairs.

When Michael and the other three got downstairs, the voices had gotten louder. They were the voices of two men talking, joking, laughing, and threatening from one side of a hallway. There were two other small rooms, but they were empty. On the other side of the hallway was a washroom, a bathroom, and a bedroom. At the end of the hallway was another door that led to the garage. Quiet was being held in the room next to the garage by Randall and Bishop. At the other end of the hallway was a rec room.

The four blacks crept down the hallway until they came to the bedroom from which the voices came. The door was open. Taylor and Young drew their pistols as they stood beside the door. "Freeze!" said Taylor as he made his quick appearance. Then came Young with a .9-millimeter automatic. Ted and Calvin with their .38s entered on both sides of the room. Bishop and Randall eased up out of their chairs and raised their hands slowly when they saw the weapons aimed at them. "Uncuff him," demanded Taylor.

"You'll be in a lot of trouble if you don't get out of here. We're cops," threatened Bishop.

"And you'll be in a lot of trouble if you don't uncuff him. This is a gun," Taylor replied.

Without another argument, Bishop reached into a pocket on his uniform belt, pulled out a key, and uncuffed Quiet's wrists. Quiet took the handcuffs and led the two officers to a water pipe hanging just below the ceiling in the bathroom and cuffed them together. "You're lucky I don't kill you both."

"We'll get you, you black bastard," threatened Randall.

"You're in no position to be threatening anyone," said Taylor as he walked up to the officers. He placed his pistol in Randall's mouth. "One more word out of you, and I'll close your mouth. Permanently."

Then Taylor, Quiet, and the other three blacks left the house through the back door and made their way back through the alleys to their cars. But just as they were going up the alley, Maulder, Marcy, Ross, Marty, and Daniels had pulled up in front of the house in their unmarked cars. When they entered the house, they heard shouting coming from the basement. "Down here!" hollered the voices. They drew their weapons and rushed to the basement. When they got downstairs, Bishop began to explain the incident as Maulder was taking the handcuffs off.

It had been over two hours since Quiet had left the apartment. After the first hour, Maraisha began to worry, but not so it was noticed. After another half hour passed, she had got on the telephone and called Clinton, who told her he hadn't seen Quiet. Maraisha called Wyatt, who hadn't seen Quiet either. The worrying began to show as she told Dino and Sharon about her concern. They also wondered what had happened.

Meanwhile, on the way back to his car, Quiet was riding in the backseat of the Corvette. *That'll be the last time they'll ever put handcuffs on me,* he thought. "Who do I owe the thanks to?" he said.

For a moment there was hesitance, but then the silence was

broken. "You knew my brother, Larry Taylor. I'm his younger brother, Michael. This is Leroy." Leroy was sitting on the passenger side. "Behind us are Ted and Calvin Renfro."

"Yes," Quiet said, "I can see the resemblance. How did you happen to be back there?"

"We've been watching you and your girlfriend for a long time," Michael continued. "She's a cop. Her so-called friends are the vigilante group that's been killing a lot of brothers. We got a few of them. Through her we can find the rest."

"What about the cops that were killed?"

"That's not us. We killed only those who needed to be killed. They killed my brother and a few other brothers. They deserved to die," added Leroy. "The police had a TIP set Larry up, then gunned him down like a mad dog."

"Larry and I went back a long way. We used to be junior high and high school running buddies. Sorry to hear about his death," said Quiet. "But whether or not you guys did them other cop killings, you'll be charged with them once the police catch up with you."

"It's that big one we want. The one who sits behind the desk downtown. He pulled the trigger that killed Larry," Michael responded.

"That's not going to be easy," replied Quiet.

"We know that," added Leroy. "But we're not afraid. If we could wipe out the whole police force, that wouldn't equal the blacks they've killed over the years."

When Michael pulled over in front of Quiet's car, Quiet got out of Michael's car, then got into his. "The streets are crawling with cops looking for you guys."

"We know that," said Michael. Then he drove away.

As Quiet sat in his car, he mumbled, "They've been in my car, too." He started up the engine and let it roar. When he pulled away from the curve, he turned the car around and headed back to the apartment.

When Quiet walked into the apartment, Maraisha rushed into his arms like he was a long-lost lover. "I was worried when Clinton told me you weren't over there," she said softly.

Quiet placed his hands upon her shoulders to keep her at arm's length. "Every time I leave, you're afraid of your cop friends picking me up. I don't like pressure, but what is it?" he demanded. "What do I have that they want? Besides the document that could send them to prison. This was going on before the document existed."

"They want to kill you and Clinton," Sharon interrupted. "They're afraid of what Clinton can do. He has the power to get blacks together. And some whites will follow."

"What has that to do with me?" Quiet asked angrily.

"You're his brother and that's reason enough. They're afraid of you also. You were in Vietnam. You learned a lot there. Your friend Larry had served in Vietnam also. He learned fighting skills. No doubt you learned primarily the same. If they kill one of your brothers, they'll have to kill you, too. Now you're in a position to really hurt them, and they can't let you live once they get their hands on the envelope."

Sharon continued, "The information the police got on you Maraisha and I gave to them, and it also mentions a few other blacks. Maraisha didn't know anything about it. Because she was black, I was supposed to keep an eye on her when she started seeing you." All while Sharon was talking, Maraisha was stunned. "Then I started seeing Dino. I didn't want to get too involved, but it was something I couldn't help. Then things started getting too far out of hand. Things they were telling me and things I saw them do confused me. Now I don't know what to do."

Sharon walked into Dino's arms. "When I saw Mack and Bill downstairs, I knew something was wrong. I was really scared. 'Cause when I got my gun out of the glove compartment, I could tell they'd been searching my car for that envelope. That's why I just got my pistol and came back up here."

With a feeling of distrust Dino grabbed Sharon by the shoulders and held her at arms' length. "Why are you telling us this now?" he asked.

Disgustedly Sharon went and sat down on the couch. "I'm scared." She looked at Dino. "I love you so much. I don't want to see you hurt. If Quiet gets hurt, you will, too."

"Did you tell anyone else about the envelope?" asked Dino as he went and sat down beside her.

"No!" answered Sharon quickly. But she thought for a split second. "Wait a minute. I told Lawrence Tanner. But I already told you that."

"How about anyone else?"

"No! No one else."

"Shep!" Quiet called. Shep barked and went and stood by Quiet's side. "Let's go, fella."

As Quiet was walking down the exit stairs, Maraisha caught up with him. "I'm going with you this time."

Quiet could see that she was dressed up. He still wore his work clothes. He just smiled as he pulled her into his arms and held her for a short moment. "Let's go out for dinner." Maraisha agreed and they went and got in the car.

Quiet drove to the Red Lion restaurant down in Chinatown. When he pulled into the restaurant's parking lot, there were two Caucasians in their midtwenties talking loudly to a Chinese parking valet. They were making fun of him because he was Chinese. Maraisha saw the expression on Quiet's face. It was one of anger. But he just parked his car and went into the restaurant. There were quite a few people there. The couple waited until a waiter came and led them to a booth.

When they sat down, a young, attractive Chinese waitress came and gave them menus. Quiet's eyes followed her as she walked away. Maraisha noticed and she dipped her spoon in her glass of water and flipped it in his face. Quiet smiled when she got his attention. Then he picked up his menu and started scanning the choices.

Quiet and Maraisha were about halfway through their dinner when the two Caucasians, leading the parking valet by his necktie, came into the restaurant. A few Caucasians already in the restaurant felt the scene was comical. Quiet became angry. Maraisha placed her hand upon his. It was cold and sweaty, but warm. Rattling nerves vibrated through his body. His muscles became tense. His eyes narrowed as the Caucasians bounced the parking valet off the wall onto the counter, with aggravating slaps cross his face. Maraisha felt at any moment Quiet was going to explode.

The Chinese waiter behind the counter, a man about in his fifties, ordered the Caucasians to release the Chinese youth. The Caucasians acted as though they didn't hear him. They seemed to have been drinking. They refused to release the valet.

The moment had come. Quiet eased up out of his booth. He walked to within five feet of the Caucasians. "Let him go," he demanded. The Caucasians ignored him. "Let him go," Quiet repeated coldly.

The first Caucasian paused for a moment, holding onto the valet's necktie. "You hear something?" he said sarcastically.

The second Caucasian grabbed a coffee off the counter that belonged to a patron on a stool and started to pour it down the valet's throat. The coffee was quite warm.

"No! I didn't hear anything."

"You keep that up and I'll kick your teeth in," threatened Quiet.

The Caucasian paused. "I think that nigga is talking to us," he said sarcastically. "Maybe we ought to teach the boy some respect, so he won't forget where he came from." He threw a punch at Quiet and followed with another.

Quiet was at a safe distance. When he saw the punch

177

coming, he backed away from it and sidestepped the next punch, then threw a couple of hooks into the Caucasian's midsection. At the same instant, as he doubled over, the other Caucasian tried to attack Quiet as he was turned to the side. Quiet grabbed him and swung him into the other Caucasian's arms.

As they started to get up off the floor, a foot, from out of nowhere, held them down. "If you know what's good for you, you'll stay down." It was another Chinese, who had come out of a nearby booth. He was about in his twenties, five feet, five inches tall, stocky, weighing about 150 pounds, and seemed to be some type of martial-art expert. "It's best you leave." When the two Caucasians painfully left the restaurant, Quiet looked at the Chinese, then went back to his booth. Many eyes followed as he sat down. When he and Maraisha finished their dinner, the restaurant owner wouldn't let them pay for it, for he was grateful for what Quiet had done. Feeling he owed something, Quiet left a five-dollar tip.

As Quiet and Maraisha were on their way to Quiet's car in the parking lot, they saw the two Caucasians standing next to it. "I can use my badge to send them away," said Maraisha.

"No!" said Quiet. "They need to be taught a lesson."

When the couple got to the car, one of the Caucasians said, "You don't have your Chinese kicking buddy with you now. Let's see what you can do without him."

Quiet kept Maraisha between himself and the car until he opened the door. The first Caucasian placed his hand on the handle to keep the door from closing.

Angrily Quiet quickly grabbed the Caucasian by his hair and bashed his head against the car top, then let a punch land in his midsection. At the same instant, the other Caucasian tried to come up while Quiet's back was turned. But Quiet put a kick in his midsection, too, then a roundhouse kick to the face.

As the second Caucasian tried to attack, Maraisha released

Shep from the backseat of the car. The Caucasian put his forearm in front of Shep's face to keep him from advancing. Shep tore the sleeve off the man's jacket, and his arm almost came with it. He screamed and hollered, "Get this damn dog off me!" Shep refused to stop. Shep forced the man to the ground.

Like when Shep was fighting the cougar, the dog was like a killer. Maraisha got out of her car. "Shep! Shep, stop! Stop it, Shep!" she shouted. Soon Maraisha realized that although Shep was used to her, he only listened to Quiet.

Then she heard Quiet's voice: "Shep!" Without hesitation, Shep stopped fighting and went to Quiet's side. The two Caucasians slowly got up and helped one another to their car, after Quiet pulled out of the parking lot.

When Quiet and Maraisha got to the house, she asked as they sat outside in the car, "Where were you? No one knew where you'd been."

"Your friends," said Quiet as they were getting out of the car, "they tried to take me on a trip."

Just then a big lump of fear clogged up Maraisha's throat but eased up as she knew that he was back with her again. They went on into the house.

"Tomorrow I want you to get the envelope and bring it down to my house. I'll find a place to hide it until Miller gets back," Quiet said.

The next morning, after Quiet and Wyatt went to work, Maraisha walked back up to her apartment. When she got there, Sharon was still in bed. "Get up," Maraisha said as she pulled back the covers. "It's time to get up."

"What time is it?" yawned Sharon as she stretched her arms out.

"Around ten," answered Maraisha. "Put your clothes on. We've got work to do."

"How about some coffee?"

"I'll make some," said Maraisha. She left the bedroom, but

as she was heading for the kitchen, the moving traffic outside caught her attention. She went to the window and pulled back the curtains. Daniels and Marcy had just cruised past the apartment. Quickly Maraisha jumped away from the window and went back into Sharon's bedroom. "Hurry up. We've got to get out of here," she said, frightened. "The guys!"

"Why?" asked Sharon as she started putting on a pair of jeans, a blouse, her shoes, and a jacket. "You don't think they'll kill us, do you? How could they kill a couple of cops and expect to get away with it? The whole department would investigate our deaths," she said, frightened. She put two extra boxes of bullets in her purse.

"Not if it looks like some type of accident. Would you want to take that chance?"

"No! Not really."

"You play pigeon. You take the car, while I'll take the envelope on foot. Meet me at Quiet's house later."

"What if they stop me?"

"Play dumb. Try not to let them know where the envelope is. But if you have to, tell them. Now, let's go."

Maraisha waited until Sharon drove their car out of the garage. But as Maraisha was about to leave the apartment, from out of nowhere a squad car began following Sharon. Maraisha recognized the two officers as they drove past the apartment. They were Daniels and Marcy. When Maraisha felt it was safe, she left the apartment. Before leaving the building, she carefully looked around. The coast was clear. She started walking down the street.

While Sharon was driving down Beacon Avenue, a few blocks away from the apartment, Daniels and Marcy forced her over to the curb. Before a crowd of people could gather, after the sound of screeching tires. Marcy got out and approached Sharon. "Come with us. We want to have a word with you."

Not knowing what to do, Sharon got out of her car and went

to sit in the backseat of the police car. Marcy got in beside her. She was taken to an isolated area where another car waited, Maulder, Ross, and Marty inside. Sharon was transferred to their car, and they drove to the warehouse out in Kent. Then Sharon was escorted from the car into the warehouse. They took her to the back office and placed her in a chair in the middle of the floor.

Munson, Morrison, Davis, Tanner, and Shatter had been waiting in the office for Sharon's arrival. Daniels and Marcy came a few moments later. Seeing the men's faces sent frightening chills through her body. They stared at her without saying a word. Spike acted as though he was guarding Sharon. Whenever Sharon made any type of move, Spike gave a snarl.

Maulder approached Sharon with a chair and placed it in front of her. He sat down. "You have something we want," he said coldly. "You tell us where we can find it and we'll let you go back to your car."

"Suppose I tell you I don't know what it is you're looking for?" she said unconvincingly. Odd expressions appeared on the men's faces. "I didn't think so."

"You came into my office and said you have proof of police misdoings in the department," said Tanner as he came into the conversation.

"Don't make it hard on yourself. I can let Spike get it out of you, if that's what you want," interrupted Maulder.

"No threats," continued Tanner. "Sharon is on our side."

Sharon looked at Spike's pearly white teeth. They showed signs of a taste for blood. "I don't have it," she said.

"I know," said Tanner as he walked around to the back of the chair, where he placed his hands. Then he leaned over. "Just tell us where we can find it. Otherwise, you're withholding evidence. And I'd hate to have to charge you with that."

If I tell them where the envelope is, that'll put Maraisha and the others in danger. But I have no room for negotiation. Quiet was right about a lot of things. *I have to tell. No telling what they have in mind,* she thought. "Maraisha has it."

"Where is she taking the document? To her boyfriend, perhaps?" added Maulder.

"Yes," answered Sharon.

Then Tanner and Maulder walked away from Sharon to a corner of the office. Sharon heard them mumbling but couldn't understand what they were saying.

"We don't need her around to bring the evidence against us," said Tanner. "After we get the envelope, kill her. Make it look like a case of rape and murder; then dump her body where the Kent police can find it. Let them try and solve this case. I want no trace leading to us."

Maulder went back and sat down in front of Sharon. "Mack and Bill are going with you to get the envelope, and they'll bring it back here. After they get the envelope, you'll be taken back to your car."

Sharon thought, *Once they get their hands on that envelope, it'll just be my word against theirs. No way they can afford to let me go. I know too much. I know what's in the envelope. There's enough information in that envelope to send about half the department to jail.* When Daniels and Marcy helped Sharon out of her chair and escorted her through the office, she decided, *This is it. Since I told them about Maraisha having the envelope, what do they need me for? They can use the force to break in on Quiet and his family. They're not going to take me back to my car. They're going to kill me. I'd better think fast.*

When they got out into the warehouse, Sharon slowed down. Daniels gave her a little shove. "Keep moving," he said. He was walking directly behind Sharon and Marcy was beside her.

Just then, Sharon gave Daniels an elbow in the stomach and quickly bashed Marcy in the face with her purse. Then she reached into her purse to pull out her pistol. At the same instant as Daniels doubled over, he was drawing for his pistol. But Sharon managed to get to her pistol first and fired a round in his stomach, just as he cleared his holster. While Marcy reached for his pistol also, Sharon put a bullet through his thigh.

When Marcy fell to the floor, his pistol fell out of his reach. Sharon ran over and picked it up as he was going for it. "Don't move," she ordered. Daniels moaned. Marcy froze. On hearing the shots from the office, the other men started to come out to see what the shooting was about. Sharon fired a couple of shots at the office door just as it was about to open. But it closed quickly. As Sharon held one gun on the office door and the other on Marcy, she said, "Don't you even flinch," while backing away. When she neared the unloading doors, she took off running.

When Sharon got outside, she entered one of the police cars, but the keys were gone. So she got out and looked through the other cars. Their keys were gone also. *What to do now?* she thought. She looked around for a place to run. There were no houses or main streets in sight, just open ground, except for the field of sticker bushes and swamp water down a shallow bank next to the warehouse. It looked messy, but it would give cover. Just then she heard Spike's barks. "Oh, no," she mumbled, frightened. "He's a killer." She took off running to the end of the building. "Get that bitch!" she heard someone holler. "Don't let her get away!" someone else hollered. For a person who didn't smoke, Sharon found her legs getting weak fast. At the same time, though, there was a good distance between her and the men. But thundering footsteps felt almost upon her heels, bullets zinging past her head. Spike was barking, but the sound was choked. Maulder held him back by his collar. While Ross, Marty, Davis, Munson, and Morrison pursued Sharon on foot, Tanner and Shatter got in their car and pursued her.

Sharon ran along the railroad tracks until she came to the end of the building. The men were still coming. She stopped and fired a couple of quick shots. But she was out of range. She put her pistol back in her purse and ran down the steep bank and into the fields. The fields consisted of swamps, soft mud, shoulder-height sticker bushes, and a pond at about the center of the field. Running north and south the field was unquestionably long. Its width was about that of a football stadium.

Each time Sharon took a step, she sank knee-deep in swamp. She clawed, scratched, and pulled her way through the swamp, tripping and falling over dead stumps, forcing herself through the bushes, crawling her way through the mud. Voices were getting louder. Exhaustion began to slow her down. Her muscles ached, as she gasped for air. Her legs felt like they couldn't take another step. But determination to prevent being killed made her use every bit of energy she had until she came to the pond. On the other side of the pond she saw a five-foot bank that led up to another road. For some reason Sharon felt her energy coming back. The sounds of the men's voices and snapping of branches breaking pushed her on. The pond was about thirty feet wide and followed along the roadway. The water came up to her waist as she waded in. Finally, when Sharon got to the other side, she tried to climb the bank, which was covered with loose gravel. She slid back down. For a brief moment she took a rest.

"I can go on no farther," Sharon mumbled. She was breathing hard as she laid her head on the gravel. Her breath blew some of the dirt away from her mouth. All of a sudden things were getting dark. Feeling dizzy, she knew her strength was gone. But as she lay there, there was a voice: "There she is," then a shot. A bullet landed just above her head. When this happened Sharon found a second wind she never knew she had and clawed and pulled her way up the loose gravel bank until she came to the top. She came to a countrylike rocky dirt road running north and south, yet there was still no sign of life. The road seemed to have no end in either direction. She started running north.

For some reason Sharon found her second wind staying with her. Strength seemed to flow back into her body. For the short time she got that extra energy, she took advantage of it by finding a steady pace and starting to run. But the men seemed to be getting closer.

Coming from the south, a cloud of dust was flying down the road toward the men. They paused to watch the cloud of dust as it came closer and closer until a blue '66 Ford Cobra came into view, then zoomed past the men. Quickly the men wondered what a car was doing on this road.

Two blacks were in the car, Ted and Calvin Renfro. They pulled up beside Sharon. "Get in," said Ted. With the policemen behind her and no place to go, Sharon felt she didn't have much room for hesitation. She got in the car; then Ted drove away. The men gave up the chase and slowly headed back to the warehouse. They watched the cloud of dust fade away.

Meanwhile, back at the apartment, Bishop and Randall had waited until they saw Sharon drive away. Then they went up to the apartment. Bishop knocked on the door. When he got no answer, he kicked the door open. A few tenants who heard the crashing of the door came out into the hallway to see what the noise was about. They watched the two police officers, in their uniforms, going through every room in the apartment. With no sign of Maraisha, they left, going outside to look up and down the street. There was no sign of Maraisha, so they got in their car and started driving through the area.

Maraisha was walking down the street when Taylor and Young pulled up beside her in the Corvette. "Get in," said Taylor. "You're going to your boyfriend Quiet's house!" At the mention of Quiet's name, Maraisha didn't ask any questions as she crawled in the backseat. Taylor drove away.

While the car was on its way to Quiet's home, Maraisha said, "My girl friend. That's our car!" as they drove past.

"She'll be all right," Young assured Maraisha.

When the car pulled up in front of Quiet's home, Maraisha got out. There were no good-byes as Taylor drove away. As Maraisha was going up the steps she heard Shep inside the house, barking. She used Quiet's key to enter. When she got inside the house, she pulled out her pistol and searched the house with gun in hand. Wherever she went, her pistol went also.

After the chase, the policemen went back into the office in back of the front office. The men waiting hadn't seen Sharon with the blacks. "Get that bitch?" coughed Daniels.

Maulder was holding his arms against his stomach, with the bullet in it. "Where is the girl?" he asked.

"A speeding car came from out of nowhere and picked her up. Two niggas," said Davis. "She got away."

"We'll get her," assured Maulder. Then Daniels was still. Maulder laid him down on the floor. "We can't let her get away."

"We'll have to move quickly," added Shatter. "But what do we do about Bill?"

"Larry and I will take care of him," Davis said. "You guys better get moving. No telling who them niggas are."

"Right!" agreed Maulder as he, Ross, and Marty went and got in their green Dart. Maulder and Marty sat in the front, while Ross and Spike got in the back. Maulder pulled the car away from the warehouse.

Meanwhile, at the Jones house, Maraisha waited patiently for Quiet, Wyatt, and Dino to come home. Three hours had passed and still no sign of Sharon. It was almost time for the men to get off work. Pacing back and forth through the house, trying to find a magazine, newspaper, or book to settle her nerves, Maraisha couldn't get her mind off Sharon.

Dino, as usual, came home first. About twenty minutes later Quiet and Wyatt came walking through the door. Maraisha was relieved to see the three men together. She had already explained to Dino what had happened that morning. As he was about to leave, Quiet walked in.

"Hi!" Quiet said. But when he saw the look on Dino's face and the tears flowing down Maraisha's face, he asked, "Where's Sharon?" There was silence. "Did they take Sharon?"

"I don't know!" cried Maraisha.

"Is that where you were headed?" asked Quiet as he turned to Dino, who didn't say a word. "Where were you going to look?" Dino looked disgusted and confused. "You were going to get yourself killed. I'm sure the police wouldn't tell you where she is. Come with me. We'll find her." As Maraisha and Wyatt started to follow, Quiet stopped them. "No! You two wait here, in case Sharon returns. Come, Shep." Quiet and Dino went back out the door, Shep following.

Quiet drove up to the Urban League office. He pulled into the parking lot. He and Dino got out and walked into the building and on to Clinton's office. Clinton was glad to see the two men. He was sitting behind his desk, talking on the telephone, when they entered.

When Clinton hung up the telephone, he said, "Hi, guys! What brings you two here?" as he cleared off his desk.

"We need your help," said Quiet in a serious tone. "I believe the police kidnapped Sharon."

"You mean her police friends?"

"I'm not sure! But if so, they may have taken her to the same place they took you. How's your memory?"

"Not that good, Bro!" said Clinton as he got up from his chair, then walked around his desk. "It was a long time ago that happened."

Just then Earl walked into the office. He had started to speak, but the other men's conversation had caught his attention.

"I want to go out there. You said once it was near some railroad tracks," Quiet continued.

"I don't know, Bro! It's been a long time," said Clinton doubtfully. "I was blindfolded. It's going to be even harder for me to remember certain stops now, as the streets may be crawling with thick traffic. That'll drown out my hearing. I don't think I can find where they took me."

"We have nothing to lose by trying. Let's give it a go," suggested Dino.

"I'll take you where they first stopped you and go from there," added Quiet.

Clinton agreed and they left the building and drove away in Quiet's car. Quiet drove to where Clinton had been stopped by Maulder and his associates, on Madison Avenue. Then Quiet placed a blindfold over Clinton's eyes. Clinton got in the back and lay down on the floor. Clinton directed Quiet as he pulled away from the curb. When they got down to the bottom of the hill, he made a right turn off Madison and went on to Empire Way, headed south. There were a couple of stops in between, but Clinton didn't recognize them. Quiet continued on Empire Way until they came to the intersection of Rainier Avenue and Empire Way. This stop Clinton did remember. They drove on across Rainier Avenue, still headed south.

Staying on Empire Way, Quiet passed all the arterial cross streets, until they were south of where Empire Way ran into the freeway. Clinton suggested they take the freeway until they came to the Kent turn-off. The drive was about fifteen minutes on the freeway until they came to the first exit. Quiet drove past the first exit but turned off the freeway at the next exit. When they came to a stop, it was a red light on Smith Avenue. Clinton told Quiet to make another right turn. They headed west until they came to a railroad crossing. A train was coming. The guardrails were down. So Quiet waited till the train was gone. Then the railguards went up, and he continued. Clinton counted the set of tracks Quiet drove across. It was the same amount Clinton had gone across before. Then Clinton told Quiet to make a left turn. When Quiet looked to his left there was no road for a left turn, only houses and backyards set away from the railroad tracks. Then Clinton said they should go back to the freeway and take the first exit.

Quiet made a U-turn and went back to the freeway. When he came off the freeway exit, he was on Central Avenue. He followed the same procedure on the first exit as he had on the second. The exits were about three miles apart. Heading west again, they went across the same number of railroad tracks. This time when Clinton said to make a left turn, there was a road that seemed to lead nowhere. Quiet made the left onto the road, and ran alongside the railroad tracks. Then it wound away from the railroad tracks and back to them. Quiet drove down the road for about three miles, until a large warehouse came into sight. The warehouse was about two blocks long, a half a block wide. There were traces of where other small warehouses had been in the area, but they had been torn down.

The warehouse had a four-foot-high loading dock which ran from one end of the warehouse to the other, four steps leading up to it. Three large doors in front of the warehouse were for loading and unloading trucks. Six smaller doors in the back were also for loading and unloading trains. Just at the top of these steps was a door that led to the dispatch office. Behind the dispatch office was another office, which was in about the center of the warehouse.

Quiet came to a stop in front of the warehouse. It looked as though it had been abandoned for an indeterminate length of time. "Shep!" Quiet called as he got out of his car. Shep jumped out from the back. "Come on!"

"Where are we?" asked Clinton as he removed the blindfold.

"I don't know," said Quiet as he noticed tire tracks on the ground. "Someone's been here recently. These tire tracks are fresh." He drew his pistol, then followed Shep into the warehouse.

Shep acted cautious as he went into the warehouse. It was deserted. Creeping through the warehouse, Shep led the men to a small puddle of blood. There were a few empty crates scattered through the warehouse. *This is the right place,* Quiet felt, as he knelt down to get a closer look at the blood.

"Think that's Sharon's blood?" asked Dino.

"I don't know," answered Quiet. "Let's hope not."

Shep continued on to the office, as Quiet, Dino, Clinton, and Earl followed.

In the office Clinton saw the chair where he had been placed. The office was dusty, the dirt deep enough to plant mustard seeds. As the four men looked for signs of Sharon having been there, Shep left the office and went back outside. Quiet followed while the others stayed behind. Shep led Quiet to the end of the warehouse. As he stood on the loading dock, he saw the swampy field. Broken bushes indicated a path through the field.

"Someone's been through there," he mumbled. As Shep started to go into the field, he called, "Shep!" Shep came back to Quiet's side. "Let's go, fella." They headed back to the car. By the time Quiet and Shep got back to the car, Dino, Clinton, and Earl were already waiting there.

7

While Quiet, Dino, Clinton, and Earl were on their way back to Seattle, Maulder, Ross, and Marty were parked just around the bend up the street from Quiet's home. They were waiting to see if Sharon was going to show. After waiting a long period of time, Ross said, "That broad is not going to show. Maybe she went back to her apartment."

"I don't think so," said Maulder. "Munson and Morrison are watching the apartment."

"Think she'll go downtown to the department and try and turn us in?" said Marty.

"No!" assured Maulder. "She'll have trouble getting anyone to believe her. Maraisha has the document. Without that, it'll just be their word against ours."

"What about Detective Miller?" said Ross. "If she reaches him that could put us in trouble."

"Yes," agreed Maulder. "That could create a problem for us. But he isn't due back until next week. By that time, them blacks will be taken care of." Maulder glanced down at his watch. "It's been quite a while. Let's get the other one." So Maulder, Ross and Marty got out of the car and started walking toward the house. Spike was left in the car.

Maraisha was in the kitchen, Wyatt and Joan in the bedroom, when they heard the front door crash open. Wyatt came running out of the bedroom to see what the noise was about but ran into Maulder. "Run!" shouted Wyatt as he grabbed Maulder by the waist and forced him back onto the porch. The envelope, in Maraisha's purse, was on the dining room table. When Wyatt tackled Maulder, Maraisha grabbed the envelope and her purse and headed for the back door. She took off running up the alley.

At the same instant, Ross and Marty grabbed Wyatt by the neck and pulled him off Maulder. "Don't worry about me!" shouted Maulder. "Get that bitch, before she gets away." Ross ran through the house while Marty ran around the back.

By the time Ross and Marty got to the back of the house, Maraisha was already at the end of the alley. They drew their pistols and started running after her. Ross fired a couple of shots at her. She dived to the ground, reached in her purse and got her gun, and returned the fire. When the two men took cover, Maraisha got up and started running, again. She ran around the corner and on down the alleyway, until she came to a fork in the road. One road led up to the neighborhood woods, where kids used to play. The other road led to the street near where Maulder had parked his car. Seeing the men come around the corner, Maraisha took the road that led to the woods. It was a long, steep, grassy hill she had to climb. Clawing and scratching her way to the top, she used the height of the grass for cover. When she got to the top she was exhausted, but she never stopped running.

While Maraisha was going up the hill, Ross and Marty were shooting. She slowed down their pursuit by returning their fire. In the woods she felt she had a better chance to elude her pursuers. On higher ground, Maraisha ran about halfway through the woods. The men hadn't made it to the top yet. So she circled back on lower ground. She stepped off the trail when she heard noises of twigs being broken and bushes rustling. Then footsteps running, getting closer. She hid behind a tree until she saw the men above run past her. Then she hurried back in the other direction.

When Ross and Marty came to the end of the woods, Ross asked, "Where in the hell could she have gone?" as they looked around. Below was the alleyway, leading back to the house. "If we had John's dog we could've caught up with her."

"You saw her shooting back, didn't you?" said Marty as he was trying to catch his breath. "That broad would have killed that dog." They looked around some more. "She's gone. Let's head on back." So the two men started taking the long stroll back to the car.

Maulder and Wyatt wrestled from one end of the porch to the other. Wyatt had his arms still wrapped around Maulder's waist. Each time Maulder tried to push Wyatt's head to the cement, he would squeeze a little tighter. Then Maulder found a pressure nerve in Wyatt's temple, which caused him to loosen his grip. Maulder dug his finger against the spot. Then Maulder got up into a defensive stance. After Wyatt got to his feet, he put his head down and tried to rush Maulder. But Maulder side-stepped Wyatt, then helped him over the banister. The fall was about five feet. He landed on his back. Just as Wyatt rolled over onto his stomach and attempted to get up, Maulder jumped over the banister and landed on Wyatt's back.

Seeing Wyatt was hurt, Joan dived from the porch on Maulder's back. With defense reflexes, Maulder flipped Joan over his back. Then he picked her up by her hair and threw a punch in her stomach. When Joan doubled over, he kicked her chin. Like a light bulb, Joan went out.

Wyatt tried to help Joan, but Maulder beat him with a flurry of kicks and punches, which almost left him unconscious. Then Maulder grabbed Wyatt by his collar and half dragged him to his car, after putting handcuffs on him. Two black neighbors across the street and a Caucasian next door saw the incident. On the way back to the car, Maulder met Ross and Marty walking down the street.

"What do we have here?" said Marty.

"Something for us to negotiate with," said Maulder as he was putting Wyatt in the backseat. "Let's get out of here. We've already aroused enough suspicion."

When Maraisha got back to the house, she reloaded her pistol before entering. The back door was still open. Cautiously she entered the house. It was empty. She thought of calling out to Joan but dared not. So Maraisha eased through the kitchen and on into the living room, checking every corner and behind every door. She crept upstairs and checked the three rooms. They were empty also, so she went back downstairs into the living room. The front door was still open also. Cautiously she went to the front door, looked outside, and saw Joan lying on the front lawn. She was unconscious. She went down and helped Joan back into the house.

When Joan finally came to her senses, she asked, "Where's Wyatt?" Her voice sounded almost hysterical.

"I didn't find him here," answered Maraisha.

"The police have him," said Joan disgustedly. "They're going to kill him."

"No, they won't," said Maraisha as she was wiping Joan's face. "They want that envelope too much for that." She showed Joan the envelope. "With this we can get Wyatt back."

"They'll kill him!" cried Joan. "I know they're going to kill him."

A little while later, Quiet, Dino, Clinton, and Earl came walking through the front door. "What happened?" said Quiet curiously, with anger in his voice.

Joan and Maraisha came out of the bathroom. "They took Wyatt!" cried Joan as she stood next to the dining room table.

"Wait a minute," said Quiet as he tried to calm her down. "What do you mean, they took Wyatt?"

Joan kept stammering her words over and over and crying at the same time as she tried to explain. But Maraisha interrupted to tell Quiet and the others about the break-in, the chase through the woods, the apprehension of Wyatt, and how he tried to fight the cops off.

At that moment anger showed all over Quiet's face. His eyes narrowed. Bitterness was evident in his low voice. "I tried to keep out of their way for the simple reason that they are cops. But cops or no cops, they've gone too far. Now I will fight back. And they won't like my way of fighting."

"You can't do that," said Maraisha, frightened. "They can get a lot of help from downtown. You're dealing with cops," she reminded him.

"Give me the envelope," said Quiet, and Maraisha handed it to him. "This is what they want. I'm going to get Wyatt back without them getting their hands on this."

"Where do you think they took Wyatt?" Dino came into the conversation. "Back to the warehouse?"

"Yes," answered Quiet.

"They'll be waiting for you," said Maraisha.

"Not really." As Quiet started to leave the living room to go upstairs, he said, "They don't know that we know where the warehouse is. We'll surprise 'em."

Upstairs Quiet pulled his drawer out and got a box of bullets. He laid his pistol and rifle on the bed.

When Maraisha heard Quiet loading his weapons, she came running upstairs. "You can't do this!" she cried softly. "They'll kill you. That's what they want, for you to try to fight back." She wrapped her arms around Quiet's body. "Please don't go."

As Maraisha seemed to be becoming hysterical, Quiet forced her arms from around his body, grabbed her by the shoulders, and shook her, hard. "Get ahold of yourself." Finally Maraisha calmed down. "They have my brother. And I'm going to get him back, whatever it takes. If they harmed him in any way, someone is going to pay."

Maraisha understood. They both went back downstairs.

When they got back downstairs in the living room, Quiet gave Dino the rifle. "You stay with the women in case them bastards come back. Clinton and Earl are coming with me." The look on Dino's face told Quiet he wanted to go. "There's a good chance Sharon may show up." When Quiet said that, Dino agreed to stay at the house. Then Quiet and his brothers left.

The sun had set, and darkness had fallen. The temperature had gone down to the fifties. A mild wind carried a breeze whistling through a few trees. The street traffic had thinned. Coming out of the cold, Sharon entered the house, using her key. As the key was turning in the lock Dino hid behind Wyatt's bedroom door. Maraisha drew her pistol and hid behind Dino's bedroom door. Joan stood behind the front door with a baseball bat. But when Sharon made her appearance, Maraisha exhaled a sigh of relief and everyone came out from where they had been hiding.

"I'm so glad to see you guys," Sharon sighed. "They tried to kill me."

Dino pulled Sharon into his arms and held her tight. "Come over here and sit down," he said as he helped her to the couch. "We've been worried about you. Where have you been?"

Maraisha sat down on the other side of Sharon. Joan said she'd made a pot of coffee and went to the kitchen.

Sharon felt nervous. She was still jumpy. "They tried to kill me," she repeated.

"Tell us what happened," Dino said as he held Sharon in his arms.

"Mack and Bill," sobbed Sharon, "they stopped me just after I drove away from the apartment. They forced me over to the curb, drove me someplace, then put me into another car, where John, Jack, and William were waiting. They took me out to a warehouse, somewhere in Kent. They led me to a dark office and sat me in a chair; then questioned me about the envelope.

I got scared and told them Maraisha had it. That's why they came here. They told me they were going to let me go if I told them where the envelope was. I didn't believe 'em but I still told."

"How did you get away?" asked Maraisha.

"Mack and Bill were leading me out of the warehouse. They said they were going to take me back to my car. I managed to break away from them and got my pistol out of my purse. I think I killed Mack. I shot Bill in the leg. Then I took off running. I got away by going through some bushes. It led me to another road. But something strange happened. As I was running down this road, a car came by and picked me up, as though they were waiting for me. In the car were two blacks I'd never seen before—"

"That's the same thing happened to me," interrupted Maraisha.

"They took me back to our apartment and waited till I took a shower and changed my clothes, then took me back to my car. I parked the car down under the viaduct and caught one bus after another. I was afraid to come back here, thinking John and the others might be waiting. So I just rode the buses from one end of the line to the other until I felt you, Wyatt, and Quiet were probably home." Sharon looked around. "Where's Quiet?"

"John, Jack, and William took Wyatt," said Maraisha. "Clinton, Earl, and Quiet went to bring him back."

"Oh, no," said Sharon, frightened. "They'll be killed. We've got to help them."

Maraisha agreed as she and Sharon started to get up from the couch.

"Wait!" interrupted Dino. "Let's wait till Quiet and his brothers get back. We'll only be in the way. They won't need any help," Dino assured the women.

Just then, Joan came into the living room with a tray of coffee and three cups. She placed the tray on the coffee table.

The road that led to the warehouse had no streetlights, so the only light came from Quiet's car. He pulled onto the roadway and parked his car about a block away from the warehouse. He, Clinton, and Earl got out of the car. Shep got out also. They started sneaking toward the warehouse. Clouds glided across the sky, obscuring the moonlight, then revealing it. There was just enough light for the men to see the large shadow of the warehouse. As they approached it, three police cars and two other cars were sitting out in front, parked near the entrance. Two men were sitting in the car nearest the entrance.

When Quiet came up to the end of the building, he whispered to Shep to come to his side. "Go on, Shep." Quiet pointed. Shep jumped up on the loading dock and walked toward the entrance. When Shep came to the entrance he was seen by the two men sitting in the car. They got out and gave chase. Seeing the men coming his way, Shep turned and started running back the way he came. When the two came to the end of the building, they ran into a .357 Magnum stuck in their faces. Their natural reaction was to put their hands up and let there be silence. Quiet ordered them to place their hands on the building while he frisked them. He took their weapons and gave one to Clinton and the other one to Earl. Then Quiet took the police's handcuffs and cuffed their hands behind their backs, placing them back to back. While Quiet and Clinton advanced toward the warehouse, Earl and Shep stayed behind to watch over the two men.

Silently Quiet and Clinton stayed in the shadows as they crept alongside the building until they came to the side of the office. The front office lights were off. But lights illuminated the warehouse, about thirty feet apart. The warehouse lights were dim, but bright enough to enable you to see where you were going. Quiet and Clinton were stooped down below the window glass. Quiet rose to peek into the office. It was empty. So he crept around to the front of the office. He slowly turned the doorknob and eased the door open a few inches. He felt a light tap. He traced his fingers up the door and found a warning bell at the top. So Quiet grabbed the bell to keep it from ringing, then continued opening the door.

Quiet entered the office and went on to the door in the back and he placed his ear to it. He heard voices on the other side, so he motioned to Clinton that he was going to kick the door open and crash in on the men inside. Clinton nodded that he was ready. Quiet stood up and took a couple of steps back. He raised his foot and let it crash the door open. Everyone in the office flinched when the door flew open. Surprised expressions spread over the men's faces when they found themselves looking down at what looked like the barrel of a cannon. Automatically they raised their hands, without Quiet saying a word.

Quiet counted nine people in the office. "Get away from him," he said to Munson and Bishop, who were standing next to Wyatt. There was bitterness in his voice. When the two men moved away, Quiet took a set of handcuff keys away from one of them, then ordered them into the farthest corner while he uncuffed the handcuffs on Wyatt's wrists. Clinton kept the men covered.

"What took you so long?" said Wyatt as he felt the handcuffs being relieved of his wrists. "I knew you'd be coming."

"Come on," said Quiet joyfully in a low tone. Wyatt wasted no time taking a gun from one of the men. "Take the rest of them." So Wyatt went to the front office and got a wastebasket, went back into the back office, and collected all the weapons from the men, then brought the wastebasket full of guns back into the front office. Then Quiet ordered the men back to back, while Wyatt paired them up and cuffed their hands behind their backs. The odd man Wyatt cuffed to an exposed water pipe. Then Wyatt ordered them to the floor. After doing this, Quiet,

Wyatt, and Clinton backed out of the office. Before leaving both offices, Quiet blocked the door with a chair.

When Quiet and his two brothers left the office, carefully they looked around as they hurried out of the warehouse. When they got outside, Quiet ordered the two men Earl had covered down the bank and made them lie facedown. Then Quiet and his brothers took one of the unmarked cars and drove it back to where Quiet had parked his car. They exchanged cars there and drove away. As they got back on an arterial street, they unknowingly passed Maulder's car and two other police cars going in the opposite direction. They headed back to Seattle.

As Maulder was driving alongside the railroad tracks, he noticed one of the unmarked cars parked a ways from the warehouse. Curiosity made him stop to investigate the car and he pulled up alongside. The car was empty. Ross got out of Maulder's car and got into the unmarked car and followed Maulder to the warehouse. After Maulder pulled up near the entrance, he got out and cautiously headed toward the entrance. But as he started to enter the warehouse, he heard a voice, "John!" almost in a whisper. "John! Is that you?" the voice came from down the bank. Maulder walked to the edge of the roadway and saw Bishop and Randall, their hands cuffed back to back, lying in a ditch.

Maulder went down the bank. "What the hell are you guys doing down here?" he asked as he was uncuffing the two men.

"That nigger," said Bishop, "caught us off guard!"

Maulder ran back up the bank and hurried to the warehouse. When he got to the entrance, he pulled out his pistol, then sent Spike on ahead. Spike headed straight to the office without any sign of doubt. After Maulder got to the front office he removed the chair and proceeded to the back office. He removed that chair also then entered the office. He was shocked to see everyone in the office cuffed the same way Bishop and Randall were. He used his key to set them free also.

Maulder sat in a chair behind the desk, where he rested his feet. "We'll have to find a way to get them guys legally and run them downtown."

"First we'll have to get that envelope," added Shatter. He sat on top of the desk. "Maybe we underestimated them niggas. They have two of our women working with them."

"Bitches!" corrected Ross.

"Yeah!" agreed Marty as he came in during the conversation. "If that's the kind of women our department hires, then we don't need any—"

"But that's not our biggest worry," interrupted Shatter. "We've got to concentrate on that envelope. No telling how much evidence Schmidt had on us."

"Right!" agreed Maulder. "We've lost our first chance to get that envelope. Next time they'll be ready for our intrusion."

"I don't know about that one called Quiet," uttered Randall. "He's very sly."

"What do you mean?" said Munson.

"I knew someone like him in the service, when we were stationed in Xunloc. About thirty-five miles south of Saigon. He might not be much to look at, but he was like a time bomb ready to go off. A few guys in the compound used to try to pick on him, 'cause they felt he was afraid. This guy never said much of anything. But when he said something, you'd better believe it.

"One day down in one of them Vietnamese villages, these five guys jumped him. Just for kicks. He went to the hospital and was laid up for about three weeks. When he came out of the hospital, on the third day, all five of them guys were dead. No one knew what happened. This guy was in the compound at the time those five guys got killed. The guys in the tent knew somehow he had done it. But they couldn't prove it. Quiet is like time bomb. Once he explodes, he could be very dangerous. The way he came in here tonight caught us off guard, and he took his brother. We lit his fuse. Now he is about to explode.

If we want that envelope, we'll have to get rid of him first, kill him if we have to. He's different from his brothers."

"If he's that good, I would like to match my skills against his," said Maulder.

"You may have to," said Randall. "He's the type can handle himself." Randall paused for a moment to see he had everyone's attention. "Think about it for a moment. He has a nose like a bloodhound. For someone that hasn't been here before how did he find this place?" In silence, everyone looked at one another. Many questions arose in their minds.

Just then, Tanner and Davis walked into the office. "We have another problem," said Davis as he sat on the desk next to Shatter.

"Meaning what?" said Shatter.

"Miller is on his way back from Minnesota. The notice came from the front office. He heard about Schmidt's death. His flight is scheduled to land in a couple of hours."

"He wasn't supposed to be back 'til sometime next week," said Maulder. "If he gets his hands on that envelope, we'll all be facing a prison term. We may have to take care of him before them blacks get to him."

"We can't do that," Davis disagreed. "We kill a cop, the department will never stop the investigation until they get us."

"That's the chance we'll have to take," added Shatter. "The department may not listen to a few blacks. But they will believe a lieutenant." There was a brief moment of silence. "Now, when Miller's flight arrives, we'll just give him a police escort out here and make it look like them militants did it."

Although not everyone approved of the idea, they all agreed to it. Davis and Tanner would pick Lieutenant Miller up at the airport and bring him to the warehouse. Maulder, Ross, Marty, Bishop, and Munson would be waiting there. They would murder Lieutenant Miller, and his body would be found somewhere in the CD filled with bullet holes. The police department was sure to blame the militants.

When Quiet got back to Seattle, he drove back to the parking lot where Clinton and Earl had their cars parked. After Clinton and Earl started up their engines they followed Quiet to his home. Quiet pulled his car near the curb in front of the house. He and Wyatt got out and headed toward the house. The lights were out except in the front room. Quiet and Wyatt eased into the house. Shep led the way as he went straight to Maraisha, hiding behind Dino's bedroom door. Then Clinton and Earl just drove up.

When Joan saw Wyatt, tears began to flow and she ran into his arms. She was so glad to see him. All she could do was hold Wyatt and cry at the same time. Maraisha was calmer as she went and hugged Quiet. She knew from the few experiences she had been through with Quiet, it would be the other person she'd have to worry about. She just placed her head on Quiet's shoulder.

Then Sharon and Dino came out of Wyatt's bedroom. Quiet's eyes met Sharon's. There was silence, but a smile on each of their faces. Everyone was together and safe again.

"We can't stay here," said Quiet coldly. "I believe the police will come very shortly."

"What do you suggest?" asked Clinton.

Quiet looked at Clinton. "Go by Clint's house and get his wife and daughter. Then go to Earl's house," he said. "Two places the police will look first are here and the apartment. Once they don't find us there, they'll be coming over to Clint's house. They'll keep looking until they find us. We'll have to stay ahead of them until we find out what to do. You guys take off. I'll meet you at Earl's house."

"Whatcha gonna do?" Maraisha asked worriedly.

"I'm going to stay here and wait till they come," said Quiet.

"No! You can't do that!" cried Maraisha. "They'll kill you."

"Not yet," said Quiet. "At least not till they know where the rest of us are. They can't chance getting one of us without the envelope. But if I figure wrong, then just come to my funeral."

"No!" screamed Maraisha.

Maraisha held Quiet tightly, trying to stop him from staying behind. "You go with them," he said as he motioned to Clinton to take her away. "I'll be all right." Clinton did as Quiet told him, Sharon and Dino helping. Everyone but Quiet left the house, including Shep.

Not long after Clinton and the others left, Maulder, Marty, Ross, Munson, Morrison, Marcy, Bishop, and Randall pulled up in front of Quiet's home in three unmarked cars. All the lights were off in the house, except a lamp in the living room and one in the hallway. When Quiet heard the cars drive up, he turned on the television set and went back and sat on the couch. Footsteps quietly came up the steps. Quiet took off his pistol and placed it under the couch pillow, then sat back as if relaxing.

The door cracked open. Slowly it opened wider. "Come in!" said Quiet as Maulder made his appearance.

Cautiously Maulder, who led the way came into the house. He looked around. "Where's the others?" he asked curiously.

As the other officers came into the house, Quiet repeated, "Others! What others?"

"You know who I'm talking about," added Maulder, standing next to the bedroom door. As he eased it halfway open, Quiet got up off the couch. Quickly Maulder pulled out his pistol. "You'd better sit back down, black boy, before you get your asshole blown open."

Quiet gritted his teeth. "You have a search warrant?"

"Don't need one." Maulder attempted to walk into the bedroom.

"No! You don't mean you're going to search this house without a search warrant!"

Just then, Marty, Ross, and Randall approached Quiet.

"Why don't you sit back down like a good boy before you get knocked down?" said Marty as he attempted to push Quiet back down on the couch.

Quiet quickly grabbed Marty's forearm and pushed him into Randall's arm, which caused them to fall backward. At the same instant, Ross tried to throw a punch. But Quiet blocked the attempt and threw a right, left, right combination to Ross's midsection and face, which sent him over the armchair. When Ross fell backward, Bishop, Marcy, Morrison, and Munson advanced. Quiet quickly jumped over the coffee table and got in a fighting position. Bishop rushed first. Quiet sidestepped him, grabbed him by the waist, and threw him over the dining room table. Morrison came up behind Quiet and wrapped his arm around Quiet's neck. Quiet grabbed Morrison's forearm and flipped him over his back. Just as Quiet was turning around to face the others, he saw Munson coming full force. But Munson's stomach ran into Quiet's foot. When Munson doubled over, Quiet hooked the side of his chin. He fell back into Randall's arms as the latter was getting up off the floor. At the same instant Marty rushed into Quiet, who rolled backward and threw Marty into the hallway. As Quiet got up to a defensive stand, Maulder made his move as he put a judo chop to the back of Quiet's head before he had time to recover. Quiet lay unconscious.

Marty, Ross, and the others had recovered and stood over Quiet. "What are we going to do with him now?" said Marty.

"Let's take him with us," suggested Maulder.

The bullet wound in his leg still bothered Marty as he limped to the front door and opened it. But as he was about to walk outside, he said, "Wait a minute, guys! Cops!"

Maulder and Ross, who had Quiet by his arms, sat him down on the couch. "Cops!" repeated Maulder. "What the hell are they doing here?"

"I don't know," said Marty. "They're coming up the stairs."

When the police knocked on the door, Maulder answered it. "We got a call about some type of disturbance."

Maulder showed his badge. "We got the same call. Everything is all right now."

The officer looked at Quiet. "What's wrong with him?"

"That's how we found him when we arrived."

The police officer went over and examined Quiet. "Looks like he's been beaten up."

"That's what we figure. But there's no one here."

Quiet started to come to. "Well! We'd better go," said Maulder. "We have other things to tend to." As Maulder looked at Quiet, he mumbled, "That guy can sure fight."

When they got outside and were inside their car, Marty asked, "What about the envelope? Think we ought to search the house after them guys leave?"

"No need," said Maulder. "If anyone was there, they'd 've showed themselves by now." Maulder pulled away from the curb. "He stayed behind to slow us up."

"We're just going to leave him there?" Ross asked.

"I didn't want to stay around with them other cops there," Maulder replied.

"We could 've waited til they left," said Ross.

"He may have come to by the time they left. Then we might've had a fight on our hands."

By the time Quiet had fully regained consciousness, everyone was gone. The door had been left open. He got up off the couch, grabbed his pistol, and went to the bathroom. He washed up. Looking in the mirror, he saw there wasn't a mark on his face. When Quiet was done washing, he went upstairs and changed his clothes, then left the house to join the others.

Meanwhile, at the Sea-Tac Airport, Davis and Tanner were waiting at the Eastern Airlines terminal. By now it was around 11:30 P.M., a half hour before Lieutenant Miller's flight was due. There came an announcement over the speaker, "Flight number

587 will arrive one hour late, because of bad weather conditions." Patiently Davis and Tanner waited in the lobby.

An hour and fifteen minutes passed after the announcement. Finally the plane came in sight on the runway. When the DC-10 pulled up to the loading terminal, 133 passengers got off the jet. Carefully Davis and Tanner watched the passengers come down the walkway until Miller came in sight.

When Miller went to claim his baggage, to his surprise, Davis and Tanner were waiting at the chute. "Hello!" he said as they shook hands. "Sidney! Lawrence! What brings you two here?"

"Shatter sent us to drive you back to Seattle," said Davis.

"I heard about Mike's death. That's the reason I came back sooner than I intended."

"We know," said Tanner. "We believe the militant group committed this crime. So far, we've never been able to get a lead on them. But something is bound to leak, sooner or later."

After Lieutenant Miller claimed his baggage, Tanner and Davis walked with him through the airport and on to their car parked outside in the passenger loading and unloading zone. Davis drove the car on around the ramp until he got on the freeway. He headed north toward Seattle, then took an exit to a dark street that led to Kent. Miller became a little curious about where he was going. Tanner kept talking to him, trying to keep his mind off of Davis's directions. The street was like a country road freshly covered with blacktop. Streetlights were about two blocks apart.

As Lieutenant Miller relaxed in the backseat, from out of nowhere a speeding car pulled up alongside the unmarked car, then cut it off and forced Davis to the curb. Calvin and Ted were in the car. Ted jumped out of the car with an automatic rifle. "Freeze!" he demanded as he pointed the automatic rifle at the officers.

Tanner was stunned. "What the hell!" he said as he was reaching for his pistol.

Staring down the barrel of that automatic weapon, Davis said, "Hold it, you fool," as he grabbed Tanner's arm. "We'll look like air filters before you clear your holster. This guy looks like he means business."

"Ah! He doesn't scare me," said Tanner as he tried to wrestle his arm away from Davis.

"These guys may be that militant group."

At that instant Tanner and Davis put their hands up.

"Everybody out with their hands up," demanded Ted. Davis, Tanner, and Lieutenant Miller climbed out of the car. "Get up against the car." As the three men stood up against the car, Calvin came from behind the steering wheel and frisked Davis and Tanner, taking away their pistols and throwing them in the backseat. Then he took their handcuffs and cuffed Davis to the front door handle and Tanner to the back door handle. Lieutenant Miller was ordered into the backseat of the Cobra. Miller didn't argue as he got in the car. Then Ted and Calvin got back in their car and drove away.

Lieutenant Miller tried to find out where he was. Without much street lighting, it was hard to read the cross-street signs. "In case you boys don't know, this is kidnapping. And I'm *Lieutenant* Miller. I'm a cop."

"We know," said Ted. "Would you rather be killed instead?"

"What do you mean?"

"Your friends!" said Calvin as he handed Miller back his pistol. "They were going to kill you."

"That's absurd. I've known them ever since they came into the department. Why would they want to kill me?"

"Some people we know have something for you to see. You can use your own judgment after that."

Leaving the back streets, Ted got on Interstate 5 and continued on to Seattle and then to the CD. Lieutenant Miller noticed the automatic M-16s. "You two wouldn't happen to the part of that militant group that's been having open season on police officers?"

"That's someone else," said Ted.

Quiet had already made it to Earl's house, where the others were waiting. But only a few moments later, there was a knock on the door. Quiet placed his hand on his pistol. Maraisha and Sharon drew their pistols. The wives became frightened, for they didn't understand the situation, as Earl went to answer the door. When the door opened, Quiet removed his hand from his pistol. Maraisha and Sharon put their pistols back in their purses. Quiet smiled a little. Michael Taylor and Leroy Young were standing on the front porch. Earl invited them into the house. Maraisha was stunned when she saw the two men. She didn't know the two men, but recognized them as the men who had picked her up. Wyatt and Michael greeted one another as though they had once been close friends.

After the introductions, Taylor said, "You've been followed."

"I know," answered Quiet. "Is that what brought you here?"

"We're on the same side," Michael turned toward Maraisha. "Your friends are going to try and kill your big boss."

"We've got to do something," said Maraisha, worried. "He wasn't due till next week."

"I don't think there's much to worry about. He came back to attend his friend's funeral."

"How'd you find this out?" asked Maraisha curiously.

Michael avoided the question. "You guys better get out of here before reinforcements come."

"If we leave, them cops will try and follow us," said Quiet.

"Remember your friend Aaron Mitchell?" said Michael.

Quiet nodded.

"Go there. We'll meet you there later."

"What about the cops?" asked Quiet as he and the others were getting ready to leave Earl's house.

"Leroy and I will take care of them. Now you guys better get going before it's too late."

Maraisha, Dino and Sharon got into Quiet's car. Joan got into Wyatt's car. Earl and Carol got into the car with Clinton and his wife. They followed Quiet as he led the way. Michael and Leroy went to their car, parked about halfway up the street. They waited til the other cars pulled away.

A squad car came around the corner and trailed Quiet and his group. Michael moved out slowly behind the police car, as Leroy reached into the backseat and grabbed his automatic weapon off the floor. When Michael came alongside the police car, the driver ducked down when he saw the automatic weapon pointed at them. Leroy opened fire, shooting out the glass windows on the driver's side. The officer on the passenger side tried to go for his gun but got hit in the hand as Michael was pulling away. The police car went up on the curb, knocking down a fence and crashing into a tree in the front yard. The crash alerted other neighbors in the area, and they came out to see what the sound was.

Quiet entered the deceased Mitchell's back driveway from the alleyway, then let Shep lead the way into the house through the back door while the others followed. The house was dark. Quiet felt his way through the kitchen and on to the basement door. There was a light switch at the top of the stairs. He flipped it on, then crept down the stairs.

When Quiet got to the bottom step, he heard low voices coming from one of the rooms down the hallway. There was a light in the hallway from the room. He drew his pistol as Dino, Sharon, and Maraisha were coming down the stairs and motioned for them to keep quiet. Then he crept down the hallway toward the room the voices came from. When Quiet reached the room, Michael and Leroy were sitting across a table from

Miller. Ted and Calvin were each sitting at either end of the table. Quiet put his pistol in his belt, then entered the room.

Lieutenant Miller stood up from his chair. "What the hell is this all about?"

Just then Dino and the two women came into the room. "Steve!" said Sharon with happiness in her voice. She ran and gave him a hug. "So glad to se you. How have you been?"

"I was all right, until I came. First two friends of mine offered me a ride to my office downtown. Then these two guys kidnapped me." He pointed to Ted and Calvin. "What the hell is going on? Somebody tell me something," he demanded.

Maraisha approached. "John, Bob, and a few others are involved in killing blacks and running rackets on the side."

Sharon pulled the envelope from her purse and handed it to Lieutenant Miller.

As Miller opened the envelope and scanned through some of the pages, Maraisha continued. "That envelope explains everything. That is part of Mike's report, the reason why he was killed."

"Sidney told me the militants killed Mike and burned down his house." Then Miller saw Davis's name on the list. "I see why Sidney told me the militants killed Mike. I'm going to make sure these guys pay for this."

For a brief moment Sharon had wondered how Lieutenant Miller got to Mitchell's house. But when she saw Ted and Calvin, she mumbled, "Why, of course." Sharon's eyes met those of the two men. But no one said a word. *Why did they help me? Who are they? What is their purpose?* She felt she should ask for the answers to her questions. But on second thought, she knew that whatever reason they helped, she should thank them for it. Then Sharon turned away and went back and stood next to Dino.

Moments later Clinton, Earl, and their wives came into the basement room, followed by Wyatt and Joan. To everyone's surprise, when Wyatt saw Ted and Calvin he walked over and hugged them, both. "Hey, guys!" he said. "How have you guys been? It's been a long time."

"Yeah! Since high school," Ted replied.

When Lieutenant Miller finished going over the document, he said, "This can't go downtown. We have someone in Internal Affairs who might intercept it. This will have to go to Special Services in Olympia. The sooner they get this envelope, the better it'll be for all of us. John and his friends won't rest until they get this report from us."

"What was Mike working on?" asked Sharon.

"He was working undercover, investigating some of our police force," said Miller. "I suspected fraud in our police department. When Olympia had me investigate, I put Mike on the case." Miller walked over to Quiet and handed him the envelope. "How much does this mean to you?"

Casually Quiet looked around at the others and then back at Miller. "Your life and mine." Evil showed in his eyes, though Quiet didn't have any hateful feelings. He turned toward Michael and Leroy. "Anyone follow you?"

"We left them in someone's front yard," answered Taylor.

"Good. But we can't stay here. When they can't find us at our residences, they'll be coming here. The streets will be crawling with cops. They know our cars, so we won't be able to use them to get out of town. But we'd better leave while we can. Dino," he called, "You'll have to get this envelope to Olympia!"

Quiet suggested, Dino assist Maraisha and Sharon taking the envelope to Olympia. By now he figured the police had made a search at the apartment and at his two brothers' houses, and they'd be combing the streets looking for them. Up to now, Quiet felt he had done all he could to keep out of the police's way, but prevent his family getting into trouble or being hurt. *What to do now?* was a question he couldn't answer. His head hung low, resting on his thumb and index finger. He was standing near the doorway when Maraisha got his attention.

"Quiet!" she called. "Is something the matter?"

"No!" Quiet walked to the center of the room. "I guess not. Let's go."

Shep led the way back upstairs. Quiet followed closely behind. Shortly behind, the others came. When Shep got upstairs, the basement door was cracked open. He pushed the door open and went on into the kitchen. But when the dog got into the kitchen, Quiet heard him snarl. Becoming cautious, Quiet drew his pistol as he motioned to the others to be silent. The moonlight glowed through the windows, giving only enough light to see silhouette figures. Although Quiet could barely hear Shep growl, it sounded like an echo roaring through. He went to the living room and dining room windows but stayed back far enough not to be seen from the outside.

As he looked through the windows he saw one patrol car after another driving up and down the street. He felt the police were looking for them. Quiet knew they had to leave the house before the police came looking. As he went back into the kitchen and started to go out the back door, he saw more police prowling among the neighbors' houses. Quickly he closed the back door and stood back. "The neighborhood is crawling with cops," he uttered. "There's another way out. Follow me."

Michael went and looked through the living room windows and saw the police also. "Wait!" he said. Everyone paused for an instant. "Those cops may not be looking for us."

"What do you mean?" Quiet asked curiously.

"If those cops were looking for us, they'd 've been in here by now. I think they're looking for the two guys who shot them two cops who were trying to follow you guys. They must have radioed in for a search."

Quiet looked at Michael. "What do you suggest?"

"If Leroy and I could get back to our car, we could lead them away from here. That would give you guys a chance to get away."

"Where did you park?"

"A couple blocks from here, around the corner in an alley."

"How are you guys gonna get past them cops? They have this whole neighborhood covered."

"Leave that to us," said Michael as he opened the back door. Then he and Leroy crept out of the house and on through the alleys and between houses. Climbing over fences and going through backyards, Michael and Leroy got past the police and made it safely to their car. Ted and Calvin left the house moments later. Their car was parked in the driveway of a vacant house just across the street. They went and got in their car and drove past many patrol cars cruising through the neighborhood, until they met Michael and Leroy coming around the corner in the Corvette. Michael pulled up behind one of the patrolling squad cars, and Young blasted it with an automatic weapon as they went speeding past.

When the police car was fired upon, the driver and the passenger wrestled for position underneath the dashboard. The police car ran into a nearby parked car. Two other police cars in the area came speeding around the corner just in time to see the incident. Without a second thought, the police gave chase behind the Corvette. At a safe distance Ted and Calvin followed the police cars. It was no contest. The Corvette put a lot of distance between them and the police cars. The officer on the passenger side in the first car radioed in for interception from other squad cars in the area. The squad cars responded.

Coming off the back streets, Michael drove the Corvette down Empire Way southbound. Then he turned onto another back street to elude the police chase. After eluding the police, Michael headed back toward the deceased Mitchell's house. He pulled the Corvette into the alley with its headlights off. Moments later the Cobra pulled in behind the Corvette. The three Jones cars were still parked in the same place, the driveway.

During the chase, when the police asked for help to intercept the Corvette, Maulder, Marty and Ross had just reached Clinton's house when they heard the call come over their radio. Six other police cars were parked in front of Clinton's house. Two were unmarked. Marcy, Bishop, Randall, Munson, and Morrison were on their way up the walkway when Maulder called them back. The other police just sat int their cars listening to the chase on the radio.

"The suspect turned southbound on Empire Way off Denny Street. All units in the area: Intercept a red Corvette. We have reasons to believe the suspects are part of the militant group that shot up two police cars in the Central District."

From another police car giving chase came: "The suspect turned off Empire Way south onto Atlantic Avenue heading east." Then there was silence. The Corvette was nowhere in sight. "We lost the Corvette. Any unit in the area spot the Corvette?"

"Negative," said an officer in the area. "That car must be a ghost."

Maulder, Marty, and Ross sat in their car for a few moments. "I wonder what they're doing in the Central District when all the action was done on the south end of town?" said Marty. Just then he, Ross, and Maulder looked at one another. "Are you thinking what I'm thinking?"

"The same two niggas who helped that Jones kid get away," said Maulder as he started up the engine, then pulled away from the curb. The other cars followed.

"He has another brother lives in the area," said Ross. "I think maybe those gunmen were at his house."

"Only one way I know to find out," said Maulder as he accelerated. Running a few red lights and stop signs, they pulled up in front of Earl's house. The officers looked up and down the block. "No one here. Their car is gone. There must be a place where they could hide."

"You mean a friend perhaps?" suggested Ross.

"Yes," agreed Maulder.

"That dog of his, I would like to get my hands on it and wring his neck. For making us chase it, then leading us to its master, waiting around a corner at the end of the warehouse," said Marty.

"Dogs!" Maulder stated thoughtfully. "There was a friend of Jones who owned pit dogs for fighting. He lived across the alley. Let's check that out."

"Why of course," agreed Marty. "That nigga named Mitchell. His house is vacant and who would've thought of looking for them blacks there?"

Maulder pulled away from in front of Earl's house and headed for Mitchell's house. When they got there, Maulder and Tanner pulled their cars into the alley. Randall, Munson, and the others parked their cars in front. The police got out, headed up the porch, then crashed through the front door, while Spike led the way through the back door as Maulder cautiously followed. The house was empty and dark, but there were traces indicating someone had been there. Spike went downstairs where the people were. Maulder turned on the lights as they thoroughly searched the house. When they didn't find anyone, Maulder thought, *Where are they now?*

8

Before Maulder had figured out the blacks were taking refuge at Mitchell's house, Quiet and the others had already left. When Michael and Leroy led the police away from Mitchell's house, Wyatt used his car to take Maraisha and Sharon, along with Lieutenant Miller, back to the women's car. Joan suggested the wives could stay with her mother until it was all over. Clinton would drive the wives there, then meet Quiet, Wyatt, and Earl at their parents' house later. Dino and Quiet were to wait until Michael, Leroy, Ted, and Calvin returned to Mitchell's house, after eluding the police, to assist in keeping the police away from Miller, Maraisha, and Sharon.

Wyatt stayed on the back streets until he got on the south side across Jackson Street. After crossing Jackson Street, Wyatt would have to do the one thing he didn't want to do. Knowing where Sharon had parked their car, he would have to drive down Rainier Avenue until he came to the Floating Bridge viaduct. Then with luck Wyatt might be able to get back on the dark streets again, which were only a few blocks off Rainier, because across Jackson the streets ran a few blocks into a dead end.

Wyatt was very much aware of the five arterial streets running north and south: Beacon Hill Avenue, which started from Jackson and ran out to the upper part of Skyway; Rainier Avenue, which also started from Jackson and ran all the way out to the valley in Renton; Twenty-third Avenue, which started a few blocks away from the University District and ran into Rainier in the valley and continued on to the Beacon Hill junction, where it ended; Empire Way, which started from the CD valley and continued on to South Renton; and, last, Mount Baker Hill, the shortest run of them all, which started from Jackson and ended at Lake Washington Boulevard. It was about three miles long.

These streets were patrolled quite frequently by the police, whether or not they were on a search. Most of the time a patrol car would sit on one of the side streets and watch a speeding motorist zoom by. Before a motorist realized it, he would be signing a citation.

While they were driving down Rainier Avenue, Sharon said, sitting in the backseat next to Lieutenant Miller, "Why can't we go downtown to headquarters and get help?"

"Every street leading to headquarters is probably being watched," said Lieutenant Miller. "How close do you think we'd get before we were intercepted? To the door, maybe? Your boyfriend was smart not to try to take this evidence downtown. This evidence is going to Olympia, where it'll do the most good. I'm sure John has thought of everything. But in case I don't make it to Olympia I want you to give this evidence to a James Adams. Tell him it's from Frank. He'll know what to do with it."

As Wyatt was passing underneath the viaduct, a police car was parked off a side street. Two police officers were sitting in the car when they recognized Wyatt's car, from the description they had received, passing by. At a great distance, the officers followed, radioing in on their CB at the same time. The squad car followed Wyatt about three blocks off Rainier Avenue until he turned into a dead end. Knowing where the street ended, the two officers parked their car about the middle of the block, just before the entrance to the dead end. They radioed their position, got out of the car, and pursued on foot. When they got to the corner, they recognized Maraisha, Sharon and Lieutenant

Miller getting out of Wyatt's car. The women's car was parked about three-quarters of the way down the street, under a streetlight.

As Lieutenant Miller was getting out of Wyatt's car, Wyatt saw two male figures sneaking down the block, staying in the shadows of the trees and bushes. He had to look twice before his eyes could focus on the two men. "Wait!" said Wyatt in a low tone of voice.

"Wait for what?" said Miller.

"I thought I saw two cops sneaking down this way."

Lieutenant Miller squinted, looking up the street. "I don't see anything." He got out of the car and went and seated himself next to Maraisha in the front seat.

While sitting behind the steering wheel Maraisha started to turn the engine over. "I just saw someone get behind that bush in front of that house up there," she pointed out in a low voice.

Lieutenant Miller got out of the car, squinting again. "I still can't see anything, but you both can't be wrong," he said, disturbed. "We've got to get out of here." Maraisha started up the engine. "We can't get past them without getting shot up. We'll have to go on foot. Turn the engine off and let's get out of here."

As Maraisha and Sharon were hurrying out of the car, one of the officers came from behind a bush. "Halt!" he shouted, then fired a couple of shots.

Wyatt grabbed an automatic weapon he got from Ted at Mitchell's house from the backseat and returned rapid fire at the officers, which caused them to fall to their stomachs. Maraisha and Sharon took cover next to Lieutenant Miller behind the women's car. They drew their pistols, then slowly started walking backward, using the car as a shield. But just as Wyatt got out of his car and started moving backward, the two officers got up and fired two wild shots. Wyatt, Maraisha, and Sharon fired back at the officers, which caused them to put their heads back to the ground. By the time Wyatt reached the women's car, the corner was swarming with police officers. He kept them at bay with rapid firing, looking for a chance to get away.

Seeing Wyatt was in trouble, Lieutenant Miller told the two women they had to get the envelope to Olympia somehow while he would help Wyatt. Sharon tried to hold him back. But Miller insisted on going and the women leaving. Maraisha came and took Sharon by the arm and led her away.

When Lieutenant Miller got back behind the women's car, next to Wyatt, he stood up. "Hold your fire!" he shouted. "This is Lieutenant Miller." Just then a bullet creased the right sleeve in his jacket. The police refused to stop shooting. "We can't stay around here too long. They'll try to get behind us."

"I know," said Wyatt. "Any ideas?"

"Yeah! Where's your brother and his militant friends?" said Miller as he drew his pistol and returned a couple of shots.

A few police officers had already circled the block and started making their way through residents' backyards. Maraisha and Sharon just got to the end of the block when they saw three police officers come out from between two houses and get behind a parked car. They fired a few shots at Wyatt and Miller. Maraisha got down on one knee, in a shooting position, behind a fire hydrant. "Stop shooting!" she shouted. One of the police officers turned and fired wildly. Maraisha blasted four rounds. Two bullets hit one of the officers in his body. The other two officers tried to go back the way they came, after seeing one of their men fall. Sharon fell to one knee and returned a few rounds, hitting one of the two officers in the back. The third officer escaped unharmed.

Maraisha took the envelope out of her purse and handed it to Sharon. "You take this and go. I've got to stay here and help them."

"No!" Sharon disagreed. "If you're not going, then I'm not either."

"No time to argue," Maraisha demanded. "Wyatt and the lieutenant don't stand a chance against our own people. Now go, before it's too late."

Sharon took the envelope and the women said their farewells, as they wished one another good luck. Then she hurried up the sidewalk toward the direction of Quiet's home, which was about two blocks up the hill and around the corner. But when Sharon got to the end of the first block, Quiet and Dino were speeding down the hill. Taylor and Young were right behind them. Ted and Calvin were just coming around the corner. When Quiet saw Sharon, he came to a screeching halt.

Sharon ran over to Quiet as he jumped out of the car. "They have them pinned down."

Quiet could hear the gunfire. He grabbed the automatic weapon and hurried to where Maraisha was. Dino grabbed an automatic weapon also and followed.

Quiet approached Maraisha. "I'm sure glad to see you," she said as she threw her arms around his neck. "They spotted us coming down Rainier."

"What happened? Where's Wyatt and the lieutenant?" asked Quiet, worried.

"Up there." Maraisha pointed. "Behind our car."

As Quiet was trying to advance toward Wyatt and Miller, Michael and Ted drove to the end of the block and made a right turn. Michael drove about halfway down the block and parked his car in a vacant driveway. There were many police officers in the area. The SWAT teams had stationed themselves between houses. Some were advancing toward Wyatt and Miller, trying to get them in a crossfire. As they tried to circle down the block, Dino and Sharon drove the officers back with bullet fire. The officers were becoming confused, because they didn't know how many assailants they were dealing with.

Ted drove his car a block beyond where the police had parked their cars. They had the dead end closed off. There was no way for anyone to get past them. Ted drove his car up the street a couple of blocks, turned off his headlights, and drove toward the police cars. The streets in the area were crawling with police. Traffic was detoured to another street. Red lights were flashing. Hearing the gunfire, people in the neighborhood raised their windows, pulled back their curtains, and cracked their doors to see what the shooting and shouting were about.

This was something new for Ted and Calvin. Most of their attacks were hit-and-run. They knew better than to fight the police toe to toe on open ground, for they could get cut down easily. They never had to face this many police officers before.

The police had most of the streets in the area blocked off. Ted pulled the car within half a block of the police cars. He felt if they got out and attacked on foot, trying to hit the police from behind, the route back to their car would be blocked off in seconds.

As Ted came closer to his do-or-die situation, he saw an officer making his first mistake. He pulled one of the cars away from the blockade and drove down to the end of the other block. This would give Ted enough space to approach the police barricade, make one good sweep, and keep on going. When Ted saw the opportunity, Calvin jumped in the backseat, rolled down the window, and got ready to fire. Ted wasted no time as he turned his headlights back on, roared his engine, and burned rubber turning the corner. Calvin made a sweep with the automatic weapon as Ted sped by. They left a few police cars with shot-out windows, flat tires, and on fire. Some officers around the inferno took coverage elsewhere just before the cars blew up. The explosions left a few officers killed and some injured. When Ted got to the next corner he made a left turn and sped up Seventeenth.

This attack caught the police off guard. They were used to pursuing their suspects. A few officers who saw Ted coming ignored his car. But when Calvin fired on them, some ducked down on the other side of their cars. Others took cover between houses. The police officers on the next street over and down at the other end of the block heard the gunfire. They looked back in the direction whence it had come. When they saw Ted's car going in the other direction, they got hurriedly in their cars and gave chase.

When Michael saw the police get behind Ted, he started up his engine and pulled out of the driveway and followed. Leroy rolled down the window, leaned over, and blasted at the police as he was speeding past them. At the same instant, the police cars went up in flames at the corner of the dead end. Wyatt saw a slim chance of reuniting with Quiet and Maraisha at the other end of the block. Lieutenant Miller tried to hold him back. But Wyatt was very insistent on escaping before the police overran their place of cover. He stooped to back away from the car. A bullet hit him in the armpit as he started to run, shot by a determined officer. Just as the officer rose and shot, the lieutenant blasted the officer with a number of shots. Then the lieutenant turned and helped Wyatt to where Quiet and Dino were.

Seeing Wyatt get hit, Quiet and Dino, behind a parked car between the women's car and the end of the block, both got up and blasted sweepingly at the officer, until Miller got Wyatt to them. Dino and Sharon helped take Wyatt to his house.

Wyatt has passed out by the time he was taken back to the house. They laid him down on the couch, then moved back away, all except Quiet. He knelt down, staring at Wyatt. For a moment there was silence. Not even Shep made a whimper as he sat down next to Quiet, resting his paw on Quiet's knee. Lieutenant Miller held his head down in shame. Sharon sniffed as tears rolled down her face. Maraisha' eyes were filled with tears, although she didn't make a sound. They noticed the anger on Quiet's face. Dino approached Quiet and patted him on the shoulder as he sat down beside Wyatt. Death spread all over Quiet's face. His narrowed eyes held the look of fighting fire.

"He'll be all right!" Dino soothed Quiet.

For a long time Quiet was still. Not so much as an eye blinked. "I'm through running," he said angrily, almost in a whisper. "They shot my brother. I tried to keep peace with them. They won't stop. Now I will fight back my way."

"No! No-o!" screamed Maraisha as she ran and threw herself on his back as he was kneeling down. "You can't do that. They'll kill you."

Quiet got up quickly and shook Maraisha by her shoulders. "Look what they've done," he said as he pointed at Wyatt, who was slowly regaining consciousness. Quiet knelt back down and held Wyatt in his arms, then tried to help him to his feet, as he was trying to stand.

"We can't stay here," said Dino. "They'll be here any minute. We have to leave now."

"Yes," agreed Quiet. "We can't stay here." As he was helping Wyatt, he called, "Dino! Give me a hand with Wyatt. Then bring my car around back."

Dino helped Quiet take Wyatt from the living room through the back door into the backyard. Then Dino went for Quiet's car and drove it through the alley on into the back driveway. Quiet and the others had taken the alley just in back of the house while Dino came around on the other alley. So then Dino drove back onto the alley Quiet was taking and met them at the fork where the alley separated in three directions, east, south, and north.

Dino pulled up just as Quiet, with Wyatt's arms resting across his and Miller's shoulders, was going up the alley that led to the lower section of the woods. "Use my car," said Quiet. Lieutenant Miller, Sharon, and Maraisha looked at him. "I want you and Sharon to take this evidence to Olympia. I'm going to stay here and see what I can do. Wyatt has a bullet in him. I'm going to take him to one of my father's friends who used to be a surgeon."

"Why don't you let me take Wyatt with us?" said Dino. "We can get him to a hospital when we reach Olympia."

"I want Wyatt with me," said Quiet.

Dino saw the look on Quiet's face. "I understand," he said as Sharon was getting in the car. They just looked at one another with sorrow on their faces. Then Dino drove away.

Quiet and Lieutenant Miller continued aiding Wyatt down the alley. The lower alley ran alongside the woods for about half a mile, then joined the pavement. About fifty yards before the entrance to the alley from the streets, a trail led upward to Fifteenth Avenue. Maraisha and Sharon's apartment was a block away from the opening.

The men came out of the alley and started walking up the back street that led to the Jones house. As they were about to cross the Dearborn Bridge, Michael and Ted were just coming down Twelfth Avenue. When Michael saw Quiet and Lieutenant Miller carrying Wyatt he got out of his car and helped place Wyatt in the backseat. Quiet and Shep got in the backseat beside him. Maraisha and Lieutenant Miller got in the backseat of Ted's car.

The shooting had stopped. The police had Wyatt's car towed away. They had combed the area looking for the suspects. With all the diversion, the suspects managed to elude the police. By this time Maulder and his associates had come upon the scene. After seeing what was explained to him, he led the police to Quiet's home. The house was empty by the time the police arrived. Spike sniffed through the house and picked up the scent leading out through the back door. The scent continued on through the alley in two directions when he came to the fork.

The police concentrated on the south end for blacks. Spike had led Maulder and the police up the alley that led alongside the lower part of the woods. When they came to the avenue, looking up and down the street, the blacks were nowhere in sight. The only place Maulder felt they could have gone, if the blacks were still in the area, was the women's apartment. Feeling the blacks had nowhere to go, Maulder and a handful of police officers went to the apartment, while the other police officers searched up the alley and through the woods.

When Maulder got to the apartment, he kicked the door open. Marcy, still limping, and Marty searched the apartment thoroughly. The apartment was empty. When the police couldn't find the blacks in the area, they met back at their cars.

Sliding through back streets, cruising on the arterial, Michael once again got past the police searching for them. They took Wyatt through the back entrance of the Evergreen Funeral Home, located on Nineteenth Avenue, in the upper part of the CD. It was a few blocks away from the Capital Hill District.

With the loss of blood Wyatt had grown weak. The mortician had Quiet and Lieutenant Miller take Wyatt to a back room where he embalmed bodies. There was a surgical bed in the room, where Wyatt was laid. The embalmer was Fred Williamette, a man in his fifties, about the same age as Mr. Jones. His hair was thin on top, with gray running along the side. Wrinkles on his face showed his age. His height was about five feet, eight inches, and he weighed about 175 pounds. He was dark-complected, his skin dark as night.

Williamette came into the back room with his surgical bag. "What happened?" he asked as he was laying his surgical instruments on another table. No one spoke. Williamette gave Wyatt a shot of anesthetic, then started prying the bullet from the bone in his armpit. When he finished digging out the bullet, he examined it. "A police bullet. What kind of trouble are you guys in?"

Quiet explained. When he was finished, the mortician said, "Leave him here. I'll take care of him." There was doubt on Quiet's face. "Don't worry! He'll be all right."

"Okay!" Quiet agreed. "May I use your phone? I want to call my brothers."

Williamette pointed to the other room. "In there," he said. Quiet went into the other room and used the telephone. He called Clinton, who was still at Joan's mother's house, and told him about Wyatt getting shot by the police and that they were at the Evergreen Funeral Home. At the words "Funeral Home," Clinton thought Wyatt was dead. But Quiet eased his tensions by telling Clinton that Wyatt would be all right. When they finished talking, Quiet hung up the telephone, then walked out into the funeral home's parking lot. He stood in front of Michael's car.

Michael walked up beside Quiet. "Whatcha gonna do, man?" he asked sadly.

Quiet's head hung low, eyes staring down at the pavement. He shook his head. "I don't know," he said in a low, angry tone of voice. "I don't want to do what I'm thinking. It may get us all killed."

"Whatcha thinking?" asked Michael.

"Find the ones responsible for this and kill them," said Quiet bitterly.

"The person you want is someone called John Maulder," Michael continued. "Your girlfriend's boss."

"Where does he live?"

"If we knew that, half of this might not have happened," said Michael as he and Quiet walked out on the sidewalk. "Ask your girlfriend. She knows."

Quiet looked back at Maraisha standing near the entrance door. Leroy, Ted, Calvin, and Lieutenant Miller were just coming outside. Although they never spoke a word, their eyes glared into the darkness. The parking lot was well lighted by the pole lights. The moon was full. Quiet turned and walked to the entrance of the parking lot and stopped. He raised his head and looked up and down the street. The streets were clear, not many parked cars. A few night owls were just getting home that night. Some had to go to work later on that morning.

Maraisha slowly approached Quiet from behind, wrapped her arms around his waist, and pressed her head against his shoulder blades. "I love you," she whispered.

Quiet turned around, no expression on his face, no feeling in his eyes. A cold chill flowed through Maraisha's body. "Where does your boss live?" he asked coldly.

At that instant many thoughts rapidly flowed through Maraisha's mind. *Why does he want to know where John lives? John and the others are looking for us. There are too many for us to face.* The look in his eyes was like a cat on the prowl. Maraisha wanted to refuse, but she could see he wasn't in any mood to accept no for an answer. "He lives in the north end," she said sadly. "I'll take you there."

Michael, standing next to Quiet, said, "Man! You know you're crazy. The cops are crawling on hands and knees to find us. That's like being in the devil's backyard with a high fence surrounding it."

"They're in the south end and CD looking for us," said Quiet. "Where's the least likely place they'd expect to find us?"

Michael thought for a moment. "Why, of course," he agreed. "Good thinking."

It was around 4:30 A.M. when Earl and Clinton drove into the funeral home's parking lot. "Where's Wyatt?" Clinton asked after getting out of his car and approaching Quiet.

"Inside," said Quiet. "Mr. Williamette is patching him up."

Clinton and Earl went on inside the funeral home. Wyatt was sitting up on the bed when they entered. "Hi, Clint, Earl!" said Wyatt.

Both brothers looked upset on seeing their brother's arm in a sling. "How do you feel?" asked Clinton.

"I feel all right," answered Wyatt. "Quiet wants me to stay here until this is over. What do you guys think?"

"I think he's right," said Earl. "At least we won't have to worry about you, because you'll be in good hands."

Williamette smiled.

The brothers visited Wyatt a few moments longer, then walked out of the back room and on outside. By the time Clinton and Earl got outside, Quiet and the others were in Michael's and Ted's cars. So Clinton and Earl got in their cars and followed Michael and Ted.

Meanwhile, Dino and Sharon had finally made it to the freeway. After leaving the alley, Dino headed northbound until he came out of the back streets, across the Dearborn Bridge, and made a left turn when he came to Jackson Street. He drove down Jackson toward Chinatown, made another left when he got on Sixth Avenue, then drove to Dearborn Avenue. He came to a red light. To his surprise, there were no police cars in sight. The light changed to green, and Dino pulled away. He turned east toward the freeway, about six blocks away. Within the six blocks he passed two police cars going in the other direction. Dino became a little nervous but continued to the freeway. When Dino got on the freeway, he headed south.

Dino noticed every car he passed on the freeway. There was very little traffic on the freeway at that time in the morning. The thought of being intercepted by the police or state patrol never left his mind. Olympia was sixty miles form the city limits of Seattle. The daylight was moving into darkness when they pulled into the state capitol. The parking lot was empty, except for a couple of security guards' vehicles. Dino pulled into the parking lot and turned off the engine.

"What now?" asked Sharon.

"Walk to the nearest phone booth and find his home address," he said, getting out of the car. Sharon went with him.

Michael parked his car near a curb a block south of Maulder's house. Ted parked his car a block north. Clinton parked on the west side, and Earl parked a block east of Maulder's house. Quiet had suggested this strategy. If anyone had any trouble escaping, there would be four directions to go

229

instead of one, for a better chance. Quiet entered Maulder's house through a back bedroom window, then worked his way through the living room to the kitchen and opened the back door for the others. The house smelled like dogs. It was a three-bedroom house with a hallway, then a living room/dining room combined.

Not knowing what they were searching for, Quiet and the others looked through every room in the house and found nothing. When Quiet went downstairs into the basement, he saw an obstacle set up for a dog. Shep gave a couple of barks. The basement was empty also. So Quiet went back upstairs.

There was complete silence as everyone sat around the living room. A large window in the living room gave a good view of the front and just beyond both ends of the block. The kitchen window had a good view of an alleyway and a few back doors of neighbors' houses. The morning was getting brighter. A few lights were coming on in neighboring houses. Strangely, there was a rooster crowing.

Maraisha was sitting on the couch. She got up and went and sat in Quiet's lap. He was sitting in an armchair. "Now what?" she asked, exhausted.

"Sit and wait, I guess," he said bitterly.

"Wait for John and his friends?" Maraisha added uneasily. "They'll—"

"This is where we'll make our stand if we have to," Clinton interrupted. He was sitting in one of the dining room chairs watching the front window. "No one has to stay. We just want the one who's responsible for Wyatt getting shot."

"Why not let the law handle him?" said Maraisha.

"The law are the ones who set my brother up to be killed," said Michael, sitting in a chair just to the side of the living room window.

"She's right, you know!" said Lieutenant Miller, sitting on the couch. "Just a handful of cops gone bad, but with you guys' help we can get all of them. This way is no good. Sharon told me she never told anyone about the envelope except Lawrence Shatter. He's the head of Internal Affairs. I didn't see his name on the list. But I feel he is part of it in some way."

"I feel that, too," added Quiet. "But here's one way we can find out. Call him." Quiet suggested that he and Lieutenant Miller go to a phone booth and call Shatter for help. Without hesitation Michael gave Quiet the key to his car. Before leaving, Quiet went to Maulder's clothes closet and pulled out a long overcoat and hat.

"What's that for?" asked Lieutenant Miller.

"Insurance," said Quiet.

Quiet and Lieutenant Miller went back through the alley to get to Michael's car. They drove to a phone booth at a Texaco gas station on Highway 99, between Lynnwood and Everette, about two miles north of Maulder's house.

Around five-thirty that morning Shatter got a phone call at his home, about three miles closer to Seattle than Maulder's home, but west of Highway 99. He was a family man, with a wife and two sons in their late teens: Jerry, nineteen, and Jim, eighteen. When the telephone rang, Shatter got up drowsily and went to the living room to answer it. "Hello!" he yawned.

"Lawrence! This is Miller."

"Lieutenant!" Shatter said excitedly. "We've been looking all over for you. I heard you were kidnapped by two of those militant blacks. Are you all right?"

"Yes! I need your help. I have to get to the department. Some cops are trying to kill me."

"Cops!" repeated Shatter, surprised. "You've got to be kidding. Why would any cops want to kill you?"

"Get me an escort to the department and I'll explain." Miller told Shatter where he was calling from. So Shatter requested Miller stay where he was and he'd send two uniformed police officers to escort him to the department. After saying good-bye, Lieutenant Miller went back to Quiet, waiting in the car.

Quiet pulled away from the phone booth and drove to a back street about a block away from the phone booth. He parked the car where he could keep the phone booth in sight. Then Quiet got out with the overcoat and hat. "Now we're going to see how loyal your friend is," he said, then walked away. On the way to the phone booth Quiet picked up a short stick to push through the arms of the overcoat and a long stick to stand the overcoat up and where the hat could sit. When Quiet got to the phone booth, he put the overcoat over the long stick. Then he sat the hat on top. Quiet wedged the garment against the wall of the booth so it would not fall. Then he took the telephone receiver and hung it over the coat as though it was being used. After doing this, Quiet went back to the car.

When Quiet got seated in the car, Miller said, "Now what?"

"Let's wait and see," said Quiet.

About forty-five minutes later, four police cars and two unmarked cars pulled up at the phone booth. The police got out of their cars, drew their pistols, and pointed them at the phone booth. When they saw the manlike figure in the coat, without a word a hail of police bullets air-conditioned the phone booth. The receiver fell off the coat. The overcoat and hat fell to the floor. Quiet recognized five of the police officers he had seen in the warehouse. The others he had never seen before.

"That's John Maulder," pointed Miller as he spoke in a surprised tone of voice.

"We've seen what we wanted to see," said Quiet as he started up the engine. "We'd better get back to the house and get the others. It won't take them long to figure out where we are." He eased away from the curb, turned the corner, and headed back to Maulder's house.

When the shooting stopped, Maulder cussed as he, Ross,

and Marty cautiously approached the phone booth. He was angry at what he had discovered. "That nigger," he said bitterly.

"What about that nigger?" asked Ross curiously.

"That nigger used my coat and hat to trick us," said Maulder. "The last place I would expect to find them. My house." Maulder turned toward the uniformed officers. "You guys go to my house and see if they're still there. So far they've managed to keep one step ahead of us. This time I'm going to wait for 'em."

"Where?" asked Ross as Maulder was going to his car.

"Their house," said Maulder. "Let's go."

The uniformed officers parked their cars in both directions about halfway down the block from Maulder's house. As though they were a SWAT team, they approached the house cautiously from the rear, the front, and on both sides. The front door was cracked slightly open. When the police entered the house, it was empty. There was evidence of the blacks having been there. They had eaten Maulder's eggs and bacon for breakfast and left behind the unwashed dishes.

When leaving Maulder's house, Quiet and Maraisha got in the front seat next to Clinton. Shep got in the back. Lieutenant Miller got in the front seat beside Earl. Michael, Leroy, Ted, and Calvin got in their cars and followed Clinton. Quiet knew of a place almost near the end of the lower part of the woods where he and a few neighborhood friends years ago had dug a cave to hide out from other neighborhood kids. Two Quiet knew were dead: Louie Albanese, an Italian who had died in Vietnam at the age of twenty-one, and Billy Williams, a black killed by police at one of Clinton's rallies. He was twenty-two. The other friends were Jerry and Tom Isaka, two Japanese brothers who had gone back to Japan during high school. They were twenty-four and twenty-five now. Each one had sworn never to reveal their secret to anyone.

Driving through the back streets off of Highway 99, taking side streets to get around town, Michael pulled his car to the entrance of the alley. A ways up the alley was a branch road that led behind some bushes into a clearing about fifty feet away from the alley. The clearing had enough space for everyone to park their cars, plus space to spare. After parking their cars, Quiet led them to the cave.

The cave showed its age. Thick sticker bushes had grown around it. The cave was located about halfway up a trail, about a hundred yards into the woods. The trail continued up onto the sidewalk on Twelfth. When they got to the cave Quiet took off his jacket and moved some of the bushes aside. Clinton and Ted helped. When they cleared the entrance, everyone went inside. The cave was as large as a small one-bedroom house. After everyone got inside, Quiet put some of the bushes back to hide the entrance. From the cave entrance was a clear view of the street below that led to Quiet's home. But there was a better view from the women's apartment. Quiet stayed near the entrance as a lookout.

Maraisha was sitting on the floor in the far end of the cave with Ted, Calvin, and Leroy. She felt as though she was getting cold. Michael and Lieutenant Miller had already gone to gather wood to build a fire. It was like being in a war zone hiding from the enemy. Maraisha got up off the ground and approached Quiet. "The first time I felt like a fugitive," she said. "Now what?"

Quiet looked at her with sorrow on his face. But it didn't hide the anger and the agony he felt at his brother being shot. "Wait for Dino," he said sadly. "Nowhere to run, no place to hide. Before long, they put enough cops and dogs in these woods," he looked at Shep, "they'll find us."

"What else can we do?" said Maraisha worriedly. "We can't call for help. We can't take a chance of going downtown due to our fear that John's friends may intercept us. What chance do we have?"

"We have a good chance until help arrives," said Clinton as he came into the conversation, standing next to Quiet and Earl.

"Dino and Sharon should be on their way back by now, with help."

"If they didn't get stopped," said Maraisha. She thought for a moment. "What kind of help could they bring back, besides legal papers to arrest someone? You see the trouble we're having just to keep from being killed. I know there's some good cops downtown, but how can we reach them? So what kind of help can Dino and Sharon possibly bring?"

"Military!" added Earl as he came into the conversation also.

"Military," repeated Maraisha, amazed. The word "military" started building up her confidence. "Why, of course."

By this time Lieutenant Miller and Taylor had brought back to the cave two armfuls of wood. They dropped the wood on the floor in the center of the cave. Taylor came back to Quiet. "There's a lot of police cars in front and in back of your house."

Quiet grunted, then went outside and gathered a handful of dry leaves and brought them back to the cave. As he was starting a camp fire, the cave became full of smoke. But most of the smoke escaped through the entrance. When the fire caught up with itself, the smoke faded away. Within moments the cave became warm. Everyone had gathered around the fire. For a short period they went to sleep, except for Quiet. He stayed at the fire, staring at the flames.

Staring down at the fire, once again Quiet had flashbacks into his younger years. He was about five years old at the time, and he and his father were on their way home from one of his father's friend's houses. It was about two o'clock that weekend morning and Mr. Jones was driving down the street from his house. There were flashing red lights ahead, and police were running everywhere, up and down the neighborhood and in between houses. The police had the street blocked off. Seeing the flashing lights and the men in uniforms, Quiet became frightened.

Mr. Jones slowly approached the police blockade and came to a stop. "What's going on?" he asked curiously.

A large, 350-pound, six-foot, seven-inch sergeant walked up to Mr. Jones's truck. "You'd better turn your truck around and take another route home, boy! There may be some fireworks," he said sarcastically.

"I live around the bend," Mr. Jones said, pointing.

The sergeant described the house the police had seen the suspect enter.

"That's my house."

"You have a man in your house we want. If he doesn't come out, we'll go in and get him," threatened the sergeant.

An angry expression came over Mr. Jones's face. "You're not going in my house," he said bitterly. "If there's anyone in my house don't belong there, I'll send him out." The sergeant had one of the officers move a car to let Mr. Jones through the roadblock. Mr. Jones pulled his truck in front of his house, got out, and carried Quiet up the stairs into the house.

When Mr. Jones got inside, one of his friends was sitting on the couch next to Mrs. Jones. Quiet's three brothers were sitting next to her. Mr. Jones's friend's name was Tom Walker. He was a young man in his late twenties, about five feet, six inches tall, weighing 150 pounds, with a light complexion.

Walker seemed disturbed. "Oh, man! Am I glad to see you," he said. "The cops want to kill me."

"What did you do?" asked Mr. Jones curiously. "They're outside waiting for you to come out."

"I owed three parking tickets from six months ago," explained Walker. "These two cops always messing with me spotted me on Eighteenth and Atlantic and followed me to your house. Man! I'm scared. Elizabeth said I should give myself up. I started to go outside. I saw a bunch of cops driving up. I came back in here. What should I do?"

"Man! You don't have to be scared," said Mr. Jones. "If the

court holds a traffic warrant against you, you'll spend a few hours in jail. When you go to court, pay the ticket. Then all this will be behind you."

Mr. Jones built up Walker's confidence, assuring him he wouldn't be harmed if he gave himself up to the police. Walker got up off the couch and walked to the center of the living room floor, as the four kids watched curiously. His chin was resting on his index finger and thumb, as though he were thinking. "Okay, Don," he said doubtfully. "I'll give myself up. But I'm still scared." So slowly Walker walked toward the front door and opened it. He stood on the front porch with his hands raised.

Mr. and Mrs. Jones were standing in the doorway watching Walker go down the stairs, as Quiet squeezed between his parents' legs to get out on the porch to see what was going on. But as Walker was slowly approaching the police, a young officer fired a round just above his head. "You said I could give myself up!" shouted Walker. Then he took off running down the street, ducking behind one parked car after another along the way. Just as Walker got in the open as he neared the corner, a hail of bullets splattered him in the back. The police were using .38s and .357 Magnums. But it looked as though Walker was hit with a shotgun blast.

The sound of the weapons and watching Walker fall to the ground shocked Quiet. For the first time Quiet felt what it really meant to be afraid of something. The police ran to Walker's body and examined him to see if he was dead. Then they spread a blanket over his face, staring up. A few days later Quiet didn't think about the incident too much, although it did cross his mind. He had almost lost his fear until the following weekend, when he went with Mrs. Jones downtown to the public market to do some grocery shopping.

After shopping at a few stores in the vicinity Mrs. Jones decided she had enough shopping bags full of groceries and it was time to go home. On the way back to the bus stop, Quiet saw a police officer directing traffic. Seeing the officer in his uniform put fear in Quiet all over again, just when he felt he was over the strange incident.

The years passed; Quiet was in his early teens. After he heard of similar incidents, the experience of seeing Walker being gunned down always came back to his thoughts. At that age Quiet didn't understand. He tried to put the pieces together but always drew a blank. So one day while he, his brothers, and Mr. Jones were in the living room watching television, Quiet asked his father about the incident that had happened that night. The look on Mr. Jones's face became angry. He explained the incident to Quiet from detail to detail. Quiet felt free to talk to his father, 'cause he never lied or tried to hold anything from them when something bothered them. A stronger relationship between father and sons grew.

In the cave Quiet rose from the fire and went back to the entrance and sat back while Shep rested his head across Quiet's feet. When Maraisha awakened and saw Quiet, she got up and walked over to him. "I guess you're used to staying awake long hours. Is that what Vietnam did to you with guard duty?"

"Somewhat," he said disgustedly.

"Ever since we've been together, you never talked about it. Why? How was it over there? Was it as bad as some people say?"

"That depends on what you've heard. Some things were good, and some bad."

"Did you feel you were serving your country?"

At the word "country," Quiet remembered when he was in the fifth grade. It was about the middle of the school year. On a warm sunny spring day he was in class while the teacher was telling the students of certain great men who had fought for their country, men like George Washington, our first president; Davy Crockett and Jim Bowie, who had died at the Alamo in San Antonio, Texas, fighting the Mexicans; President Lincoln, who freed the slaves; General MacArthur and General Patton, who fought the Germans, among others. Quiet wondered if there were any great black men who made history but dared not ask.

Later that evening Quiet was sitting at the dining room table doing his homework after everyone had eaten. He asked his father, who was sitting on the couch reading a newspaper, while the brothers were watching television, "Daddy, were you ever in the army?"

"Yes, Son!" answered Mr. Jones. "Quite a few years ago."

"Have you ever fought for your country?"

Mr. Jones put his newspaper aside. "I want to tell you, Son, all of you, and I don't want you to forget," he said, "you kids are getting older now, so you'll understand certain things. Blacks don't have a country. Only Africa. Our heritage is from Africa. The blacks who had a country were those who were brought here as slaves, by the whites. Africa was their country. Through the years whites mixed our blood with that of almost every nationality. So now we're not classified as Africans. Only blacks. Africans don't have mixed blood.

"In the fourteenth and fifteenth centuries, the Spanish had blacks as slaves. But when they came to the New World, to places such as Cuba, Jamaica, Tahiti, Peru, and other parts of Central and South America, the Spanish set the blacks free.

"When the whites left the old country and came to America, one of the first things they tried to do was make Indians slaves. But they couldn't adjust to the southern heat. Most of them got sick and died, while others escaped. The Indians gave part of their land to the whites. But that wasn't enough. They wanted more. So they took the Indians' land and put them on the reservations in deserts.

"Blacks don't have a country because they were used as slaves. The first blacks were brought over here by the Pilgrims on a ship called the *Mayflower*. There were twenty of them. South Africa is a hot country. The heat didn't bother the blacks, so they were forced to work in the fields. The whites raped our

239

women and killed our forefathers. Now our blood is mixed. Africans don't want us anymore because we're no longer considered Africans. We're not Americans because our skin is dark. An animal has more classification than a black man or woman. So now we're forced into being a race of our own, like the Chicanos and the Mexicans."

Quiet looked at Maraisha with narrowed eyes as they scanned the view from the cave. "Blacks don't have a country," he said coldly. "Just a place to live. I don't feel I was in Vietnam fighting for my country, but fighting to keep money in the rich man's pocket. His price was the lives of blacks and poor whites. Whites with money, their sons were placed in offices around the States or had some special type of classification so they didn't have to fight in Vietnam. At times, I wish I could take this feeling out of my system. But when I see what's happening the feeling grows stronger."

"You don't like it here?"

"I love this country. I wouldn't want to go anywhere else. I live here. Although it wasn't theirs, this is what the whites gave us. I'll fight for this country because this is the only home I know. But I won't accept anymore of their torments."

Maraisha leaned over and lightly kissed Quiet on the lips. "You're full of hate, but I love you for what you are."

Lieutenant Miller, who was lying on his back in the far back of the cave, listening to the conversation, got up and walked over to Quiet. "You must be awfully bitter," he said.

"I thought you were asleep," said Quiet.

"I was," said Miller. "But I couldn't help overhearing what you were saying. You must have been through a lot of hell. I'm not black, but I can imagine what kind of hell you went through. Just by being in this predicament. I apologize for whites, but I know that's not enough. People like John will always keep blacks in bondage."

"You don't apologize for people like John," said Quiet.

"There's blacks I had trouble with, too. I know the ones. People are people, regardless of what race."

"When we get out of this, I'll see that you and your brothers are not disturbed by the police department anymore," assured Miller.

"What about other blacks?" said Quiet.

"Them, too. Unless they break the law," Miller stated. He looked at Quiet. "Why don't you get some rest? You look like you can use some. I'll take over here for a while."

Quiet agreed and went to go lie down.

"I'll wake you if I see anything."

Shep laid his head across Quiet's stomach. While Quiet, Clinton, Earl, and the militants slept, Maraisha and Lieutenant Miller stayed at the entrance. Lieutenant Miller looked back at Quiet and his two brothers. "Those boys were raised well," he said. "They had a father. I wish I had a father who had the time to teach me things."

"But he's so full of hate," Maraisha noted.

"Anger, danger, maybe, but not hate," Miller disagreed. "He needs an excuse, whereas some people don't. He's awfully wise for one so young. He'll live a long time."

"You understand his kind? I've been with him two and a half years and still I don't understand him."

"Don't try. Just give him your love and respect. He'll do all right with a good woman."

An odd expression came over Maraisha's face.

"I mean you, of course."

"Of course," repeated Maraisha doubtfully.

9

Stray police cars were driving up and down Rainier Avenue, but when a police car drove down the street Quiet lived on, "Look!" said Maraisha, astounded. She pointed. "That looks like Josh's car. Think they found us?"

Another car drove down the same street. Marcy was behind the wheel. "If they found us, they'd be here," said the lieutenant. "No! They're still looking for us." He looked at his automatic rifle. "This is a fine weapon. I like it," he said as he examined the weapon. "I wonder where they came from?"

"Maybe this is what we need on the force," added Maraisha.

"No-o! Not really. I'd hate for someone like John to get his hands on them."

Meanwhile, Dino and Sharon had managed to find out where James Adams lived. From the parking lot Dino drove to Adams's house, which was located in a highly taxed area just on the east side of Lacy. James had spent a weekend in his cabin on the Olympia Peninsula, with his wife and two sons. He just happened to come home that morning around eight-thirty. Sharon was sleeping on the couch. Dino was sitting back in Adams's armchair dozing off and on. When Dino heard a key turn in the door lock, he got up and got behind the door. When the door opened, Adams's two sons ran right into the house and were stunned when they saw Sharon sleeping on the couch.

"Dad! Dad!" the oldest cried out.

Just then, Sharon awakened as Adams and his wife rushed into the house. For a split second Adams was shocked, but then, "What the hell are you doing here?" he shouted angrily, but curiously.

Drowsily Sharon looked around for Dino. But he was nowhere in sight. "I wanted to see you."

"I can have you arrested for this," threatened Adams.

Then a voice came from behind the door. "Don't do that." The door closed. Adams saw a black holding an automatic weapon pointing at him. He dared not make any motions for fear of being shot. "We have enough trouble without adding any more," said Dino as he approached Adams. "We came because we need your help."

Adams looked at the automatic pointed at him. "You ask me for help with that gun in your hand? You won't get much help that way."

Dino walked up and put the rifle in Adams's hands. "We were sent here by a Lieutenant Miller. We need your help. He said you can help us."

There was doubt on Adams's face as he looked at the expression on Dino's face. It was the look of a serious man. "For some reason I believe you," Adams said as he examined the automatic weapon, then handed it back to Dino. "What kind of trouble is Frank in?"

Sharon went into her purse and pulled out her police badge. "I'm a cop," she said as Dino went and sat beside her on the couch. Sharon began to explain as she handed Adams the document. He started scanning some pages. A few pages he took the time to read thoroughly. The document seemed personal, so Adams sent the boys upstairs to unpack, then asked his wife to make some coffee.

"We have no time to waste," said Adams. "I'll call for the National Guard immediately." He went to pick up the telephone. He dialed a number and called Fort Lewis and asked to speak to General Whitehead, the commander of the fort. When Whitehead answered the telephone, Adams identified himself, then explained the problems Lieutenant Miller was having in Seattle.

"How soon can you get here?" asked Whitehead.

"In about a half an hour," answered Adams.

"Good!" said Whitehead. "I'll have truckloads of troops ready to leave before you get here. We'll be lined up on Interstate 5."

Adams, Whitehead, and Lieutenant Miller had gone to the same high school in Tacoma. They were in the same age bracket. Tacoma Highlands used to be their old stomping grounds.

By the time Mrs. Adams came back into the living room with a tray of coffee, Adams, Sharon, and Dino had already left in Quiet's car.

When leaving Adams's house, Dino made his tires squeal. Running a few red lights and stop signs, he got on Interstate 5 and headed north. In about ten minutes Dino pulled up near the entrance gate at Fort Lewis. Trucks were still pulling out of the gate. Dino counted eleven two-and-a-quarter-ton trucks loaded with troops and six military Jeeps. General Whitehead was sitting in a Jeep parked just to the side of the entrance gate with a driver behind the wheel and two military police officers sitting in the backseat. This operation was called Red Alert.

When Dino pulled up, General Whitehead got out of his Jeep and sat in the seat next to Adams. "I thought you said you'd be here in about a half an hour. You're early."

"I didn't know this was a hot rod," said Adams.

"How bad is Frank's situation?" asked Whitehead.

As Dino took off at high speed and whizzed down Interstate 5, Adams said, "Pretty bad." Then they started talking about old times and comparing experiences with different girlfriends and the fun they used to have.

Military Jeeps tried to keep pace with Dino but were no match for Quiet's car. Speeding down the freeway, two state patrol cars gave chase as Dino zoomed past. They had been sitting on the side of the road between Seattle and Tacoma. General Whitehead told Dino not to stop but put more distance between them. Dino did what Whitehead told him. Dino began to pull away farther and farther.

On the freeway the traffic was pretty thick. Dino zigged and zagged his way through the traffic, passing every car. His speed averaged between 90 and 130 miles an hour. When Dino came to the Renton and Burien turnoff, four more state patrol cars were sitting on a ramp, as though they were waiting. As Dino went zooming past the exit, the state patrol cars gave chase. Not knowing whether or not Quiet and the others had been apprehended or killed, Dino violated every traffic law ever made to get to Seattle.

"Do you always drive this fast?" asked Whitehead, in the backseat, as he almost swallowed his cigar.

"Only when I'm in a hurry," said Dino.

Adams never said a word. He just had his eyes closed and braced himself between the back and the front seat.

Although the state patrol cars couldn't catch Dino, they did manage to keep him in sight. But Dino felt somewhere up ahead the state police had called in for an intercept. Dino's feelings didn't lie to him because just beyond the Empire Way exit traffic was beginning to slow down. There were flashing blue and red lights. The state patrol had closed off two lanes just ahead of the traffic.

"Looks like the state police have a roadblock ahead," said Dino as he let the car coast to cruising speed.

The Empire Way exit was just to the right of the freeway about fifty meters ahead. "Take that exit." Adams pointed. "And go through town. I'll take the responsibility if we get stopped."

"We won't get stopped," said Dino as he accelerated. "We're about five minutes away."

Weaving and bobbing through traffic, Dino got on the Empire Way exit. About two blocks past the exit he caught a green light, but four blocks away, on Henderson, a street crossing Empire, Dino ran through a red light. Two motorcycle police officers were sitting on the corner when Dino came zooming by. They put on their flashing blue lights, then gave pursuit. Seeing the police in his rear view mirror made Dino put on more speed.

Averaging between sixty and ninety miles an hour, Dino cut through the traffic. Adams groaned. Whitehead chewed half of his cigar, then swallowed the rest. Although they couldn't keep pace, the military Jeeps followed the state patrol cars. The state patrol cars kept the motorcycle police officers in sight. They were picking up other police cars along the way. When Dino got to Rainier Avenue, traffic was thick on both sides of the street. This caused him to slow down as he maneuvered on both sides of the street. Then finally he came to Massachusetts Street, where he made a left turn. Now he was only a few blocks away. Within seconds he'd reach his destination.

When Dino finally pulled onto the street where Quiet lived, police cars were parked up and down the block and in front of the house. Dino stopped at the intersection. Without warning, when the police officers saw Quiet's car they opened fire. Dino quickly backed the car back down the block and around the corner. Then he got out with the automatic weapon and fired at the officers when they came to the end of the block. The officers took cover. Sharon, Adams, and Whitehead tried to duck under their seats.

Just then, the two police officers on their motorcycles pulled up behind Dino. Then came other officers and the state patrol, and behind them came the military police. The military wasted no time in blocking off the whole neighborhood. Trucks took other routes to get around the neighborhood to block off the other end. There were only two ways in the neighborhood, and the military was in the process of cutting off any type of an escape.

At the first sight of other police officers and the military, Ross, Marty, and a few other police officers ran to Quiet's house. Maulder, who was already in the house, let them in. Ross tried to explain about the authority but wasn't making much sense. He was talking too fast and stammering over his words. Maulder looked out the window. When he saw the military getting in position, he wasted no time going out the back door, escaping through the alley.

At the cave, by this time a couple of hours had passed. Quiet was still asleep. Lieutenant Miller was sitting in the back of the cave resting his eyes. Maraisha and Clinton were standing lookout at the entrance. Ted, Calvin, Michael, Leroy, and Earl were sitting around the fire playing cards, tonk. All of a sudden there was a humming sound that seemed far away. At first, the men disregarded the noise, because they felt it wasn't important. But the humming sound was getting closer. Soon the noise vibrated the earth.

"What's that?" asked Maraisha.

The humming sound had attracted the men's attention also. "I don't know," said Clinton.

The noise woke Quiet up. He got up and walked to the entrance of the cave. "See anything?" he asked Clinton.

"Just cops patrolling up and down the streets," said Clinton.

Quiet eased behind a bush at the entrance. "Sounds like trucks," he said. "I wonder." An army truck drove down the street. "I hope it's what I'm thinking."

"What's that?" asked Maraisha.

"Our help!" added Clinton.

"Maybe we ought to check it out," said Quiet.

The sounds of the truck engines alerted Michael and the

others, except Lieutenant Miller. He was still resting his eyes. Quiet said, as Michael was the first to approach him, "Let's use your car to see what this is all about. If this is what Dino brought back, you can come back here and get these guys." Michael agreed and he and Quiet alertly went back to the parked cars.

Slowly Michael drove through the alley, hitting every hole and ditch in the roadway, until the paved streets came into view. Army troops patrolled the neighborhood, apprehending other police officers in the area trying to escape. When Michael came to the entrance to the alley, Quiet got out of the car and started walking down the street. He was confronted by two military men as he came to the front of his house.

"Quiet!" cried Sharon, standing at the bottom of the stairs near the sidewalk. She ran and threw her arms around his neck as she exhaled a breath of relief. "I'm glad you're all right."

Dino walked over and wrapped his arms around Quiet. "Glad to see you," he said. "Where are the others?"

"In the woods waiting for you two to get back," said Quiet.

Adams, General Whitehead, and the militia men collected names and badge numbers of the captured police officers and watched Sharon and Dino talking to Quiet. They wondered about the blacks. When the state patrol officers came up to Quiet, he explained the situation when they asked. Quiet looked for Maulder among the apprehended officers, but he was nowhere in sight.

"Where's your friend John?" asked Quiet.

"We saw a few of them go into your house," said Sharon. "I think John was in there already."

Quiet hurried up the stairs and into the house. Adams, Whitehead, and two military officers followed. When they got inside, the house was empty. The back door had been left wide open. But still Quiet, Dino, and Sharon made a thorough search upstairs and downstairs in the house. The military police made a thorough search outside and around the house, in the alley,

248

and around the area. There was no sign of Maulder and the police officers who had left with him. Quiet left the house and went up the alley. The military police were already up the alley where it turned heading back to the street. When Quiet got to where it turned, Michael's, Ted's, Clinton's, and Earl's cars were coming down the hill below the woods.

Adams approached. "You must be Quiet," he said. "I heard quite a bit about you." As the cars were coming closer, he asked, "Who are they?" Quiet didn't answer.

"Friends of ours. Those are the guys we were talking about," answered Sharon. "Including Frank."

When the cars came to a stop Lieutenant Miller got out of Michael's car. "Am I glad to see you," he said joyously as he shook Adams's and Whitehead's hands. "There was a time I gave up hope."

Whitehead presented the large envelope to Lieutenant Miller. "Is this what this is all about?"

"Yes," answered Lieutenant Miller. "It almost cost us our lives. But thanks to him," he pointed to Quiet, "we're here now. A couple of days ago I might not have been able to say anything."

"This report has some strong accusations in it," said Adams.

"It's all true," Miller confirmed. "We have work to do."

While the conversation was going on, Quiet went to Michael's car and pulled his automatic rifle out of the backseat. He checked the magazine clip. It was full of ammunition. By doing this he caught Lieutenant Miller's, Adams's, Whitehead's, and the military police's attention. When Maraisha saw Quiet get his weapon she got out of Clinton's car, ran to Quiet, and threw her arms around his waist.

"Let the police finish this," she said softly.

"This is something I have to do," he said.

"She's right, you know," said Lieutenant Miller. "We can take it from here."

"You're gonna try and stop me?" said Quiet.

249

"No! I just want your word that you'll let the law try him."

Quiet paused for a moment as he and Lieutenant Miller looked at one another. "If I can," he said.

"What's up?" asked Michael, who was still sitting behind the wheel.

"The main ones are still at large," said Quiet angrily. "I'm going after them."

"Any ideas where they might be?"

"My guess is the warehouse."

"What if they're not there?" Leroy came into the conversation.

"Then we'll go back to his house and wait, before he leaves town," said Quiet.

"Leroy and I and Ted and Calvin will go back to his house. If they're not there, we'll meet you at the warehouse," said Michael. "By us splitting up we can check both places at once."

Shep jumped out of Michael's car. As Quiet started to walk away, Maraisha grabbed him by his collar. "You guys are talking crazy," she said, frightened. "Let the law pursue them."

Quiet removed her hands from his collar. "They shot my brother," he said coldly. "Now, we must go." He took his rifle and started to walk back down the alley.

Dino approached Quiet. "I'm going with you. He is my brother, too," he said seriously.

Quiet saw the serious look on Dino's face, knowing he wouldn't take no for an answer. "Okay. Let's go."

Quiet got between Michael and Clinton's car. "You'd better listen to her," said Whitehead, standing next to Adams and Lieutenant Miller in the roadway. "That weapon is going to get you into serious trouble. You'd better let me have it." He held out his hand.

"You're not taking my weapon," Quiet refused.

The military police officers assisting Whitehead got in a ready firing position and pointed their weapons at Quiet. Just then, Michael and Leroy, Ted and Calvin, and Clinton and Earl got out of their cars with their weapons and pointed them at the military police.

As Dino and Sharon drew their weapons and ran to Quiet's side, Maraisha drew her pistol also and pointed it at Whitehead. "No-o!" she screamed. "Frank! Don't let this happen."

Weapons were cocked, guns pointed. Seeing how the blacks were close together and knowing they had been through a lot and were ready to fight, Lieutenant Miller looked at Whitehead. "You'd better let them go. They mean business." Then he turned and walked on down the alley.

At the first sounds of the weapons being cocked, Adams's legs shook, which went on until his knees began to knock. The military police, the state patrol officers, and the few uniformed police officers started looking at one another in fear of getting killed. Slowly, they began to move backward, leaving General Whitehead to face the blacks alone. "I admire people like you," said Whitehead. Then he also walked away.

"Shep!" Quiet called as he went and got in Clinton's car. The others did the same, getting back in their cars, except for Maraisha and Sharon, who walked on down the alley trying to catch up with Lieutenant Miller. Clinton drove his car down the alley alongside Lieutenant Miller as he was still walking. Miller walked over to Clinton's car. "I'll give you a half-hour start; then we're coming." Quiet gave no response as Clinton pulled away. Earl and Dino followed.

Marcy, Maulder, Ross, Bishop, Randall, Munson, Morrison, Davis, and Tanner had a good forty-five-minute head start on Quiet. At first sight of multiple authorities, they had escaped in three awaiting police cars parked in the alley and driven past the military before they had a chance to close off the area. The rogue cops headed back to the warehouse. When they got there, Bishop, Randall, and Marcy stood watch outside while Maulder and the others went to the office. Occasionally Bishop, Randall, and Marcy walked around the four-block-long, one-and-a-half-block-wide warehouse to make sure there were no intruders in the area.

Lieutenant Miller, Adams, and Whitehead, along with four military police officers and the militia, escorted the captured police officers downtown. They were taken into custody. Then Miller, Adams, and Whitehead went upstairs in the elevator to the detective bureau. When they entered Shatter's office, Miller dropped the envelope on his desk. "It's over," said Miller. "You're under arrest. This is proof of your conspiracy and payoff system. You, Maulder, Bishop and others will soon be under indictment."

Shatter, talking on the telephone when Miller entered his office, was stunned at the sight of him. The telephone was still in Shatter's hand while Miller was talking. When he saw the envelope fall on his desk, there was denial on his face, but he dared not speak.

Lieutenant Miller continued, "This whole department is under investigation until I get to the bottom of this." He reached down and opened up the envelope. He took the papers out of the envelope. "There are names, dates, and activities on this document. Your name is on one of the sheets." Just then Sharon entered the office, with Maraisha trailing behind her. "You know Sharon and Maraisha." Shatter just looked at them, still holding the telephone receiver. "Who's on the telephone?" Shatter didn't answer as he gently laid the receiver down. "John Maulder, no doubt. It's best he and his friends come in and give themselves up. It'll make my job easier. Or I'll put an APB on him with an arrest warrant. I told you when I was coming back here, when I heard of Mike Schmidt's death. You sent two of your men, Sidney and Lawrence, to dust me."

Shatter casually opened his desk drawer. "Let me clean out my desk," he said. Then he pulled out a police revolver. "Don't move," he demanded as he got up out of his chair. "I'm going out of here, and you're going to help me."

Everyone moved away from the desk except Miller. "How far do you think you'll get?" he said. "Uniformed officers are out in the secretarial office, waiting to take you upstairs. If you get out of here, you'll be on the run. It'll just be a matter of time before we catch up with you. You're a cop. You know that as well as I do."

"You're right," said Shatter calmly as he sat back down, then turned the revolver to his head and squeezed the trigger, before anyone could stop him.

"That might have been the easiest way out for him. Twenty-two years wasted on the force," mumbled Miller. He turned toward Sharon and Maraisha, who were also stunned by the incident. "Take us to your boyfriends." Everyone left the office.

By this time, after taking the freeway, Clinton had pulled his car to the entrance of the roadway. Quiet and Shep got out of the car. Earl pulled his car up behind Clinton's. Quiet leashed Shep; then he and Clinton crept toward the warehouse along the bottom of the embankment, while Earl and Dino went to the other side of the roadway down the other embankment to approach the warehouse from the rear. As Quiet and Clinton neared the warehouse, three unmarked police cars were parked in front. Two men were in view patrolling the front of the warehouse. Quiet unleashed Shep, sent him farther down the embankment, then let himself be seen on the roadway at the far end of the warehouse.

The three men were standing near the cars when Bishop said in an astonished voice as he saw Shep, "Hey! What's that?"

As the other two men looked, Randall said, "That nigga's dog. He must be around here somewhere."

"Maybe we ought to tell the others," said Marcy.

"Let's follow him. He might lead us to his master," said Randall.

"Remember what happened last time?" Bishop put in.

"That's why I have a score to settle with that black. Let's get that dog," said Marcy.

First the three men slowly started approaching Shep. But when Shep felt they were getting too close, he started running. As Shep took off, the three men started running after him. When they turned the corner around the warehouse, Shep led the three men into Earl's and Dino's weapons, waiting at the far end. Without any arguments Bishop, Randall, and Marcy carefully dropped their pistols from their holsters and raised their hands. Then Dino and Earl put their handcuffs on their wrists behind their backs and escorted them to the cars where Quiet and Clinton were waiting. Randall and Marcy cursed themselves at being tricked into being caught off guard. They showed signs of disgust with themselves. Quiet ordered them into the backseat of the first car. He gave Dino his automatic weapon and took the police shotgun and ammunition out of the police car, then advanced toward the warehouse.

In the back office, at that instant, Spike alerted Maulder and the others with a couple of barks and scratching at the door. "What's wrong with him?" said Ross worriedly.

"Probably excited," answered Maulder.

"Maybe someone is out there," added Morrison.

"Bill, Bob, and Josh are standing watch. If anyone is out there, they'll let us know," assured Maulder.

"Remember when we had that nigga's brother and he caught us off guard and took his brother back?" said Marty, frightened, as he came into the conversation.

"Well, if you're worried, go out there and take a look," said Maulder.

Marty was sitting at the side of the office desk next to the door. "I'll go," he said. He got up and left the office. When he got to the dispatch door, he opened it and looked toward the open double doors. Everything was quiet. There was no sign of movement. Marty called out. He got no answer. Then a worried look came over his face as he drew his pistol and slowly advanced toward the open doors.

In the office, when Maulder and the others heard Marty call Bishop, Randall, and Marcy by their first names, they came out into the warehouse. "Maybe something is wrong," said Maulder in a low voice. He was standing next to Davis.

"Let's check it out," said Davis. Cautiously they moved behind Marty with weapons drawn. Maulder, Davis, and Tanner had shotguns. Spike was being led on a leash. He gave a couple of challenging barks. From outside the warehouse Shep returned the barks. Hearing Shep's barks, Maulder and the others took cover, behind brace posts, beams, empty crates or whatever. But there was still no sign of movement.

Munson and Morrison started making their way toward the doors, ducking behind one post after another. Marty, who was already ahead of the group, made it to the doors and was standing to the side. He peeked around the doorway. The cars were gone. As Marty started to go outside, a bullet hit the frame of the doorway just to the side above his head. This caused Marty to duck back behind the doorway.

"At least that tells us someone's in front," said Maulder. "I'll try the back doors." The back unloading doors were closed. Maulder went to an exit door directly behind the dispatch office. As he eased the door open, there was gunfire from an automatic weapon. Quickly he ducked back behind the door, then went back to where he had been. "We can't stay here. The back is covered also." As Maulder moved cautiously toward the entrance doors, he came up behind Marty. "See anything?"

"No!" said Marty. "But they're out there somewhere."

"It must be them niggas," said Maulder. "If it was the force, they would have a blowhorn."

"The force is probably on their way," said Marty.

"These guys are amateurs," said Maulder. "We should be

able to take care of these guys with no problems before their help arrives."

"We can handle the rest, but what about that one?" added Marty. "He's no amateur. He led them here the first time."

"I just know if we stay here we'll be outnumbered within minutes," assured Maulder.

"We don't know how many are out there," said Marty. "Your dog can flush 'em out."

"We have two choices: take our chance with these niggas or give ourselves up to the force, when they get here."

"I'm not giving myself up to no nigger," said Marty angrily. "If we rush out we'll have a chance of making it to them bushes, then getting away through the woods."

"They have automatic weapons. Remember?" said Tanner as he and Davis came up behind the others. Williams, Ross, Munson, and Morrison spread themselves through the warehouse, behind the other doors.

"They can't cover all the doors," said Williams. "Let's make a break for it."

"There can't be any more than three or four of them. If we can draw their fire, maybe a couple of us can make it to them bushes and even up the situation," said Maulder. Maulder suggested that he and Ross try to make a run for the swampy field, while Williams, Morrison, Marty, Tanner, and Davis gave them cover by blasting wildly at the open field.

When the police fired upon the swampy field with their pistols and shotguns, Maulder and Ross hurriedly jumped off the loading dock onto the ground and rolled down the five-foot embankment, then crawled into the bushes. Spike led the way. When the police stopped firing, there was no return fire. Then Morrison tried to follow, but Quiet put two shotgun blasts in his chest. Williams had already started to follow Morrison. But seeing Morrison getting shot up, Williams got back inside behind the door. Tanner, Davis, Marty, and Munson returned the fire. But still they couldn't see where the shots were coming from.

Quiet saw Maulder and Ross go into the bushes, ordered Shep to stay, then moved toward the wooded area. When he got to the woods, he saw a few bushes in the swampy area moving. Quiet blasted in the direction of the movement and hit Ross in the chest and face as he tried to return the fire. When Ross got hit, Maulder quickly got up and ran toward the woods, about fifty feet away. Quiet got up and tried to fire, but the shotgun was out of shells. While running Maulder fired a couple of shots at Quiet. But Quiet had already gotten behind a tree and started reloading the shotgun, while at the same instant Maulder had sent Spike to attack.

At the sound of Spike's growl, feeling that his master might be in trouble, Shep disobeyed Quiet's command and went to find him. Shep galloped through the swampy field until the woods came in view. Then he saw Quiet using the shotgun as a stick, swinging at Spike. Shep gave a challenging bark, then advanced. On hearing Shep's bark, Spike backed away from the shotgun to meet the challenge. When Shep got to the bottom of the hill, Spike was coming down at full force. Shep heard Quiet tell him to go back. But he kept coming. Halfway up the slope, from a flying leap, Spike was all over Shep. Like two wolves deciding which one would be the leader, they went round and round, until they got to the bottom of the hill and a small clearing.

Spike, with his speed, pursued Shep, not giving him a chance to gain his balance. Spike kept the pressure on, staying on Shep's back, trying to take a chunk out of his neck. But Shep kept his head low and spun around, trying to get a grip on one of Spike's front legs. When Spike lowered his head to defend his legs, this gave Shep the opportunity to regain his balance by spinning around and standing up on his hind legs to face the beast. As the two dogs stood up on their hind legs, they began to snap at one another.

In spite of Spike's speed, Shep's strength wasn't to be denied as he forced Spike backward. But Spike was as swift as the wind. While going backward Spike shifted his body to one side, causing Shep to land on all fours. Before Shep had a chance to regain his balance, Spike got back on Shep's back. Instinctively Shep dropped his head, spun around, got back upon his hind legs, and faced Spike. Once again the dogs began to snap at one another.

In the few other fights Shep had had, never had he faced another dog with speed such as Spike. He knew some way he had to find a defense. Most of his fights had been with other shepherds, collies, and Labradors, but none of them had Spike's swiftness. After a few rallies Shep could see that this was no average neighborhood dog he was fighting. This dog was a killer. Shep knew he had to put all his experience together and fight this brute. Along with Spike's speed, his strength was equal to Shep's.

When Dino heard the dogfight, he felt Quiet might be in trouble. So he made one good sweep across the entrance of the warehouse, then left his position to investigate. At the same instant this gave Munson, Davis, and Tanner a chance to get away from the pressure put on them from the rear by Earl. From the embankment Clinton fired at the three men. But they managed to escape down the embankment into the swampy field. Like infantrymen they got down on their elbows and knees and crawled among the bushes, heading toward the woods. Coming through the rear entrance, Earl met Clinton in front. From the loading dock they saw moving bushes going toward the woods.

Spike matched his strength against Shep but still found himself being pushed backward. In the process Spike put a cut across the bridge of Shep's nose. Shep reached down and tried to bite Spike's neck. But Spike challenged his fangs against Shep's. Like a raging bull Shep almost caused Spike to fall from under his feet. But Spike maneuvered his body to one side, again causing Shep to land on all fours.

Once again Shep found himself in the same position he was in before. Spike was up on Shep's back. Whenever Shep tried to spin, Spike would try to get a hold on his neck. But Shep kept his head low, trying to get a grip on Spike's back leg. When Spike moved back to keep his leg from getting bitten, Shep turned and rose back up on his hind legs. Again the two dogs were in the air snapping at one another.

Spike got a hold on the side of Shep's mouth and started tearing at it as though it were a piece of raw meat. Shep used his front leg to push Spike to the side. Spike went to the ground but left a gash in Shep.

The fight became bloodier. This time the tables were turned. Shep was all over Spike as he tried to get back on his feet. Shep hooked his fangs into Spike's ear and began to tear away at it. Furiously Spike struggled to his feet, his ear almost torn in half. Pulling and tugging, he tried to force Shep to release his grip. But the grip was too tight.

When Spike managed to get back on his feet he hooked his fangs in Shep's shoulder. Quickly Shep released the ear, then tried to hook his fangs in the back of Spike's neck. But Spike reared up and both dogs got back on their hind legs. Shep seemed more determined as he used his strength and weight to keep Spike off balance. But Spike shifted his body to one side as Shep kept charging. This time when Spike shifted, Shep maneuvered to the opposite side and came up on his back. Shep wrestled Spike back to the ground. Blood covered Spike's face as he fought his way back to his feet.

As the dogs stood up on their hind legs, Spike tore a piece of meat out of Shep's shoulder, bit him across the nose, and left a scar on his back. Shep had torn half of Spike's ear off, bit him around the neck, and left a wound in his shoulder. Blood covered both dogs as exhaustion was getting the best of them. But still neither wanted to give in.

Spike stood straight up as he tried to bite down on Shep. But Shep, being underneath, again forced Spike backward, causing him to lose his balance. This time as Spike tried to get back on his feet, Shep hooked his fangs into the side of his adversary's neck. Spike struggled to free himself, but the grip was too tight. Each time Spike struggled, Shep dug his fangs deeper and deeper into the flesh, with a deadly grip on Spike's neck. Blood squirted out of the wound rapidly. Spike began to lose his strength. Like a mad beast Shep began to tear at the wound. Spike yelped. Then, soon, the struggle stopped.

Michael and Leroy and Ted and Calvin arrived at the entrance road to the warehouse at the same instant as Maraisha, Sharon, Adams, Miller, and Whitehead, along with the military police and a few army troops off of two trucks. They saw Clinton's and Earl's cars parked off the road. Continuing up the roadway toward the warehouse, they came to the three police cars parked just away from the warehouse to the side of the roadway. Maraisha and Sharon got out of the police cars they were in and investigated the three police cars, finding Bishop, Randall, and Marcy lying in the backseat with their hands cuffed behind their backs. When Maraisha mentioned who they were, Whitehead ordered two military police to take them into custody.

From a distance there was a yelp. "What's that?" asked Sharon curiously.

"It sounded like it came from over there." Michael pointed. With weapons ready, he and the others hurried to investigate. When they got there, Shep had just killed Spike. Blood was all over their bodies.

"Oh, no!" said Maraisha as a sad look came over her face. "I knew them two had to meet."

Shep was lying down, but on hearing the voices of the people he raised his head, looked at them, then put his head back down. Maraisha walked over, pulled a handkerchief from her purse, and gently wiped his wounds. But the thought of Quiet entered her mind. "Where's Quiet?" Shep raised his head again and whined, then put it back down.

From the woods came the sounds of gunfire. Everyone became alerted. "Over there!" motioned Michael. Then he, Ted, Leroy, and Calvin dashed off in the direction of the gunfire. Lieutenant Miller, Sharon, and Whitehead followed. After laying Shep's head to the ground, Maraisha went also. When they came to a fork in the path, Michael, Leroy, Ted, and Calvin took the path to the left. Maraisha, Sharon, Miller, and Whitehead and the other military men went up the other path.

When Maraisha saw Clinton helping Earl, a bullet wound in his left leg and having suffered a great loss of blood, back to the car, she asked, "Where's Quiet and Dino?" There was fear in her tone.

"They're after your friends." Clinton pointed.

Sharon took off running in the direction in which Clinton had pointed. Whitehead had two of his military men give Clinton help carrying Earl, while the others followed Sharon.

As Quiet was moving cautiously among the trees, the bushes from the pathway reminded him of his rare search-and-destroy missions in Vietnam. Searching for Vietcong with the infantry units was like searching for a panther in the dark. Whenever the infantry felt they were going to surprise the Vietcong, they would walk into an ambush.

The running footsteps ahead were fading away, then stopped. The shooting had stopped. There was complete silence. Like a soldier, Quiet paused in his tracks, listening for any sound and watching for any movement. There was none. *Ambush,* he thought. Quiet knew it was dangerous to walk on low ground in pursuit of an enemy, for the hunted has the advantage over the hunter then. He backtracked about fifty feet until he came to a path that led to a higher level of the woods.

When Quiet came up over a ridge that overlooked a good portion of the woods below, he carefully looked at every tree, every bush, but still no sign of any movement. As he stood there for a moment he remembered an old sergeant he met in Vietnam, a deer hunter from Kentucky. Quiet remembered him saying when hunting deer you looked for signs of tracks, trails, broken bushes, and trees where they'd been eating the bark. You could also look to see where leaves fell and birds suddenly left their resting places. But it's more dangerous to hunt man. Man can think. The woods can be your worst enemy, because they have many dangers. The woods can also be your friend. The woods have life; life can survive there. There are many places a person can hide in the woods for safety. It depends upon the person knowing how to use the woods.

As Quiet turned to look in another direction, he saw a crow quickly take to the air, giving out a warning cry. There was a slight movement behind bushes below. "It's John," Quiet mumbled.

He started to come off the ridge, but just then he heard voices. "John! John! John, where are you?" It was Davis and Tanner running through the woods. Maulder came out from his hiding place when he saw his friends. Quiet wondered what had happened to Dino as he looked back toward the entrance of the woods. About the length of a football field away Dino was coming up a trail, moving cautiously. Maulder, Tanner, and Davis had hidden in some bushes to set up an ambush. So Quiet left the ridge to go down and warn Dino.

The woods were about as thick as a forest, with a small creek running through them. The woods ran for an indeterminate number of miles, passing highways and roads. These woods once were occupied by deer, raccoons, feral dogs, and other wild animals. Police had been called in to kill off the feral dogs, because farmers in the area complained about their livestock being raided. Kids on their way to school were being attacked. In spite of the disappearance of the feral dogs, the woods were still occupied by a few wild species.

Sharon came up on higher ground and saw Munson. She scanned below to find Quiet or Maulder. They were nowhere to be found. Then a head rose up from behind a bush. "Dino," she whispered. Just ahead were Tanner and Davis, waiting. "They're going to kill Dino," she mumbled. Quickly Sharon came off the higher ground and rushed through the woods. When she came into view, Munson had just put a bullet above Dino's left lung. "No-o!" she screamed. With a burst of fire, Sharon emptied her pistol into Munson's body. The gun was still clicking as Munson was falling to the ground. Michael came from out of nowhere and eased the pistol out of her hand. A surprised look came over his face as she knelt down and held Dino in her arms. Tears ran down her face.

From the direction Sharon had seen Tanner and Davis, there was a movement of bushes and a trampling of twigs. "Someone is coming," said Michael. He got behind a tree. Sharon laid Dino back down, then grabbed his automatic weapon. The footsteps were coming closer.

"Move it!" shouted a voice.

Recognizing the voice, Michael came out from around the tree until the person the voice belonged to came into view. Leroy, Ted, and Calvin were marching Tanner and Davis back to the entrance of the woods.

Sharon asked worriedly when Leroy approached, "Where's John? Quiet?"

"We didn't see 'em," said Leroy. Then he saw the bullet wound in Dino's shoulder. "What happened?"

"He'll be all right," said Sharon.

Finally Maraisha, Miller, Adams, and Whitehead and the other military men made their appearance. On seeing Dino was wounded, Whitehead had two military men take him back to their vehicle.

Unaware of all this, Quiet and Maulder had left the woods. Whitehead and Miller went back to their cars and called for a search team with dogs. The military police escorted the prisoners to their vehicles. Ted, Calvin, and Maraisha waited in the woods until the search team arrived. Sharon went to the warehouse with Michael and Leroy, who carried Dino, to wait for an ambulance.

On the way back to their own vehicles, Miller noticed two unmarked police cars were gone. Whitehead picked up the microphone and started to call in for a search team.

"Put that down," said Miller. "We're not going to need it."

With a curious look on his face, Whitehead asked, "Why's that?"

"They're not here. Just call for an ambulance," said Miller as he was getting into Quiet's car. "Two cars are gone."

Maraisha had used Quiet's car to get to the warehouse. Then Miller fired two shots in the air. Michael and Leroy came running out of the warehouse. Ted, Calvin, and Maraisha came running out of the woods heading toward the vehicles, ready for action as they approached the vehicles.

"What's the shooting about?" Michael asked.

"Quiet and Maulder are gone," said Miller.

"How do you know?" said Maraisha.

"There were three cop cars here when we drove up. Now there's only one," he continued. Everyone looked but didn't say a word. "I think I know where they might have gone." Maraisha was getting into Quiet's car. "To Maulder's house, before he leaves town."

Maraisha started up the engine, drove to where Shep was, and called him, and he got up and crawled in the backseat. Michael, Leroy, Ted, and Calvin had already left when she took off.

Meanwhile Quiet had parked the police car about a block away and around the corner from Maulder's house. Quiet made his way through the alleyway, checking closely to see that he wasn't noticed by the neighbors. Then he entered the house through the basement window. When Quiet got inside the house, carefully he searched the basement and upstairs. The house was still empty. Quiet went through Maulder's bedroom closet and found his clothes and baggage there. "He hasn't gotten here yet," he mumbled. So he went to the kitchen and pulled out a jar of instant coffee from the cupboard, then went to the stove drawer and pulled out a boiler, ran some water in it, and set it on the stove. When the water heated up, he fixed himself a cup of coffee, then went into the living room and sat back in the armchair facing the front door with the police shotgun.

A short time after Quiet sat in the chair, he heard a car coming to a screeching halt in front of the house. Quickly Quiet got up and from a safe distance, looked out the window. Maulder had just pulled up near the curb in the other police car. He got out and hurried up the stairs toward the house. Seeing him coming, Quiet went into the bedroom and stood behind the door. When the key turned in the lock, the front door opened. Footsteps ran toward the bedroom.

Walking past the kitchen, Maulder noticed the boiler on the stove had steaming water. He became cautious, feeling he wasn't alone in the house. Maulder looked around as he continued to the bedroom. When Maulder got to the bedroom he eased the door open and caught a glance of a figure through the crack as he was entering the bedroom. Instinctively Maulder pushed the door wide open with his shoulder, knocking Quiet up against the wall, causing him to drop the shotgun. But Quiet pushed back on the door, forcing Maulder away.

Maulder reached for his pistol while falling off balance. Quickly Quiet dived on Maulder, grabbing his wrist, as the pistol was in his hand. Quiet shook the wrist and the gun fell to the floor. From the floor the two men wrestled back onto their feet. Quiet kicked the pistol under the bed. Maulder grabbed Quiet by the waist and flipped him across the other side of the bed. Quiet tried to go for the shotgun, but Maulder dived on top of his back. He put a choke hold on Quiet's neck as they struggled to their feet. Then Quiet flipped Maulder over his back. But Maulder rolled back onto his feet.

As the two men squared off, Maulder got into his defensive stance. At that split second, Quiet thought, *Kung-fu*. The slight pause took Quiet back to Vietnam, to the time when he had trained with the Koreans in hand-to-hand combat. A Korean instructor in his early forties said one day, "Defense is a matter of psychology. It puts fear in an opponent. The fight is halfway over before it's begun. But it doesn't matter what the name of your defense is. If you know how to fight, you fight. Anyone can lose. There is only one victor. Defense controls mind and body control, which is one."

Maulder attacked Quiet, first with a double kick, and a fist followed. Instead of challenging, Quiet rolled to the other side of the bed, grabbed a pillow, and threw it in Maulder's face as he tried to follow. The moment the pillow blinded Maulder's vision, Quiet grabbed him by his shirt collar and threw him against the wall, he landed upside down. Without giving Maulder a chance to recover, Quiet went and tried to put a flurry of kicks in his face. But as Quiet came to him, Maulder put his feet in Quiet's chest and pushed him back. He fell back on the bed. Quickly Maulder got back on his feet. But as he attacked, Quiet rolled back to the other side of the bed.

As Maulder was coming across the bed, Quiet grabbed the blanket and pulled it from under him. He landed back down on the floor. As Maulder was rolling back to his feet, Quiet jumped up on the bed and down on top of him. Once again the two men wrestled on the floor, trying to get leverage and throw punches. When they struggled back to their feet, Maulder grabbed Quiet by his collar, kneed him in the stomach, and let an uppercut send him to the other side of the bed. But Quiet quickly rolled to his feet, as Maulder came leaping. But as Maulder came flying across the bed, Quiet sidestepped, and let him go into the wall.

Quiet jumped on Maulder's back and tried to put a choke hold on him. Quiet was unaware of Maulder's experience as he felt an elbow in his rib, which caused him to loosen his grip. Then the twist of a body sent Quiet rolling just to the side. Maulder tried to give Quiet a karate chop, but Quiet blocked the attempt by placing his foot on Maulder's stomach, then pushing him back toward the end of the bed. Quickly Quiet got to his feet and attacked. Maulder had already regained his balance as he waited for Quiet.

Quiet came with a quick kick attempt to the head, and a straight punch followed. Maulder moved back from both attempts through the doorway into the dining room, then countered with a straight kick, landing in Quiet's chest. Quiet fell back up against the wall just to the side of the doorway, then, raising his foot, kicked Maulder in the chest as he tried to follow through. Quiet followed through, throwing one punch after another, until Maulder stumbled over the coffee table. Losing his balance, Quiet fell on top of him. Again the two men wrestled.

In the living room the two men knocked over the lamp that had been sitting on the end table. Quiet broke a dining room chair swinging it at Maulder, but it hit the wall. The shelves of flowers were knocked over in the fight. The television set sitting on a stand was smashed. Maulder grabbed a flowerpot and threw it at Quiet, but he ducked, and the flower pot went out the window.

When the two men wrestled back to their feet, Maulder kneed Quiet in the midsection and landed a punch across his chin. Quiet went back toward the fireplace, picking up a handful of ashes, and threw it in Maulder's face as he was attacking. Then Quiet grabbed a leg of a dining room chair, as Maulder put his hands over his eyes and bashed him on the forehead. Quiet tried to make another attempt, but Maulder blocked with his forearm, then grabbed him by the waist and threw him over toward the couch. Maulder advanced. Quiet threw the chair leg as Maulder ducked, followed behind it, then pulled Maulder back into the bedroom.

During the fight both men were badly bruised. Quiet's left eye was swollen, the side of his face was puffy, and he had a split lip and a bloody nose. Maulder's eyes were bruised also. He also sported a cut on his forehead, a gashed lip, a cut across his nose, a puffy jaw, and a split lip.

When they got back in the bedroom, Maulder, being the shorter of the two, swung Quiet to the side, then threw a couple of rotated kicks. Quiet ducked under the kicks and grabbed Maulder's leg as he was making a third attempt and flipped him on his back. Then Quiet dived across the bed and grabbed the shotgun. As Maulder quickly got to his feet and started to attack, Quiet cocked the shotgun and pointed at him.

"Let's see if your defense is faster than buckshot," said Quiet.

Maulder eased back with his hands raised. "Wait a minute, brother," he said, frightened. "We didn't harm you or your brothers."

"You caused one to get shot and you have harassed my family for the last time," said Quiet angrily. "Now I'm going to blast you wide open."

As Quiet eased his finger on the trigger, Maulder saw the death look in his eyes. *This nigga is really going to shoot me,* he felt. "Hold it, man! You don't want to do this. You'll be in trouble," pleaded Maulder.

Just then a voice came into the bedroom. "Don't do that.

He's our property, now," said Miller as he came into the bedroom. Quiet paused when he saw Maraisha. Then Adams and four military police came into the bedroom.

Quiet held the shotgun to Maulder's stomach. "He's not going to get out of this," he said.

Just then Michael and Leroy and Ted and Calvin came into the bedroom behind two uniformed officers. But when the two officers saw Quiet with the shotgun pointed at Maulder, they drew their pistols and pointed them at him. At the same instant Maraisha had her pistol in her hand in a position ready to fire at the two officers. Michael and Leroy and Ted and Calvin cocked their automatic weapons and pointed them at the two officers. Looking at the weapons pointed at them, the officers looked at Miller, then at Adams. They got no response. So the officers eased their pistols back in their holsters.

"Well, the choice is yours," Miller said as he walked over and stood in front of Maulder. "Either you use it or put it down. Hasn't there been enough killing?"

There was burning hate in Quiet's eyes as he looked at Miller. Maraisha had sadness and anguish written on her face. Quiet walked up to Miller and put the shotgun in his hand. "Yes, there has been enough," he agreed, disgusted. Then he walked out of the bedroom with his arm wrapped around Maraisha's waist. Michael and Leroy and Ted and Calvin followed.

Miller placed the handcuffs on Maulder's wrists behind his back. Then he walked outside, with Adams trailing, and stood on the front porch, as Quiet and Maraisha was getting in his car. "Quiet!" he called. Quiet gave Miller his attention. "I hate to have to come after you," he threatened. "Besides, the D.A. might want to talk to you."

Maraisha was already seated. Quiet stood with the driver's door opened. He looked back at Miller. "You can tell your duckass, I said he can shove it," he said. Then he seated himself in the car and drove off.

He watched Quiet driving down the street. "He's unthankful, isn't he?" said Adams who was standing next to Miller.

"What's there to be thankful for? He's been through a lot," said Miller.